Café Merle – Book Tw

CAFE MERLE

Neil Argue & Anita Hewlett

COPYRIGHT

Copyright © 2024 Neil Argue & Anita Hewlett

Cafe Merle
Book Two

The Rage of Chaos

ISBN: 9798300416966

First eBook edition: November 2024

This is a work of fiction. All the characters, organisations, and events portrayed in this novel are either products of the authors' imagination or are used fictitiously. Any resemblance to actual persons, living or dead, is entirely coincidental.

© Neil Argue & Anita Hewlett 2024.
All Rights Reserved.

Neil Argue & Anita Hewlett assert the moral right to be identified as the authors of this work.

No part of this publication may be reproduced, stored in a retrieval system, or transmitted in any form or by any means without the prior written permission of the publisher, nor be otherwise circulated in any form of binding or cover other than that in which it is published and without a similar condition being imposed on the subsequent purchaser.

DEDICATION

For J & T

CONTENTS

COPYRIGHT ii
DEDICATION iii
CONTENTS 4
ACKNOWLEDGMENTS 5
PROLOGUE – A GIRL & HER DOG 7
CHAPTER ONE - A QUIET, WET DAY AT HOME 26
CHAPTER TWO - EIGHT DOLLARS & A BLANKET 57
CHAPTER THREE - ARRIVAL 83
CHAPTER FOUR - KIPPERS & KERFUFFLE 119
CHAPTER FIVE - COFFEE, CAKE & PENELOPE T 145
CHAPTER SIX - SEA BREEZES & OLD FRIENDS 184
CHAPTER SEVEN – CAPER & CONFUSION 215
CHAPTER EIGHT – PLYMOUTH HARBOUR 246
CHAPTER NINE – SNAKE & DAGGER 269
CHAPTER TEN – COLD & DARK 307
CHAPTER ELEVEN - THE POND 338
CHAPTER TWELVE - HELLO 357
CHAPTER THIRTEEN - NO LOOSE ENDS 399
EPILOGUE - ALMOND BISCUITS 407

ACKNOWLEDGMENTS

The cover design is our own, but it was only possible with the help of the following: Please support these wonderful, creative people in any way you can.

The French-themed graphic elements and backgrounds were courtesy of:

https://www.frenchkisscollections.com

The character illustrations were drawn by our friend, Kitty McEwan.

http://kittymcewan.co.uk

I would also like to thank Monica Byrne for her help and advice in the early stages of this project when I needed to figure out how to begin. She was gracious and patient in her assistance.

https://www.monicabyrne.org

Finally, our grateful thanks go to Kelvin Butcher for proofreading so enthusiastically and comprehensively.

"Whatever will be, will be." – Doris Day

PROLOGUE – A GIRL & HER DOG
Bickley, Seven Miles North of Plymouth, Devon, England

"Alfie!"

Little Jayne Brewer hurried to catch up to her friend, who seemed to know where he was going and wanted to get there as fast as possible. The hem of her dress was already damp from the wet, clumpy grass that got deeper as her dog ran further from the road. They'd only been this far from Plymouth twice before, and both times, it had been when Papa had visited Father Hopper at St Mary's Church. Mama had said he wanted them to move there, work the grounds, and help keep the church tidy, but Jayne loved Plymouth and the home where she had grown up. The idea of leaving Wimple Street and the cheery bustle of Plymouth worried her. Bickley was on the edge of Dartmoor, where the wind blew hard, and it always seemed to rain. She liked the people there, but the barren, wide-open spaces that stretched to the horizon held little interest to a young girl.

"Puppy!"

The black and white collie stopped briefly and looked back at her. Ears half a second behind the movement of his head, he bounded off again down the muddy lane. A hundred yards further on, he stopped once more to look back at her. She was no closer to him when she stopped to catch her breath.

"You have never been here before, you silly dog! How

could you be in quite such a hurry to get somewhere you have never been?"

Alfie barked and ran off again, tearing around a bend in the road and out of sight. Jayne looked down at her wet, dirty shoes, knowing they would dry before the fire but would never be truly clean again. Sighing heavily, she ran after him. Deep down, she knew it was not his fault to be curious and excited at new sights and smells, but even though he was almost five - a gift on her tenth birthday - the idea of losing him so far from home was too much to bear.

"ALFIE BREWER! WHEN I CATCH YOU, I WILL TIE YOU TO A TREE UNTIL THE VERY MOMENT WE CLIMB ONTO THE CART TO GO HOME!"

His bark didn't seem any further away than before, and when she turned the bend in the road, she saw him barely fifty feet ahead, nosing and sniffing about a dreadful scene. Her happiness at finally catching him up quickly disappeared when she saw the carriage on its side, broken and still. One horse was trapped on the ground by the weight and complexity of its harness; the stream of hot breath from its nostrils and tired, quiet cries of frustration told her it was alive, though. The other stood close by on the far side of the road, loose of its reins and eating grass as if it were a day like any other.

She ran quickly, covering the short distance, coming to a sudden stop when she saw two still bodies covered in mud at the side of the road. She had seen death before - when her Grandpapa passed away last year. He'd laid in the parlour the night before the funeral, his pale, still-handsome face looking out from the open coffin. She had sat with him for a while, Papa holding her hand while they talked about his life and what death meant to those left behind. She had tried her best to understand, but Grandpapa had been old her whole life, growing forgetful, weak and impatient as she grew up. By the time he died, he barely spoke unless it was in anger or frustration, and this was why his passing didn't upset her in the way she expected. She had saved her tears for happier memories - walking on The Hoe and watching the fishing boats together in the harbour.

Now, she knelt on the grass, unwilling to get any closer to the bodies, and called to Alfie. He looked up and happily wandered over, tail wagging. When he reached Jayne, she put her arms around his neck, and as always, his breath warmed her cheek, and his nose wet her ear. She closed her eyes and held onto him until she was ready to look at the people again.

"What shall we do, puppy?"

What would Papa want her to do? He would want her to go to him and be sensible and not be upset; after all, these people could not be helped, and she was not strong enough to help the horse by herself. In her head, she could see the loving face of her father and almost hear his firm, sensible voice.

Jayne climbed to her feet, letting go of Alfie, who ran to the other side of the carriage, barking as he went.

"Alfie! We must go to Papa, come here!"

He barked but, once again, didn't do as she asked. When she looked around the carriage, she saw him sniffing at another body and any frustration she felt disappeared. The man was dressed in a smart grey suit, unlike any she'd ever seen, which was now covered in grass and mud. Unlike the other two, he looked unharmed, and in the few moments before resting her palm on his chest, she clung to the hope that he was still alive. Regretfully, his body was unmoving and cold, leaving her nothing to do other than touch his cheek with the tips of her fingers.

"Oh, dear sir..."

A few feet away, Alfie was sniffing at the low drystone wall, blissfully unaware of the grim situation and happy to have found another interesting scent on a patch of ground he had never visited before. How she envied his ignorance at this moment.

"Oh, Alfie, you silly dog."

The soft grey hairs of the gentleman's moustache and sideburns brushed against her fingertips as she wondered about his life and if there was a family who would miss this kind-looking man. She was trying to imagine his smile and the sound of his laughter when she noticed his arm outstretched to the side and a pocket watch just inches from his open hand. It would be the slightest kindness, but her family had taught her that such things mattered, so she leaned over and picked up the watch.

The sudden, violent stab of pain took the breath from her lungs, knocking her backwards onto the grass. She tried to stand, but only her back straightened, snapping into painful rigidity, stretching every muscle in her body and pushing her arms out to the side almost to the point of breaking.

She cried out, but there was no sound, only a voice in her head and the brightest white light that made her eyes cry. It hurt so much that she could barely focus on what it said.

"Lah!"

It sounded desperate and upset – loud, but only in her head, and had a strange softness.

"Lah!"

Jayne's vision began to clear as the pain lessened; her body was exhausted as she tried to get to her feet, stumbling twice before standing. The voice was still there but quieter now - the same word, over and over.

Jayne pressed her fists to her temples.

"Quiet...please be quiet!"

For a moment, everything went silent as she gasped and wept quietly. The voice briefly returned but faded away as she finally opened her eyes.

"Ahsoof gid on...gid on...ahs..."

Now that she could focus, she felt her skin tingle and itch, but that, too, was fading. She was still unsteady, but she felt much better than before. Had she fainted?

"Alfie?"

Looking around her, everything had vanished - the carriage, the horses, the bodies, and her dog. The grey clouds were now white, and the sun was warm on the parts of her face not shaded by her bonnet.

"Alfie!"

Confused, she rested her back against the nearby drystone wall and rubbed her eyes with still-trembling fingers. Was she sick? Last Winter, she had been unable to leave her bed for a week, with a cold so heavy that her parents thought it was The Influenza, but even then, her body did not ache like this. She wanted her Papa and Alfie, too. The idea of him returning and not finding her made her cry.

"ALFIE! ALFIE!"

All her life, she had been told she was very grown up and sensible, but at this moment, she felt lonely and afraid enough to run away down the road to the village and her Papa. He would know what to do - he would hold her and tell her everything would be well. Mama would be upset about her dress and shoes, but that would be tomorrow. For now, she ran as fast as her legs would carry her towards the village.

By the time the church tower came into view, the running and sobbing had weakened her already tired body. As she got closer, she saw that the clock showed that it was almost four in the afternoon. How could this be? She had left for her walk not long after breakfast, and surely it hadn't been all day?

"Jayne! Miss Brewer!"

Father Crispin Hopper ran towards her, holding his cassock to his knees and moving with more agility than she would have expected from a man of his years. He reached the end of the path, opening the church gate so hard it slammed against the wall and dislodged some of the stonework. As he reached her, almost breathless, he flung his arms around her, kissing the top of her head. He smelled of wine and tobacco, and, most disturbingly, he was crying too.

"Praise The Lord! Praise him to the heavens! He gave you back to us!"

Jayne politely and gently extracted herself from his enthusiastic grasp.

"Father Hopper! I am quite well, thank you. Where is my Papa?"

"Oh, my child, we searched, and we searched. The whole village looked for so long, but we couldn't find you. Your Papa is at home with your dear Mama, both bereft of hope that you would ever return. Oh, Jayne, what a joy it is to have you back. Where did you go? Did someone take you? Are you injured?"

He continued to fuss, holding her at arm's length, looking her up and down, then fumbling at her body in a most inappropriate manner. She struggled against his touch, trying to step back against his strong arms, her impatience and frustration now evident.

"I am quite well, Father. I do not understand. After breakfast, I left for a walk with Alfie; we walked until we reached the Tavistock Road, then turned back down the farm road towards the village. Papa told me it was a mile and as far as we should go."

Jayne suddenly remembered the carriage and the bodies. How could she have forgotten? Her voice became eager and quick as the emotions and fear returned.

"There was a carriage! It was on its side, and there were people...they were dead, and a horse was trapped in its harness!"

Crispin Hopper's eyes were full of wonder and sadness, darting from side to side as she explained. He squeezed her shoulders gently, looking down with his kind, pale eyes as what little grey hair he had blew in the light breeze.

"Shhhh...calm yourself, Jayne, calm yourself. The carriage accident was some nine months ago. It was a tragedy, but such things happen. The carriage driver and his poor passenger are buried in the churchyard behind me. I assure you that both horses are uninjured and quite well in the lower field."

Jayne's face was suddenly pale, and she began to tremble, only faintly aware of Father Hopper's continuing tale. He continued, under the mistaken impression that to do so would calm her further.

"Today is the 23rd day of May, child. The evening sun is warm, and you have returned to us; that is all that matters. Louise will make us some supper, and tomorrow, I shall take you home to your family. I would send Noah to tell them now, but Solomon has thrown a shoe and cannot be ridden until it is mended in the morning. In any case, were he to leave now, he would not arrive before dark, and one does not travel the Tavistock Road after dark, no matter how glorious the message they carry. Now, let us wash your face and get some food inside you."

He led her to his cottage, just outside the church gate, where his housekeeper Louise would make them some hot stew. He was deeply troubled by her sudden reappearance and fragile state of mind. Food and a good night's sleep were what she needed, and while she slept, he would give the matter more serious consideration. She would see her parents again tomorrow, and things would begin to mend.

Inside the cottage, Louise embraced Jayne with possibly more enthusiasm than Father Hopper, praising God for quite what, Jayne still wasn't sure. Her stew was hot and filling, but their joyful conversation was confusing and did little but make her eyelids heavy. It was still light when Louise took Jayne upstairs to bed, hurriedly spreading new bed linen on Father Hopper's spare bed and warming the mattress with a pan of coals from the parlour hearth.

"No one has slept here since Father Gilbert on his way to Exeter last Easter, and I fear the stench of his tobacco will hang on the curtains long after I am in my grave. I will add a little lavender to your candle, Jayne. That may help."

"It is of no matter, Louise; it reminds me of my Papa's pipe."

Louise smiled a little awkwardly, pouring water into the

bowl on the oak dresser.

"Wash yourself, Jayne, and sleep. Tomorrow, you shall see your Mama and Papa."

Louise kissed Jayne on the forehead and rubbed her shoulder before leaving and closing the door behind her. Jayne looked at the door for a moment, the adults' conversation beginning before Louise reached the bottom of the stairs. She couldn't hear clearly, and when the parlour door closed, it became nothing but a dull murmur. What they were talking about was hardly a mystery, but she didn't care for now. She undressed, climbed into the musty, warm bed, and lay quietly until exhaustion overwhelmed her, and she fell asleep.

Just a few hours later, her eyes opened again. She lay there - warm and sad, remembering a cold winter's day - mist and frosty grass, running and laughing with her puppy.

"Alfie?"

By the sound of the third bark, she was out of bed and down the stairs, barefoot and dressed only in her white shift.

"Alfie!"

Louise had long since left for her own cottage on the other side of the green, but at the sound of Jaynes's footsteps, Father Hopper was soon after her down the stairs, lantern in hand.

"What is it, child? What is the matter?"

Hurriedly, Jayne slid back both door bolts and pulled the door open, the cold morning breeze blowing on her face.

"Puppy!"

Alfie jumped at her with enough force to push her back into the house, covering her face in licks and saliva. She giggled, half-heartedly pushing him away as he pawed at her. Father Hopper laughed.

"Twice in one day. We are indeed blessed!"

Who or what was genuinely responsible for Alfie's return didn't bother Jayne for now. All that mattered was her dog, his sniffing, his wet tongue, and the joyful tippy tapping of his claws on the wooden floor. Father Hopper closed the door, and they returned to their rooms. Alfie waited for Jayne to climb back into her bed before jumping up, bouncing, playing, and covering the blanket in dirty footprints.

"Go to sleep, you silly dog. Go to sleep."

At the slight change in her tone, he settled at her side, resting his head on her tummy and looking up at her face. She reached down and stroked his head, letting him lean into her hand.

"Oh, puppy, what has happened to us both? I want Mama and Papa, but I am not sure they will understand any more than Father Hopper or Louise."

Alfie looked up, unable to answer but happy to be with her again. Jayne stroked the top of his head, and within a few moments, they were both fast asleep.

Bickley, Seven Miles North of Plymouth, Devon, England

Outside, behind the trees on the village green, Elizabeth watched the happy reunion, remembering what it felt like to have a home, family, and people who cared. Hidden from view, she watched the door close and then the upstairs window until the happy voices went quiet, and the front bedroom light was extinguished.

"Goodnight, Jayne Brewer," she whispered.

Running her fingers through her long red hair, she turned away, strolling down the quiet, dark lane to the Tavistock Road. Her boots tapped on the dry mud beneath her feet. Once polished and black, they were now dirty and worn down by roads that couldn't get better quickly enough as far as she was concerned. She walked with both hands in the pockets of her long coat, the front undone, revealing the lace dress beneath. She had only walked a short distance when she looked up at the moon, smiled and spoke quietly in words that so few apart from her closest friend would understand.

"Proxime."

There was a rustle of leaves, a quiet growl and the padding of large, soft feet came from not far behind. Aramis was particularly adept at staying out of sight for such a large dog, but he was practised and knew how he must behave. He was at her side a few moments later, matching her pace.

"Now, where have you been? I told you to stay out of sight, not vanish from the face of the earth. I trust that whatever took your interest was worth the time. Was it a rabbit?"

She stroked his head, and he came as close to smiling as a dog of his noble bearing could ever do. He growled quietly, nuzzling his wet nose into her hand and licking her palm.

"I am pleased for you, but next time, restrain your curiosity and stay close by. I am all you have."

She winked at his shiny-eyed, happy face, confident that he knew the reverse to be true. He'd had a friend to play with for almost eight months, but now Alfie was back where he belonged.

The night was cold now, colder than usual for May, but their walk into Plymouth would be pleasant enough. Back at the boarding house, Mrs Thornton would grumble at the late hour of their return, but there was little Elizabeth could do to change that unless there was a cart going their way, which was unlikely at this time of night.

On reaching the Tavistock Road, she reached into her pocket, taking out an apple and a carrot. She took a small bite out of the former and passed the latter to the dog, who crunched at it quickly until only the green top was hanging from his mouth.

"You strike fear into the hearts of men with such ease, Aramis. If only those men could see you now, my love."

He looked up at her as he finished his snack, then suddenly looked past her, pricking his ears. Moments later, she heard a voice in the distance and a loud, tuneless song. The moon was bright—not bright enough for her to see the singer clearly yet, but he was getting closer. Aramis sniffed the air, growling quietly.

"Just once, it would be nice to enjoy a quiet walk home, would it not?"

She scratched his head with the tips of her fingers as she watched the man approach. Keeping her eyes on the lumbering, slightly unsteady figure, she spoke quietly.

"Circulus."

Aramis disappeared into the bushes and walked parallel to the road and Elizabeth. The dog's soft, heavy footfall was loud enough for the sober but lost in the gentle breeze to the drunk who approached. He still sang to himself, pausing only to put a large clay jug to his mouth.

She slowed her walk, wondering how long it would take him to notice her silhouette against the moonlight. He stopped less than 30 feet away, holding the jug against his leg, swaying slightly and looked her up and down, undressing her with his eyes. Unable to avoid his path, Elizabeth made the first move.

"Good evening, sir. Do you have enough cider to share?"

Now that he was close, she could see that he was a large, heavy-set man, broad at the shoulder and almost a foot taller than herself.

"I might. Who asks?"

"A thirsty traveller, a long way from her bed, sir."

He paused, taking a large swill of his drink, most of which poured down his smock.

"My bed is close by, maid."

"My father would not take kindly to a man who said such things."

"Then perhaps we shall not tell him."

He belched out a laugh that turned into a deep, guttural cough. Had he been sober, he would have wondered at such confidence and lack of worry in one so young, but for now, all he saw was a young girl, just shy of womanhood, alone on a dark road.

"It is a brave girl who walks this road alone at night."

"What I fear is none of your concern, sir, as I am sure the reverse is true."

Some of the confidence had left his voice, replaced with confusion. He tried but failed to hide it well.

"Nothing much around here scares me, least of all a girl who should know better than to talk to a man as you do."

She watched Aramis emerge from the hedge a short distance behind the man and stand silently on the road, unseen and unheard. She almost felt sorry for the drunk. Had he just walked by, she would have nodded and smiled

—even if his words had been ignorant and disrespectful. He was poor—possibly a farm labourer, enjoying what little his income could afford at a nearby Inn.

"Would that you had enough sense to offer a stranger a little courtesy, sir. Instead, you come crashing into my little world unbidden. Please let me be on my way."

Aramis growled more loudly this time, enough for the man to hear and precisely as required. He knew the part he must play on such occasions, and he played it well, baring his teeth and narrowing his eyes.

Elizabeth smiled as the drunk turned his head to see her handsome and loyal companion.

"Aramis is quick, sir. A surprising display of speed may see you to the end of the lane, but I wouldn't wager a farthing on the chances of you getting home to your bed, no matter how close it may be. Let me pass, and we shall both be on our way."

As he staggered forward, she sighed but remained rooted to the spot. It was quite literally the last thing he had expected. Elizabeth never looked for trouble, but it had a habit of finding her at the most inopportune moments. In a few hours, Mrs Thornton would ask how her evening went, and once again, she would lie. She always had to.

He took another drunken step forward, a hateful, familiar look in his eye, clearly having decided that there was nothing left to say.

"Oh, you foolish man. Is what you think you may take from

me truly worth what it will cost you?"

She sighed again, calmly running her fingers through her long hair.

"Aramis...sedeo."

Aramis sat down, tilting his head to the side, still and silent. Unlike Arthur Blundy, who was about to learn a simple but important lesson, he would watch and not be frightened. The drunk saw the fingers on Elizabeth's right hand stiffen and stretch for a moment; then, a bright orange glow grew slowly in her palm. Her whisper was too quiet for anyone else to hear, but that didn't matter. It was nothing but a memory from long ago, but it gave her strength and always made her smile.

"Run from me...and do not look back."

There was a silent flash of fire, and she was engulfed. She continued to stare at him, intense and constant, her head tilted forward and a slight smile on her lips. Arthur's screams were shrill - not loud enough to be heard at a great distance, but enough to take the breath from him and cause his heart to hammer, almost to the point of bursting in his chest. He stumbled backwards, falling onto his backside, the sharp stones in the road cutting through his threadbare trousers. Behind him, Aramis sat patiently, his eyes reflecting a familiar scene—flashes of colour and movement, stumbling and fear. They didn't always scream, but they always ran. Aramis knew he wasn't allowed to run after them unless she let him, and that wasn't very often.

Terrified, Arthur scrambled to get to his feet, dropping the jug of cider as he fled and taking with him a memory that would stay with him until he drew his last breath. He ran until his throat was dry and his limbs ached, but he never stopped or looked back. Patiently, Elizabeth and Aramis watched him go as the flames shrank to a brief flash in her palm. She wiggled her fingers, shaking off a feeling she had never gotten used to, and put the hand back into her coat pocket.

"I believe your home is in the other direction, sir..."

Arthur was too far away to hear, but a dear friend had once shown her the value of an acerbic comment, even at the most inappropriate moments.

The jug of cider still wobbled on the ground next to her, only steadied by her foot just before it would have toppled over. She reached down and lifted it to her mouth, smelling it briefly and taking several large gulps. It was thick, strong and not particularly well strained, causing her to gag briefly as bits of apple clogged her throat. When she had taken her fill, she wiped her hand across her mouth and threw the jug into the ditch.

"Oh, that is quite terrible."

Aramis stopped watching Arthur Blundy run away and stood, walking back slowly towards Elizabeth and rubbing against her leg when he got close enough. She scratched the top of his head; the sudden intake of alcohol made her chuckle and stumble a little as she did so.

"Good dog. You may have the next one, I promise."

She was mostly joking, but it was a joke for herself more than him. He understood her tone, mood, and sometimes her intent, but despite their many years together, he did not yet understand her sense of humour. He had brought down those who had threatened them more than once, but it was at her instruction and always as a last resort. Aramis was a large and imposing friend with a deep growl; often, that was enough to deter. When they lay asleep, and she felt his warm, comforting presence, it was difficult to imagine him capable of violence, but they had been as one for so long, and each would die for the other without a moment's hesitation.

Today had been a long day coming, but things had gone well. They still had a fair walk ahead of them, but like her dog, she didn't tire easily, and as her diary was clear for a while now that events in Bickley were concluded, they both had plenty of time. Inhaling deeply of the fresh night air, she slowly spun around, eyes on the moon and arms out to her side. Aramis barked and jumped backwards and forwards, feeling the joy return to his friend.

"Come, faithful hound, let us to Plymouth wander, where there is a kind but impatient woman, a warm bed, drink and maybe even a hot pasty for us to share."

Aramis barked loudly at the moon. He liked Pasties.

CHAPTER ONE - A QUIET, WET DAY AT HOME
Café Merle, Paris - Sunday, June 7th, 1908 - 4.14 am

The dirty, stray mongrel bared its teeth at the wet kitten. It wasn't angry or hungry; it was just being a dog, and the two large green eyes that stared back at it wouldn't change matters. The soft drizzle had soaked them both now, their coats glistening in the light of the nearby streetlamps.

With its shoulders dipped, the dog menacingly walked forward and barked twice, the force of which almost knocked the kitten over as it backed into the corner of the café steps. It was cold, wet, scared and had nowhere left to run on what would probably be the last day of its life.

High above, Francois lay in bed, now awake and seriously considering opening the bedroom window and shooing away the barking hound. Were he not so comfortable and warm, he may have done so, but not this morning.

The kitten was afraid and did what it could - rising on its toes, tail stiff and upright to appear as large and intimidating as possible. At less than eight weeks old, this was not very impressive and barely worth the bother of the stray dog, who was now only a few feet away, teeth bared, growling and focused. The kitten screeched in a desperate last attempt to scare the dog away, but the sound was lost in the rain.

The dog took one final step forward but unexpectedly saw only feathers and claws. Suddenly, it felt pain on its face and heard the screech of an angry crow. Again and again,

Boreas filled the space between the kitten and the dog with feathers and fury, quickly becoming too much for the dog to endure. In just a few seconds, its snout was covered in blood, forcing it to run away, whimpering as it crossed the square away from the bird.

Boreas landed, leaving his back to the kitten until he was sure the dog had gone. He turned around, tilting his head in an entirely unintentional impression of Imogen DiRossi. There was understanding and curiosity rather than concern in Boreas' black eyes as he took a few hops closer to the wet, furry animal. The kitten squeaked, apprehensive but less afraid now.

Boreas squawked, and the kitten replied, even though neither understood the other. Then, the bird spread its wings, and for a few moments, the kitten's feet no longer felt the wet cobbles, only a short, sharp pain on its back. As quickly as it had happened, the pain was gone as Boreas landed on a nearby table, sheltering them both from the rain under the café awning. The rain was gentler now, but the kitten still shivered in the cold. Tucking his wings tighter, Boreas felt it purr safely under his feathers. Patient and brave, Boreas tucked his head down and waited for her to come.

Grateful for the silence, Francois turned onto his side, found Monica's hand under the blankets and inched closer to her. Another hour and he would have to leave and go back to the concerns of a Café owner - the wine cart, the leaking kitchen window and the complaints of a rain-soaked vagrant, but not just yet. He was not one to fall asleep again easily once he had woken up, but he was happy to lie there and be satisfied with his life.

Still half asleep, Monica sighed and squeezed his hand.

Café Merle, Paris - Sunday, June 7th, 1908 - 6.45 am

Belle Veilleux skipped happily across the square, clutching a basket of white roses and smiling at everyone she passed. Smoke rising from the chimneys of Café Merle was one of many things that made her feel at home and ready for a busy day. Inside, there would be bread, coffee and the company of her friends, and she knew of no better way to start her day. As she got closer, she saw Boreas sitting on a table next to the door, looking not unlike a small loaf of bread.

"Good morning, Boreas. Are you well? Is it not past time for your breakfast?"

Comfortable in her cheerful presence, he allowed her finger to stroke his head, opening his beak alarmingly close to a smile. She giggled and made for the door when there was a muffled squeak, causing Belle to turn at the noise and search for the source.

"Boreas?"

The crow squawked, turning his head to face her, but he remained in place, almost as if glued to the table. As she walked back, she realised his left side bulged more than the right. Carefully, she lifted his bulging wing, cautious that Boreas was injured. She was unprepared for the small, furry, black face peeking up at her.

"Oh, my dear thing!"

Boreas stood, reassured by her tone, revealing the kitten. He stepped away, alternating his gaze between Belle and his new friend. She picked it up, cradling it in her free hand and pushing the café door open with her knee. At the last moment, she turned back to Boreas, who hopped about like a concerned parent on the table.

"Come, Boreas, I think our new friend is hungry."

Boreas squawked, waited for the door to open wide enough, then flew in, landing on the counter. As usual, his claws caused him to slide a short distance before coming to a stop against the arm of Belle's best friend, Bryonie Jewell. Even after three months, few café customers were entirely used to Boreas' frequent appearances inside, but Bryonie was more used to it than most. Despite this, she still spilt a little of her coffee and squealed, causing Boreas to jump backwards in surprise. For a moment, they both stared at each other, Bryonie's friendly raised eyebrow and Boreas' open beak in something of a deadlock.

"You clumsy, handsome bird! Were I not completely in love with you, I might be upset."

Boreas squawked and hopped closer, bowing his head to her stroking fingers.

Belle and Bryonie had been friends since school, but their lives had taken a very different direction. Despite their friendship, Belle understood little of Bryonie's chosen profession, and apart from an occasional stray comment, her friend was the picture of discretion, as were all of the girls who lived and worked at The Flaming Tiger - Madame Amelie Bonheur's establishment. Few disapproved of what went on there - certainly no one in the café, but it was seldom the topic of everyday conversation. Belle knew that her friend was happy, and that was enough. Bryonie was still stroking Boreas when she noticed the kitten in Belle's arms.

"Belle, who is this?"

"This is a new friend and a hungry, wet one at that! Anton? Maria?"

As Belle passed the kitten to Bryonie, who held it to her chest and tickled the top of its head, Maria appeared from the kitchen, her eyes widening as she saw their new guest.

"A towel, please, Maria and perhaps something for..."

Belle paused and lifted the kitten's tail.

"...her to eat."

A few minutes later, three doting women gathered around the kitten as it tucked into a plate of cheese. Anton appeared from the kitchen, having finished sweeping the backyard, squeezing his wife gently around the waist and looking over her shoulder at the hungry animal.

"I am not sure Francois would approve, my love."

"Approve of what?"

Francois wiped his feet on the doormat, removing his hat as he did so. It was still raining, and his coat glistened after his short walk from next door. He heard a squeak, noticed the kitten and sighed at the idea of yet another animal moving into his home. Then he saw what remained of his finest Camembert on the small plate. Before he could speak, Imogen emerged from what was, until recently, Francois' office. Behind her, the casual observer would see a tidy, cluttered pile of equipment and plants swiftly hidden by the closing door. Shortly after she had entered into a partnership with Francois, her need for more space became evident, and he happily agreed to vacate his office. With the help of Jacques LeGrande, the room would soon suit her requirements completely. At the sight of Imogen, Belle leaned around Bryonie.

"Lady Imogen! We have a new friend!"

She picked up the kitten to show Imogen, squeezing its now full tummy. Protesting, the kitten opened its mouth and belched loudly. It blinked slowly, fascinated and curious, as its eyes met Imogen's. Tilting her head slightly, Imogen smiled as the kitten mirrored her movements. Putting the tip of her finger close to its nose, it flicked its tongue against her skin, and that was that. Everyone knew that the little creature had found its forever home. Francois looked closer at the kitten and put his hat back on his head.

"It seems that I must restock my larder. We have a new mouth to feed and one that shares my taste for the finer things in life."

Imogen looked up briefly.

"You make that sound like a bad thing, Francois. Be of good cheer. A welcome to all."

Francois doffed his hat at the group and favoured Imogen with a raised eyebrow as he left. Bryonie stepped down from her stool, adjusting her dress as she did so.

"I shall perhaps see you all again tomorrow. Madame Amelie expected my return almost an hour ago, and I must prepare for my evening. The Flaming Tiger hosts several important guests; we must all look our best. Councillor and Madame Lemaire always insist that I wear fresh blue stockings, and it is not for me to question those that put food on my table and these charming earrings on my lobes."

She tapped one earring, kissed Belle on the cheek and half-curtseyed to everyone else before leaving. As usual, the bell above the door failed to tinkle as it shut, but Francois had long since stopped worrying about it. The kitten cared little for Bryonie's parting comments, but the others wondered in their own way at Bryonie's evening and life in the city they called home. Belle climbed onto the recently vacated stool and stroked the cat's head with her finger.

"What is her story, do you think, Lady Imogen?"

Imogen furrowed her brow a little.

"On several occasions over the last few months, I have noticed a pregnant cat on the back road. I attempted to catch it to ensure its health, but it ran into the park. If this is one of its offspring, I fear the mother is long gone or worse. A mother does not usually abandon her child without reason. In any case, we have milk and Francois' cheese."

Belle chuckled, easily impersonating Jacques' oft-heard greeting.

"A welcome to all!"

Imogen stood, nodded politely and scooped up the kitten. As she turned away, she was already in deep conversation with her new friend.

"Indeed. Now, Madame, let me have a good look at you, away from the gaze of others…tell me, little one, are you quite well? Are you?"

There was a quiet squeak as the study door closed behind her, leaving Belle to place a fresh rose in the vase on each table, twirling slowly and singing quietly to herself as she did so.

After kissing his wife on the cheek, Anton took his broom outside to sweep away the debris of last night's rain from the front cobbles, leaving Maria to wipe the counter before returning to her oven to check on the first batch of bread.

Café Merle, Paris - Sunday, June 7th, 1908 - 9.55 am

Francois sat on a recently emptied packing crate, barely recognising what was, until recently, his office. Not long after Imogen had decided to make her home at the café, she'd sent several telegrams, and a few weeks later, the first heavily loaded cart appeared outside. Yesterday morning, the last of three such carts had arrived, and what little free space in the cellar there was had now been lost to books, crates and all manner of mysterious items.

No sooner had Francois vacated his office than Jacques LeGrande had covered the bare walls with sturdy shelves and racks. As Francois sat watching, Imogen carefully and quietly arranged bottles and flasks in what seemed to be a very specific order. The room smelled fragrant and strange and was decorated with many unusual ornaments and hangings - the largest of which was an old wooden sign, half a meter in length, hanging high on the wall opposite her desk. The red lettering was faded but still readable.

Great Danger - Keep Out

"Imogen, is all this quite safe?"

"Safe? Whatever do you mean?"

Francois pointed to the sign.

"I am rather fond of my...our...the café, and I would hate to see it vanish in a puff of yellow smoke."

Imogen tutted and walked over to the sign, nudging the bottom left corner with a finger and then taking a step back to consider its alignment.

"It is a memento, nothing more. It was a gift from Nikola many years ago—generous but impractical, something of a habit in his case. It has been in storage for almost five years, but now I have sufficient wall space on which to hang it."

"It is a little…out of place with everything else here."

"It was displayed outside his temporary workshop almost twenty-three years ago, on the day I first met him. To my young mind, such a sign told of something I had spent my entire life looking for. Its presence here is a reminder of things hoped for."

Francois smirked at the image of an eager young Imogen, throwing caution to the wind.

"So young and yet so sure. Why am I not surprised?"

Imogen turned around and smiled, cheered at the memory, and even more cheered at having someone with whom to share it.

"Nikola leaned around the door of his workshop very suddenly and terrified the breath from my lungs. My mother leapt to my defence, and there was something of a scene."

"I can only imagine."

"You could try, but I doubt you would succeed. My mother

howled like a wolf and struck him with a small copper shovel, rendering him unconscious for almost thirty minutes. The scar is still with him today, as is, he claims, an ability to know when it is about to rain. He is convinced the two are connected."

"Oh my."

"Indeed. Fortunately, all was eventually settled over a pot of herbal tea."

"That sounds very civilised."

"One of my mother's more…relaxing blends. I believe there was rather a lot of cocoa leaf powder in it."

"Imogen?"

"It was laced with Cocaine, Francois. My mother drugged one of the finest scientific minds of our age in the hope that he would forget that she attacked him with a shovel."

"Did it do the trick?"

"No, it did not."

Imogen picked up another flask, sniffed the open top, pushed in a cork stopper, and wrote something on the label.

"To this day, I wonder what astonishing and vital invention the world has been denied because Nikola Tesla wasted three days of his extraordinary life dancing about his workshop like an excited gibbon."

It was a striking mental image, and Francois took several moments to dismiss it. She turned her back to him once more and continued tidying as Francois stood, peered closely at a bubbling flask of purple liquid, and tapped it with the tip of his finger. Immediately, it belched, and white smoke poured over the rim. Imogen's slap on the back of his hand was gentle but arrived with the suddenness of a slamming door.

"Leave it! When my study is more settled, I shall give all those here a suitable induction. Until then, you must be cautious. There are things in here best left to those who possess a firm grasp of botany, chemistry and the sciences in general."

"I shall endeavour to stay out of the way whenever possible, Imogen."

"Francois, this is your home; I merely wish you to remain well. Armed with a cautious manner and a keen mind, life-threatening injury is unlikely."

"Unlikely?"

There was a squeak. Imogen tutted quietly, chuckled, and turned around, holding a happy kitten by the scruff of the neck.

"Please, Francois. It seems you are not the only one in an overly curious mood today."

Francois awkwardly took the kitten and grasped her in the manner of one who had never held a living creature before.

"Ow! The beast is feeding on me."

"Oh hush, she is merely experimenting with her teeth. How else will she learn to make her way in the world if she cannot playfully feast on your plump digits? Besides, it is scarcely her fault that you taste of cheese, is it?"

He sat back down on the crate, the creature's small, sharp teeth still clamped to his thumb. Imogen nodded with satisfaction at his obvious discomfort, and all was once more merely unusual. Increasingly, this was the best that Francois could hope for. With her back to him, Imogen continued about her business, talking to herself as she arranged the items on the shelves. As the weeks passed, they had both grown more used to each other's ways, and any discomfort or awkwardness in silence had long since vanished. After almost fifteen minutes, during which Francois had managed to make the kitten fall asleep, Imogen spoke.

"In answer to your previous enquiry, Francois - yes, this is all quite safe."

As he watched, Imogen wrote the word 'Poison' on a large bottle of blue fluid and described an elegant skull and crossbones underneath. She placed the bottle on the shelf with the other bottles, stepped back, and again nodded with satisfaction. Then, she walked through the open patio doors, returning almost immediately with a large plant pot. She put it down on the floor, just next to the desk and began to trail the long vine and its white and green leaves along the shelves above.

"That is quite impressive, Imogen. What is it?"

"Epipremnun Aureum - more commonly known as Pearl and Jade or The Devil's Ivy. It will thrive in relatively low sunlight, requires surprisingly little water, and generally keeps itself to itself."

She fussed about, fanning out the leaves until she was satisfied.

"The Devil's Ivy?"

"When dried, finely ground and combined with several other powders, the leaves make a particularly foul tea that will induce violent and uncontrollable vomiting even in those possessing of the sturdiest constitutions. However, as you can see, for now, it is content merely improving the ambience of my study."

"Do you often have cause to make people vomit?

Imogen continued to pull at the leaves, talking to them as much as to Francois.

"If administered promptly, vomiting will eject poison from the body with sufficient rapidity to prevent serious harm or even death."

"It works quickly?"

She spun around, smiling, wiggling both eyebrows and holding up a small glass vial of pale green powder.

"Yes, very, and as you have probably surmised, it can be used to incapacitate. A body convulsing and bent double can do little else. It is not ideal, however - first, you must ensure the recipient inhales or swallows enough. It has a strong flavour and tends to turn food a rather obvious shade of green."

After holding it up to the light for a few seconds, she lifted her dress and inserted the vial into an empty leather slot in her leggings, just below the knee, then let the dress drop again.

"Imogen, you told me that your mother helped the sick and ailing from the back of her cart, but I have seen so much more from you. You have always spoken of her with something less than fondness, but it seems she taught you well."

Her smile lessened, eyes looking past Francois as if lost in the past for a moment. To his credit, Francois had not mentioned her mother often, but she still felt strange and a little uncomfortable when he did. Since deciding to make the café her home, she had grown to trust him, but she was still not used to someone other than Nikola Tesla knowing her even slightly well. Nikola was precise, factual and only occasionally sentimental.

"My mother did not need such things, but a curious young woman making her way across Europe alone is another matter entirely. I was equipped with what she had taught me, and I met others who added to my knowledge, but for the most part, I learned to protect myself. The forests and the plants therein were almost all I needed; the rest could be obtained relatively easily."

Imogen's focus returned, and she picked up a nearby bowl of white powder, stirring it slowly with her index finger.

"It has always been easier to frighten or confuse than actually harm anyone, but some are not easily scared."

In less time than it took to blink, she threw a pinch of the powder into the air, and it exploded with a bright yellow puff of smoke. It made almost no sound and was gone as quickly as it came; the only indication that it had happened was a gentle shower of black soot. Francois was startled enough to wake the kitten, but not as much as he would have been three months ago.

"Very funny, Imogen. What is that?"

He pointed at her left wrist, presumably the source of the flame. Imogen turned her hand over to reveal what looked like a small brass bracelet, from which now protruded a short metal spike. A wire ran from the bracelet down to a tiny thimble over her thumb. She moved her thumb ever so slightly; there was a loud click, and a small, bright yellow flame appeared at the end of the spike. She moved her thumb again, twice more, and a flame appeared each time.

"Not quite up to Nikola's standards, but it possesses a simple elegance. Potassium Chlorate and Red Phosphorus, a spark and a few items salvaged from my glove."

Imogen pulled her sleeve down a little, covering up the bracelet, then reached over and took the kitten from him, stroking its head with her finger as Francois brushed soot from his trousers.

"Imogen, as you know, I defer to no one in my admiration of your technical proficiency, but a box of matches would seem a far simpler solution."

"I agree; however, my device offers two distinct advantages over Monsieur Pasch's crowning moment."

"Pasch?"

Imogen tutted gently.

"Gustaf Eric Pasch, inventor of The Safety Match. Sweden. 1844."

"Ah."

Francois nodded, already well on the way to forgetting that tidbit of information.

"Advantages?"

"Firstly, my device is waterproof, and secondly, I will no longer have to visit Monsieur LeClerc's tobacconist's shop and endure his mumbling appreciations."

Francois tried and failed to stifle a laugh.

"Ernst LeClerc is 81 years old, Imogen."

"Yes, and despite his years, it seems the fires of amorous passion still burn hot within him."

"He has a wooden leg and only one good eye, Imogen. A sudden step to the left and a brisk walking pace will see you safely escape his attention."

"Perhaps."

Imogen frowned and brushed soot from her chest as Francois watched and considered the extraordinary woman before him.

"Are there any others out there like you, Imogen DiRossi? Is it likely the chairs outside our café will one day give comfort to another?"

"I should hope not. Your life is more than interesting enough already."

Francois moved to the bookshelf on the opposite side of the room. The books were a mixture of the factual and the frivolous - the scientific brushing shoulders with the likes of Jules Verne. As he neared the end of the lowest shelf, Francois pulled out a large book that didn't seem to belong. On opening it, he discovered what appeared to be a diary, full of clippings and juvenile scribbles. He slapped it shut quickly.

"Forgive me, Imogen; I did not intend to pry."

Imogen took the book from him, opening it as she did so.

"I have no secrets here, Francois. This is one of my scrapbooks - my first, in fact. My childhood was a solitary one for the most part, so when something took my interest, I tended to obsess a little."

She turned to the first page, running her fingers over the elegant script. Francois read the words aloud.

The Crimes of Jack the Ripper, Whitechapel, London, 1888. A Comprehensive Thesis on The Subject of Evil and

The Violently Disturbed

"I was almost twelve.", said Imogen, "which perhaps explains the absent definite article. My English grammar was not all it could be."

"English?"

"Yes, my mother considered it wise that I learn it as soon as possible, and as more than half of my books were in English, I agreed. We met many English speakers on our travels, and I had ample opportunity to practice."

Francois smiled at the idea of a precocious twelve-year-old girl already on her way to understanding the world.

"How long was it before you were fluent?"

"Almost six months. I was a child far too easily distracted."

"It took me almost a year, surrounded by the good people of Place St Genevieve, to grasp conversational French. I have been told that English is particularly difficult to learn - present company excepted, of course."

"There are some things I find difficult, Francois; language is simply not one of them."

"Such as?"

"I once took Cello lessons."

Francois waited for further explanation, but none came. Imogen took a pencil from her waist pocket, wrote the word "The" in front of "Evil", and made a slight noise of satisfaction.

"So…Jack The Ripper…a rather gruesome topic for a young girl."

"Yes, but I was twelve years old and already determined to protect my mother and myself from such men. I was not entirely sure how to do such a thing or how likely it was that we would encounter such a creature on the muddy roads of northern Italy, but…"

"I have no doubt your study was thorough. Did you reach any useful conclusions?"

Imogen chuckled.

"No. I must confess I wasted my blossoming intellect on the more lurid stories and sketches, but essentially, it was those that taught me the most. It seemed that the poor women were either surprised and quickly overwhelmed or so desperate for their next meal that they risked everything."

Her voice drifted away, Imogen's thoughts elsewhere for a few moments.

"No man will ever put a knife to my throat or threaten those in my company without consequence."

Francois watched Imogen's face, waiting for the right moment to respond, and remembered the dagger slipping into her hand and twirling around her fingers that night by the fire months ago. She seemed somewhere else for a short while - somewhere Francois didn't feel like he belonged. After a moment, she sighed and patted his back as if to tell him she had returned.

"For the entirety of The Ripper's campaign of terror, I found out what I could, mostly from newspapers and word of mouth. As you say, it was a somewhat gruesome fascination for a young girl, but I do not consider it time entirely wasted."

"Neither do I, Imogen."

"Quite so."

Francois put both hands behind his back and casually wandered over to the other side of the room, keeping a respectful distance from the many and varied items. He recognised José Garcia's journals, now neatly piled and sorted, remembering the musty château cellar and that exciting, exhilarating few days following Imogen's arrival at the café. A caw from Boreas brought Francois back to the present. He flew in through the open patio doors and landed on the end of Imogen's desk, dropping a small piece of lavender. Imogen picked it up, smelled it and dropped it into a small vase on the shelf, which already contained several other small plants and flowers. Francois noticed a small label on the vase - 'Boreas'.

"Thank you, kind sir."

Boreas squawked, then looked at Francois with his usual curious intensity.

"Hello, Boreas. Another gift for Imogen?"

Her back to Francois, Imogen smiled.

"At least twice a day. It is not unusual for an intelligent animal to do such a thing; crows are especially cooperative with those they trust."

"He seems to regard you with a lot more than trust, Imogen. He has done as you asked on more than one occasion - you have spoken, and he has complied. At first, I thought it was a coincidence or some trick, but…"

Boreas stared intently at Francois, tilting his head this way and that and shuffling his feet on the desk. Imogen looked at him, across to Francois and then back again.

"Boreas does as he pleases, Francois. It just so happens that our lives walk a similar path, nothing more."

Francois was unconvinced, but it was apparent he would make no headway with this discussion, for now at least. Imogen put her hand flat on the desk, and Boreas walked up to her shoulder until they were both looking at Francois with uncomfortably similar expressions on their faces. For the moment, defeated, he turned his attention to a bowl full of dark pink powder. He leaned in and thoroughly sniffed, causing a small rose-coloured cloud to puff into his face.

"What is this, Imogen? It looks and smells rather potent."

Imogen crept up behind him, looking over his shoulder at the bowl. Boreas, too, leaned in, effortlessly maintaining his grip on Imogen's shoulder.

"That is a preparation of my own invention. 'Juliet's Whimsey' is a delicate blend of flower extracts and sundry minerals, the ingestion of which will cause an individual to hopelessly and irresistibly fall in love with the next person they encounter, regardless of any existing romantic attachment."

Francois stood up straight with almost enough force to snap his spine. Turning around, he found Imogen staring him in the face and close enough to smell her breath. His look of abject terror and the small amount of dark pink powder around his nostrils were almost enough to make her smile.

"It is a nutritional supplement for my Orchids, you ridiculous man."

Francois suddenly sneezed, covering Imogen's chest, Boreas and the kitten with nutritional supplement. As she stepped back, just in time to avoid the second sneeze, Boreas flew out of the open door.

"Proof, if proof were needed, that you must take care when you come through my door."

Francois looked up at his usually dignified friend, her chest, face, and hair lightly dusted with pink powder.

"I shall do as you ask."

"Thank you."

With her free hand, Imogen picked up a small pile of books and walked past Francois through the open study door. He followed her up the stairs, both pairs of shoes tapping on the wood as they went.

"I will keep these in my room. Now that I am more settled, perhaps I will find the time to catch up on my reading. I fear the time wasted on Conan Doyle's latest drivel is lost to me forever, though."

Francois felt the first inklings of a tirade as she continued.

"I realise that your request that I revisit his inexplicably popular detective was well-intentioned, but once again, I lost interest long before he lit his first pipe."

"I understand the lighting of his second pipe is where the narrative usually takes flight."

"I shall have to take your word for it, as I have neither the time nor inclination to 'learn all that is learnable' at the feet of Mr Sherlock Holmes. Quite honestly, I am surprised you have the patience to endure the tedious, meandering prose. Doyle sacrifices brevity and clarity on the altar of needless verbiage. Why should he limit himself to three words when he has fourteen at his disposal?"

Francois wasn't even sure if she was still speaking to him at this point, but he was enjoying the almost manic display of displeasure and frustration.

"Can you imagine a life such as theirs, Francois? The pompous intellectual leading the eager, charming and supportive friend about the world as they stumble from one adventure to another?"

"It sounds ghastly, Imogen."

"Indeed, it does."

Francois stopped at the top of the stairs as Imogen wandered down the hallway and entered her room. Out of sight, she lowered the kitten onto the bed. After walking in a small circle several times, it lay down and yawned.

"I ask you, Francois. Listen to this."

As he walked slowly towards her door, she emerged again, flicking through the pages of the book he had only recently recommended. She slid her fingertip across the words, searching for the relevant phrase.

"Ah. Here we are...."

Francois steeled himself, still wondering why this particular author frustrated her so. Her clipped, precise attempt at the accent of a stiff, intellectual detective did not disappoint.

"How often have I said to you that when you have eliminated the impossible, whatever remains, however improbable, must be the truth?"

Francois poked the angry bear with a large stick.

"I have always found that a reasonable and somewhat fascinating conclusion."

Imogen slammed the book shut and disappeared again into her room just as Francois arrived in the doorway. She dropped "The Return of Sherlock Holmes" onto the bed from such a height that it caused the kitten to bounce three times. Still mumbling to herself, she lifted her skirt from her ankles and stepped onto the only chair, having pushed it close to the shelves above her bed.

"It is perfectly acceptable to simply not know. The phrase 'we do not know' has led to landmark discoveries in all branches of science. Doyle is a buffoon, and I will not be convinced otherwise, even by you."

Francois opened his mouth to speak, but she quickly twisted around and looked at him over her shoulder.

"I intended that as a compliment."

"I took it as such."

Imogen stepped down to the floor and opened a second book with a plain white cover and sizeable black lettering. She skimmed through the first few pages, her recent mood disappearing as quickly as it had arrived.

"A favourite, Imogen?"

"This belonged to my late husband and was a permanent fixture on his bedside cabinet. I never saw him read and often wondered at his attachment to it. As I left that night, something made me take it."

"A memento?"

"Not of him, but possibly of the room or the house. Perhaps it is a connection to the last place I called home. I am not normally one for sentimentality, but I kept it, nonetheless."

She closed the book and held it out, briefly looking around the room before returning her gaze to Francois.

"Please. I have no further need for such a reminder."

"Imogen?"

"Perhaps it will find a home on your bedside cabinet."

Francois took the book, smiling at the title, then looked up and saw Imogen do the same.

When The Sleeper Wakes - H.G. Wells

"Why, Imogen DiRossi, what is left of me that remains hidden from that keen eye?"

Imogen closed one eye, put a small magnifying glass over the other, and glared at him through a comically enlarged eyeball. He had no idea where the magnifying glass had come from. The overly clipped accent returned.

"One may not quantify the unknown or know what is…not laid out before us, Wilson."

"Watson."

"Pardon?"

"Sherlock Holmes' most trusted friend is Doctor John Watson. Aside from that small fact, your pastiche was most impressive."

She lowered the magnifying glass, slipping it into a pocket on the hip of her dress.

"Thank you; however, I was overconfident and stumbled at the conclusion."

"I shall share your embarrassment with no other."

Imogen bowed her head slightly, resting her palm on her heart.

"You are the soul of discretion, sir."

Francois opened the book and flipped through the first few pages. It smelled a little musty from years in storage but seemed as crisp as the day it was first printed. Imogen sat on the bed, stroking the sleeping kitten and looking up at Francois as he closed the book.

"I know him to be a favourite of yours. You must have most of Wells' works on your shelf, but I have not seen this."

"No, but I intended to purchase a copy at some point."

"Then you will be a few Francs richer, and I will have more room on my shelves. This is a satisfactory outcome for us both."

Francois looked around her room, recognising almost nothing of what was formerly Anton and Maria's room. Imogen had only replaced the last of the two pictures this week, stamping her unique presence on the walls. Three weeks ago, Anton and Maria had moved to a small apartment across the square, above Madame Tomas's Bistro. They had insisted that it was only appropriate that Imogen take their room at the cafe, and she did not object.

However, she insisted on paying their rent - a logical and obvious solution for Imogen. For their part, Anton and Maria loved their new accommodation. It was far more extensive and luxurious than they had experienced in their long lives. Of course, they still opened the café just after dawn and walked home together long after dark, but as they often said, the café was their life as much as it was Francois', and he was powerless to change this.

"I struggle to recognise what once was, Imogen. Life moves on apace, does it not?"

"I trust you approve of my alterations."

"Yes, but the café is as much your home as it is mine now. Your room is yours to do with as you please."

Imogen nodded, still unused to such freedom and unsure what to say. It had only been a few months, but she felt at home here.

"I am happy here, Francois."

Francois answered with a broad smile, understanding what it meant for Imogen to say such a thing, and looked down at the sleeping animal.

"As it seems, is our newest friend. She is staying with us?"

"Yes, she seems content to do so and clearly has nowhere else to go. Unless you object?"

He looked down at the peaceful pile of fur on Imogen's bed, well aware of the comfort it gave her.

"No, of course not. She is one more mouth to feed, but a small one. In return for her board and lodging, we shall no doubt be free of mice and other vermin."

"Have you seen any such vermin since I arrived?"

He thought for a moment.

"Actually, no. Now that you mention it, the traps have been vacant."

"A delicate blend of cinnamon, cloves, peppermint and chilli is usually enough to deter the most determined intruder. After a brief period of observation, I selected the most appropriate locations to deploy my countermeasures. I made no secret of my movements, Francois. I am surprised you did not notice."

"I find it best not to enquire as to your every move, Imogen. I'm not particularly eager to fuss, as you know. However, you will have seen me pointlessly checking my traps each morning."

"Mmmmm."

Imogen brushed a small amount of dust from her dress front, doing her best to hide her amusement, and quickly changed the subject.

"I think the time has come for electricity in the upper two floors of our home, and I believe our business accounts are healthy enough to justify the expense despite Monsieur LeGrande's continued abuse of our generosity."

"I haven't the heart to turn him away, especially since

recent events at The Château. He is old, Imogen, and lives in a shack. I find myself less and less willing to be bothered by him with every passing day."

"It was not a criticism. His work continues to be satisfactory and more than justifies his salary."

"You have been paying him? The devious old fool! He continues to plead poverty at our counter, and I assumed his continued assistance in moving your belongings deserved a daily meal at the very least."

They walked out of Imogen's room and past the bathroom. Francois paused briefly to consider that the lavatory lay directly above Imogen's study and her arsenal of potions and chemicals. A violent, fiery death whilst taking his first ease of the day was an uncomfortable thought at best.

"Despite what you may think, Francois, Jacques LeGrande is a proud man and is not one for charity for the most part. It seems, in your case, he makes an exception."

"Henri Maison was fending Jacques LeGrande off with a broom long before I first set foot in Place St Genevieve, Imogen; his fascination is with the café, not me. I am confident he will end his days near or indeed inside our home, probably dining on one of our baguettes."

"Very probably."

At the foot of the stairs, Imogen disappeared into her study, already planning the locations of electric lamps on the landing and in their rooms, whilst Francois put another pot of coffee on the stove.

CHAPTER TWO - EIGHT DOLLARS & A BLANKET
Café Merle, Paris — Wednesday, June 10th, 1908 - 2.26 pm

For the third consecutive day, the rain outside fell heavily on Place St Genevieve, something Imogen found peaceful and calming, along with the deep, pungent odour of coffee, her fresh newspaper and the comforting crackle of the open fire behind her. To her side, on the blue and white checked tablecloth, lay the newest member of The Café Merle family, its eyes closed, its belly rising and falling slowly, and a gentle purr on its lips. Boreas rested on top of the coat stand, his dark eyes watching the café and the patrons within, but mostly the small furry animal on the table.

All was well in the world of Imogen DiRossi. Almost.

Across the table, Francois Meyer sniffed, blew his nose, and returned the crumpled handkerchief to his waistcoat pocket.

"Pick a card, Imogen, any card."

He was attempting to look sophisticated and mysterious as Imogen peered over pages four and five of her newspaper. She reached out and took a card, keeping the face to herself.

"Please memorise it."

"One card? I believe I can manage that."

She narrowed her eyes, aware of several more acerbic responses that would result in the sort of gentle tutting she had come to find so endearing in the months since she had arrived at the café. Instead, she favoured her friend with a wink and prepared to be underwhelmed. She was well aware that this latest obsession would further hinder Francois' study of Latin, but she lived in an imperfect world.

"Return it to the pack if you please."

Imogen did as he asked, and Francois shuffled the pack with surprising skill, dropping only three cards. Their recent evening at the theatre, witnessing the illusional stylings of "The Great Strombo", had sent Francois into a whirl of childish excitement and instilled a newfound enthusiasm for the magical arts. She was confident it would only be a matter of time before he affected a garish turban adorned with a giant question mark.

He lay the pack face down before him, forcing her to lower the newspaper to see. Not possessing a wand, he had improvised with a silver cigarette holder from the lost property box and tapped the deck twice, triumphantly turning over the top card.

"Your card is the three of hearts."

Imogen was outwardly calm as she quietly replied, but Francois could hear surprise in her voice.

"Yes...yes, it was..."

"Voilà!"

Francois' chest swelled, and he patted it with both palms

as if he had just eaten too much chocolate cake. Imogen quickly but tidily put down her newspaper, taking care to avoid the sleeping kitten, and picked up the deck, fanning out the cards with a mixture of surprise and frustration. Her voice, though, was as calm as ever.

"Francois...that is somewhat impressive."

"Calm yourself, Imogen; please do not make a scene. Think of our customers."

Jacques LeGrande snored at the far end of the café, his head face-down on his usual table next to a cold, half-cup of coffee. As he had yet to pay, it would be premature to consider him a customer, so Francois' moment of triumph was wasted on a small animal and one of the hardest women in all of France to impress.

Imogen continued to examine the cards, eventually reshuffling them with all the skill of a casino croupier and handing them back.

"Please. Again."

Francois feigned a polite refusal, waving his hand gently.

"We magicians never repeat our..."

"Hush. Again."

As before, she chose a card and returned it to the deck. This time, however, Imogen leant forward, her fingers steepled and her eyes watching every movement of his fingers.

"The six of clubs!"

She sat back in the chair with enough force to wake the kitten, who lifted its small head and squeaked. Francois flashed it a look, and it squeaked again, getting to its feet and stretching its front, then back legs. Finally, it rested its bottom on the clean tablecloth and stared at Francois intently. Imogen quickly rummaged through the cards, muttering to herself. This alone gave Francois more than a little satisfaction. After the third performance, Imogen was no closer to understanding.

"Francois, I am intrigued. I must know how..."

Once more, Francois interrupted.

"No, Imogen. I will not give up my secrets. Not all of us are granted the ability to mystify. Perhaps you must accept that I am gifted and leave it at that."

Once more, her eyes narrowed, and she picked up the kitten, nestling it against her chest and stroking its head with two fingers.

"Perhaps, Francois Meyer, perhaps..., however, if you would be so kind, please think of a number between 1 and 1000."

Francois smirked. Imogen wasted not a second more than necessary.

"37."

"I was not ready."

"Francois, it is an established fact that a significant majority of those asked to choose a number between 1 and 50 will choose 37 on the first attempt. I allowed you a mental canvas sufficient to indulge your imagination, and you failed to seize the moment. Choose again."

He stared at her, reasonably sure that he had not been insulted but not entirely sure. An endless stream of random and numerous digits ran through his mind. All the time, she calmly studied his face and stroked the black furry belly that now presented itself to her fingers. Francois' face calmed, and he placed both palms on the table before him. Imogen leant a little closer, their noses no more than six inches apart, her gaze threatening to drill two small holes in his forehead. After what seemed like an eternity, she spoke.

"742."

"Oh, for heaven's sake, Imogen…"

Imogen smiled and wiggled her eyebrows.

"The café seems filled with those skilled in the mystic arts today, Francois. Perhaps we should wake Monsieur LeGrande and see what bafflement he may offer."

Francois sighed, picked up both empty cups and walked towards the counter

"Cherry cake, Imogen?"

"Please, and 14."

His back to her, he sighed, and his shoulders slumped. For

the moment, defeated, he entered the kitchen. As he moved out of earshot, Jacques' voice drifted towards Imogen. His head remained comfortable on the table, and his eyes closed.

"Dear Francois is a man easily frustrated, I think, as are you, Lady Imogen. What will happen now? Who will surrender first in the battle of wills, I wonder?"

"There is no battle, Monsieur LeGrande; it is merely two intelligent adults engaging in intellectual activity on a wet afternoon."

"His mind is more open than he suspects. There is no magic about you, Lady Imogen."

"Most reveal more than they wish without even being aware. Often, the more they try to hide themselves, the wider their doors open."

The older man chuckled, sighed and dozed off again with his usual ease as Francois returned to Imogen with two refilled coffee cups and two slices of cake. As he sat, he slid her cup and plate across the table, then reshuffled the cards as Imogen stroked the cat.

"What was Jacques mumbling about?"

"He was speculating on the nature of our current battle of wits."

Boreas squawked loudly from the top of the coat stand, reminding everyone but Imogen that he was still there. At the far end of the café, a startled Jacques bolted upright in his chair and knocked his coffee cup onto the floor.

"My card trick is bothering you, is it not?"

"Bothering me? No, but I am curious about your method. The explanation is merely an intellectual exercise when stripped of the obvious theatrical embellishments. However, you seem more than a little perplexed by my own expertise."

"Imogen, I know how the card trick works, but honestly, I cannot fathom how you can see into my mind."

She leant a little closer, her eyes staring deep into his as she chewed. He leant back slightly, intimidated by her close proximity and delicate scent.

"Stop looking at me as if I have a number tattooed on my forehead."

Her eyebrow raised, but she said nothing. Francois did his best not to think of a number, thinking instead of tonight's dinner. The corner of Imogen's mouth curled slightly.

"451."

"Chicken casserole! I was thinking of chicken casserole with broccoli and sautéed potatoes!"

"I know, but you were also thinking of the number 451."

Crumbs of cherry cake fell from her mouth as she tried to eat and not laugh too readily at her frustrated friend. Francois stayed seated, mopping his brow with his tea towel.

"You imp! I have opened my home to a mystical creature possessed of powers from beyond the veil. Perhaps I should fetch Father Edwin and have our café exorcised of the demons within."

Imogen's eyes widened, as did her smile.

"With every passing hour I spend in your company, I discard another layer of the onion skin that is your character, Francois Meyer. I am confident you will be free of secret and artifice by next Wednesday at the very latest."

She folded her newspaper, so it appeared never to have been opened, drained her coffee cup and stood, picking up the kitten as she did so.

"Do not be concerned. I shall share my keen insights into your character with no other."

The kitten squeaked in obvious approval as Imogen winked at the tiny black face.

"Quite so, Inglenook."

For a moment, Francois stared past Imogen into the roaring flames that filled the dark, comforting fireplace, then looked up.

"Inglenook?"

"After much consideration, I believe we have chosen a most suitable name."

"We?"

"Yes. I present Madame Inglenook DiRossi."

Francois smiled awkwardly at the tiny face, inwardly surprised that she had bestowed her own name on the small animal but deciding to find it charming.

"Hello, Inglenook. Welcome to our home; I hope you will be very happy here."

She cradled Inglenook closer and walked towards the stairs, but even as she turned away, the kitten kept its eyes locked on Francois. At the last minute, Imogen turned and leant down, her eyes and Inglenook's intimately close to his. He made a surprised noise as his nostrils filled with her familiar scent. She put her palm on his forehead, pressing lightly and looking deep into his eyes.

"Despite your recent protestations of good health, you have a temperature, and I suggest you take to your bed."

Francois glanced to one side, meeting Inglenook's intense gaze, and then back to Imogen.

"You fuss, Imogen. I am quite well."

"No, you are not. You sniffed forty-two times in the last hour, and if you were indeed quite well, perhaps your mind would be focused enough not to let me in so easily. 598."

She straightened and walked away. Francois swivelled in his chair just as she put her foot on the bottom step.

"I wasn't even thinking of a number."

She was already on the eighth step and out of sight when she replied.

"Yes, you were."

Less than one second later, Inglenook squeaked in agreement.

Café Merle, Paris — Thursday, June 11th, 1908 - 9.14 am

The following morning, the rain had stopped, and the sun shone down on the wet cobbles of Place St Genevieve. Inclement weather did little to change life in the square except to keep the many benches free of anything other than crows. Upstairs at the front of Café Merle, overlooking the cobbles, was Francois Meyer's bedroom, where he currently lay - feverish and not in the best of moods. Imogen dabbed a damp, herb-infused cloth on his forehead, causing his bedroom to smell much like hers. He was well aware of the futility of his resistance, but nevertheless…

"Please, Imogen. I am temporarily forced to my bed with a heavy cold, nothing more."

Despite being confined to his room since yesterday afternoon, he had risen at his usual hour, washed, dressed and then slumped back down on his bed, exhausted by his own stubbornness. His apron lay half tied across his waist, brought up to him by Maria along with his breakfast coffee, but he didn't have the energy to put it on properly.

"Hush."

Imogen pressed two fingers to his damp, fevered temples and stretched her thumb to the bridge of his nose. Francois had never seen anyone, doctor or not, do such a thing before and wondered at the diagnostic properties of his nose. After a few moments, she tapped her fingers lightly across his skin as if playing the piano, made a noise of curious satisfaction and took her hand away. His eyes, which had crossed to follow her fingers, gradually returned to focus as she made a quick and comprehensive diagnosis.

"Your temperature has been elevated for two days, and I believe you also have the beginnings of a chest infection. However, under my attentive care, you will soon be quite well - perhaps a little more quickly, if you would be sensible enough to undress and use your bed and blankets more traditionally. Why on earth do you still have your shoes on?"

Francois looked down at his gleaming shoes. Anton had insisted on cleaning them, as he did every evening, and it seemed ungrateful not to wear them.

"I prefer to be dressed and in a state of at least minor readiness, Imogen. I am a man of some responsibility. What if I am needed downstairs?"

She stood and opened his bedroom window wide, inhaling the cool air of Place St Genevieve. Boreas immediately flew from a nearby tree and settled on the balcony, cawing in what Francois now accepted as a greeting. He replied, having long since accepted the bird's constant presence.

"Good morning, Boreas. Are you quite well?"

Imogen frowned, suspicious of gentle mocking and winking at her feathered friend, who caw-cawed in response.

"If I enter your room to find the windows closed again, Francois, I shall remove them both from the hinges until you are well."

His handkerchief once again muffled Francois' words.

"Maria insists that I must drown in my own perspiration. Fresh air, it seems, will take my last breath."

"I will speak with her."

"Thank you."

Imogen sat back down on the bed and took his pulse as Boreas flew the short distance to Francois' bedside cabinet. The handsome, dark bird eyed him with some intensity as if preparing his own diagnosis but remained quiet as he hopped from one claw to the other. Francois had no idea whether his pulse rate worried or brought joy to Imogen's heart as she only made a brief, non-committal noise and let his wrist flop slowly onto the bed. He watched it fall and then returned his gaze to her, ready for further discussion. At that moment, she opened her mouth to speak but was interrupted by a knock at the door. Imogen and Francois both spoke at the same time.

"Come in."

Jacques LeGrande entered, dressed in the dirtiest overalls

Imogen had ever seen, and his welding mask lifted away from his face.

"Lady Imogen, do you wish for your study doors to open outwards or inwards?"

Imogen pondered the idea for exactly four seconds, giving the illusion of consideration when, in fact, she had decided several days ago. The one thing she disliked more than a rushed decision was other people thinking she had made a rushed decision.

"Outwards, if you please, Monsieur LeGrande. I prefer to launch myself onto an unexpectant world rather than beckon it in."

The old man peered around the door at Francois, putting his hand over his mouth and nose.

"Mr Meyer still breathes, Monsieur LeGrande. I predict a slow, troublesome recovery, but I am confident he will be quite well within the month."

Francois prepared a reply, but his words were lost in a cough and a damp handkerchief.

"I am sure he is in the very best of hands, Lady Imogen."

Francois frowned; the bottom half of his face still buried in the handkerchief.

"I have not yet breathed my last, Jacques. You may address me directly."

Jacques chuckled and left, Imogen pushing the door closed

behind him.

"Imogen, my friends seem convinced that I am close to death. Your comments do not help matters."

"Happy Birthday, Francois."

Francois tried to speak, failed, then cleared his throat and tried again.

"Thank you. Can I assume there is some event planned?"

"Monica has devoted her time to little else recently. I would suggest it appropriate that you show both gratitude and some surprise when events unfold in the manner she expects."

"I feel old, unwell and not in the best of moods to enjoy cake and the enthusiastic affections of others, but I will rehearse a suitably effusive reaction."

Imogen reached into her skirts and passed a small box to her friend. He smiled and tried to raise himself higher on the pillow. She reached out and helped him to move, temporarily covering his face with her hair and pleasant scents. She returned to her previous position, resting her hands in her lap as he unwrapped the small parcel. There was no card, label, or message, just a simple box wrapped in white tissue paper. He removed the paper and opened the box to reveal a golden pocket watch. A stab of emotion almost punctured his ill heart, and his throat dried.

"Oh, Imogen."

Imogen tilted her head and smiled.

"It seemed fitting that I replace it. I was able to salvage the rear half of the case, but the remainder was too damaged. I trust that it retains a sufficient connection to your father."

Francois turned the watch over in his hands, opening the case. Inside the lid were the words "The Adventure & The Caper" in neat, engraved script.

"Monsieur LeGrande insisted, and I chose not to resist his kind offer. I did, however, remain close by. His ability to spell does not match his enthusiasm or the quality of his steady hand."

Francois rubbed his thumb over the fine engraving, remembering the moment in the château when Imogen used Tesla's glove to pull an antique shield from the wall and protect them both. As the bullets had thumped into the thick wood, the watch had been crushed under his own weight - something he found an acceptable exchange at the time, but as the days passed and he thought of his father, he felt less certain. Francois had seen his father take out that same watch every morning just before he opened their grocers' shop, and it was one of the few connections to him that remained.

"Thank you, Imogen."

Imogen started to speak, but he interrupted gently.

"...and please do not tell me it is of no matter. It is an act of kindness that I will not soon forget."

Imogen's half-begun, quiet words disappeared in the

morning breeze through the window as he patted her hand.

"I am still not used to your naked fingers, Imogen."

She looked down at her fingers and palm, criss-crossed as they were with light blemishes and tiny scars, all testament to a life of event and occasional mishap. She had disassembled Tesla's glove to fashion a suitable storage container for the strange metal she had found among Jose Garcia's treasure. The power source lasted long enough for the short journey to the university, where Madame Curie had taken the metal to store in the relative safety of her vault. What was left of the glove lay in her desk drawer downstairs. She slowly pulled her hand away from his, twisting it in the bright sunlight that poured through the open balcony doors.

"I had grown somewhat used to compensating for its weight, and it is still...unsettling to be without it."

"There is so much more to you than that device, Imogen. It surely is of little matter."

He was trying to reassure her but could quickly recall at least three occasions on which Tesla's glove had saved either or both of their lives.

"Quite so, but one gets used to those things that become familiar."

"Yes, and that is why I do not enjoy lying here when there is work to be done."

"Our business is in safe hands, I promise you. Belle is surprisingly efficient, particularly when Monica is absent. Together, there is something of a battle of wills. However, they are under my constant supervision, so do not be concerned."

"Constant? Should you not return to watch over them?"

"No, that will not be necessary…"

Imogen tilted her head and whispered to Boreas, who took his eyes off Francois and looked back at her. She jerked her head slightly in the direction of the open window, and he flew out. Flying high in the air, he looped around out of sight and flew back into the open door of the café.

"…a watchful eye is a watchful eye."

Francois smiled at the idea of café life continuing without him. He had heard light fussing through the floor all morning and knew that Belle and Monica had helped to keep things going in his absence. He felt grateful and a little proud that they struggled to achieve what he found so natural. As if on cue, there was a slight noise from downstairs, followed by a sudden curse of surprising crudity. Monica had clearly dropped another plate.

"Indeed, I have noted several modifications to the café routine that would improve efficiency to the nth degree— the discussion of which can wait until you are fully recovered. I must confess that you have given a most relaxed impression of your work. I am more than slightly impressed."

"Heavens, Imogen. I gladly accept your compliment. If only it would lessen my boredom. I miss life, conversation, and interaction. I feel my brain is growing as stagnant as I am."

Francois saw Imogen's expression change briefly. She made a quiet, thoughtful noise and left, leaving the door ajar. He had neither the energy nor inclination to close it after her, especially as he had already learned that she only shut the door on rooms to which she had no intention of returning. Less than ten minutes later, she returned with Jacques, a folding table and a small leather bag. It rattled and clanked as she re-entered the room. Jacques waited as she unfolded the table and set the bag down next to it. She pulled the dresser chair over, and once she was seated, she patted the tabletop with both palms. Jacques placed the clock in front of her.

"Thank you, Monsieur LeGrande. Please tell Maria that Francois and I will have coffee and cake up here at 11 O'clock."

Jacques bowed, looked from Imogen to Francois, and smiled. As he straightened, he winked solicitously at Francois and then left, closing the door. Imogen reached into her bag and took out a small selection of tools.

"The clock is broken, Imogen?"

"I am not certain."

Francois knew how she hated uncertainty but also knew that she loved a mystery with equal passion. He watched quietly, idly shuffling his deck of cards, as she tapped the glass front with the tips of two fingers and raised her eyebrow, turning to face Francois with it still raised.

"It is keeping excellent time, but the chimes do not. I had difficulty sleeping last Tuesday, and while preparing some tea in the kitchen, I heard the clock chime. It was 2.20 am. Its correction has not been a pressing concern; however, your boredom and desire for stimulating interaction give me an ideal opportunity."

Imogen looked at Francois' quiet face. She understood it was for her benefit, but as she had repeatedly told him, it was seldom necessary.

"Please feel free to engage in conversation. I am quite capable of working simultaneously. Let us waste not a moment."

With no preamble, she reached inside the top of her dress and retrieved the small clock key. Francois had no time to look away, but if Imogen expected him to, she gave no indication, merely unlocking the glass front and making a slight noise again.

"I am forty years old, Imogen. In only seven years, I will be as old as my father ever was."

She did not look up when he spoke. Instead, she reached into the bag for her spectacle frames and dropped two clear, thick lenses into them. Her nose wrinkled as she leaned closer.

"I am approximately thirty-one years old. My mother was unsure of the exact date, and it seemed to matter little when I was a child. By the time I became sufficiently curious, she was no longer part of my life, so I chose a specific day myself.

The clock made a soft click at the end of her small tool.

"The 14th day of August 1876. A Monday."

"Was there a particular reason for your choice?"

"None that I am aware of, but it seems a sturdy day, one situated away from the more popular celebrations at the end of the year and the playful exuberance of early Summer."

She moved closer to the clock face, lifting the spectacles and resting them on her forehead. Exactly why, Francois had no idea.

"You tease."

She flashed him a look, wiggled both eyebrows, and the glasses fell back onto her nose.

"Yes. In fact, I was reading a newspaper over a light brunch at a small café in Madrid on what I estimated to be close to my 29th birthday. The date on the top of every page was the 14th of August. I have since ascertained that quite literally nothing else of note occurred on August 14th, 1876. Nothing. One might say that I filled an obvious historical vacuum with my own significance."

Francois grasped the conversation and continued as she began to unscrew the clock face.

"I drew my first breath at eighteen minutes after six in the morning, in a cold corner of my parents' bedroom. I was wrapped in the best and only woollen blanket my parents owned. There was no nurse, just my father and my mother."

Francois stared ahead, lost in the past.

"She squeezed his hand so hard that it bled, but he told me years later that she never cried out. I arrived with little fuss, but I suspect that may be a father's perspective rather than a mother's. He bathed her tired face, washed me, and then walked down twelve stairs to open the shop. 11th June 1868 was a day much like any other, except for the arrival of one Francois Wilberforce Meyer."

"A strong name."

Francois felt his cheeks redden a little.

"Most of it."

Imogen's mouth curled up at one side as she squinted at the clock face.

"Mmmm. Although, I venture to suggest that the middle portion is best left for those in your confidence."

"That would be myself, Monica and now you, Imogen. However, I suspect Monica has taken Belle into her confidence. In turn, Belle may well have shared it with Jacques when conversation by the fountain became slow."

"I am flattered by your trust. You may assume I will take the information to my grave, whenever that may be."

"Long after me, I fear."

At his sudden remark, Imogen stopped fiddling with her tools and looked over at him through the top of her spectacles.

"Death is something that happens, Francois. When and where are not for us to know, so discussing them is of little benefit. We should make the best of each day and waste not a moment worrying about things we cannot possibly know."

When she used the word "waste," Francois became overly conscious of his location and prone position. He sat up higher on the cushion, watching Imogen work.

"It is an odd thing, the blanket - the one I was first wrapped in."

Imogen made a quizzical noise. He recognised this as her "I am busy, but please continue" noise.

"My father told me many years later that a small package was left on our doorstep the night before. It contained the blanket, eight dollars, some milk in a muslin-clad clay jar and a woollen hat that would not fit me until I was almost nine".

"No doubt the lifelong possessions of a forgetful vagrant."

"Possibly. The items were clean, though, and the milk fresh."

"I dare say the money was of use."

"My parents regarded it as something of a talisman, and despite our circumstances, it was never spent."

He raised his finger and pointed at the wall opposite the bed, where a miniature painting hung—at least, that is what most would assume. Imogen stood and regarded the painting more closely. They were banknotes, and she had never noticed them before despite being in this room several times."

"A five and three ones."

Imogen turned back to Francois, clearly intrigued and effortlessly concealing the calculations in her head.

"Eight dollars would be a considerable amount of money for your parents. Were they overly superstitious?"

"Not that I remember. Sentimental, possibly, but it was a long time ago."

Imogen continued to work on the clock, storing the shared information for future use. She knew Francois would love to hear more about her own life, but it paled in comparison to the simple charm of his story.

"We owned a horse. His name was Alfonse, and I liked him very much. He pulled our cart about Italy, and he liked carrots and radishes. With one brief exception, he was my only friend for most of my early life."

Francois listened carefully, as always, when Imogen revealed something new about herself. It didn't happen very often and nearly always took him by surprise.

"One exception?"

"There was a girl - Janis. She stayed for a few days, and then we moved on. Despite her assurances, I never saw her again."

"I'm sorry, Imogen."

"You are? Why?"

"A child should have friends."

"I had my books and the countryside. Perhaps I was more particular than most."

Francois loudly blew his nose.

"Then I must consider myself most fortunate."

"Oh, hush."

It was evident that Imogen was growing quietly frustrated with her inability to ascertain what was wrong with the clock. As she stared at the source of her irritation, it chimed. It was 9.43 am. Francois disguised a chuckle by sneezing into his increasingly damp handkerchief, but Imogen wasn't fooled and favoured him with a slight frown.

"I must venture behind the faceplate. It seems that simple cleaning and lubrication will not be sufficient."

Again, Imogen tutted, frustrated by her inability to do four things simultaneously.

"Francois, please hold the small hand in place while I remove the faceplate."

Happy to be helpful and no doubt improve his friend's mood, Francois rolled off the bed a little too quickly. His head swam for a moment, and the sight of his friend blurred for a short while.

"I fear I leapt into action with too much enthusiasm."

"There is a first time for everything, Mr Meyer."

Francois steadied himself, ignoring the tease and moving next to the small table. He grasped the small hand of the clock while Imogen started to unscrew the centre. Another small tut, and she took off her glove, allowing herself to hold the large hand more firmly.

Suddenly and with no warning, the moment and Francois Meyer's world fell in on itself. There was a rush of silence as all around him vanished. A cacophony of a thousand insects sounded all at once, followed by nothing.

There was pain, noise and then a hand holding his. Not for the first time, he regained consciousness to a loud whisper with a faint Italian accent.

"Francois? Are you quite well? Francois! Francois!"

He felt a cool hand on his forehead as he tried to focus.

"Imogen?"

"You have hit your head, but it is not serious. Are you otherwise well?"

A ship's foghorn almost completely drowned out his reply.

CHAPTER THREE - ARRIVAL
Somewhere Else

The sound of the foghorn faded, replaced with the dull murmur of nearby, hushed conversation and the occasional cough. Francois tried and failed to move quickly.

"Almost every part of me hurts, but I will do for now."

Imogen's kind, concerned face finally came into focus.

"Yes, you almost certainly will. Now, listen to me very carefully, Francois. Something has happened to us, but we are not in any immediate danger. We were unconscious and now are not. We were in your bedroom at the café, and now we are not. Until we know why, I need you to focus and do what you do best."

"You would like me to make you a chocolate cake?" said Francois groggily.

"No, not just now. I was thinking more about your sensible, good-humoured, and honest nature, as I suspect you are more than aware."

Francois smiled through considerable discomfort.

"I am always at your service, Imogen, and once again, I have the bruises to prove it. Imogen I…"

"In a moment."

She cut him off, far more concerned with their immediate situation and peered over the plush furniture that concealed them. They were close to a roaring fire behind a curved, high-backed hearth seat. She saw a luxuriously decorated room, not unlike a London Gentleman's Club. As expected, there wasn't a woman in sight, just a dozen or so men, smoking, drinking and talking. A steward moved between them, but he was attentive and had no reason to look over at the fireplace where Francois and Imogen were hiding. Francois crawled over and also peered over the seat.

"Everyone is speaking English."

"Yes, and until we know why, so shall we. One mystery at a time, though. In the meantime..."

Imogen turned around and sat on the floor, leaving Francois to observe the room. She pulled her dress up to the knee, removed a small metal tube from a pocket in her leggings and tapped two tablets into her hand.

"Swallow these. They will help with your pain."

She passed him the two tablets, turned her back, grabbed a discarded half-glass of gin, and handed it to him.

"What are they?"

"Acetylsalicylic acid."

He looked puzzled.

"Aspirin—purchased from the Avenue de la Bourdonnais pharmacy when we walked home from the park last Tuesday."

He frowned, still looking puzzled. It wasn't vital that he remember, but Imogen was concerned at his sudden lack of recall and worried that he had hit his head harder than she first thought.

"You also purchased a bag of bonbons and some hair creme. Then, as we left the premises, you politely raised your hat to a woman in a frightful yellow dress and told her that her small, yapping dog was exquisite."

Francois's face remained blank as she cupped his cheek and looked into his eyes. She saw enlarged pupils and a slight glassiness. She was sure it was nothing serious, but it would be one more thing to worry about.

"In any case, not everything about my person is scavenged from the forest floors of Southern Europe, Francois. Now, swallow the tablets and gather your wits. I need you."

Imogen patted his arm. He smiled and swallowed the tablets, followed by a gulp of warm gin and the soggy remains of a cigar tip. She was already peering over the seat again when he spluttered and spat it into the fire, making it sizzle and spit loudly. As Imogen looked at the men, most reacted to the noise and looked up.

"It is time to leave, Francois."

Imogen stood, straightening her skirts and meeting the gaze of the gathered gentlemen with a look of polite defiance, and not for the first time wishing she could still throw lightning across a room and shock the pomposity from every disapproving face that now looked at her.

"Come on, quickly now. My stoic demeanour and withering gaze will only intimidate and baffle for so long."

Francois stumbled as he tried to get up, causing him to lean on the soft, green upholstery of the hearth seat. Imogen bent down and put his arm around her shoulder, taking some of his weight and lifting his body high enough for the assembled men to see. As his head appeared above the seat, the steward saw someone at whom it was appropriate to raise his voice.

"Sir! This is the first-class smoking room, and ladies are not permitted!"

Imogen helped Francois towards the nearby door, ignoring events from across the room. She turned around and put her shoulder to the revolving door, seeing the steward and a large, round man walking quickly towards them. The door opened, sending them falling to the floor on the other side. They found themselves in a small, empty café which opened onto the deck through two sliding doors at the far end. A solitary steward stopped wiping the table and looked at them in surprise.

"Are you quite alright? Sir? Madam?"

He moved towards them, eager to help, but Imogen spoke quickly and decisively.

"Leave. Now."

The young man threw his cloth over his shoulder, picked up a small tray of used crockery and left through the far doors. Imogen tried to help Francois to his feet, but again, he stumbled halfway between the doorways. Stabbing pains in his leg forced him down on one knee.

"Francois?"

"My leg, Imogen, it has never hurt like this. The pain is quite…remarkable."

She knelt, facing the door they had just come through, half turning Francois and pressing his face into her shoulder just as their pursuers came through the door.

"Close your eyes.", she whispered against the top of his head.

He heard the glass crack in her hand, and even with his eyes tightly shut, he saw the brightest white flash. There was a dull thump, not unlike someone punching a cushion, and he felt the air rush from all around them. When sound returned, he could smell sulphur and singed cloth. Imogen released her grip on him, but he remained still, breathing heavily against her shoulder. Life had been more eventful since Imogen arrived, but the last few minutes had been almost too much for him. She held him there for a moment, then whispered to him again.

"You may release me now, Francois. The moment is passed."

She gently patted his back, and he relaxed. He opened his eyes and turned to see the two men on the floor. The steward lay face down, moaning into the carpet, while the other man slumped silently against the leaves of a nearby trellis.

"Imogen?"

"Sulphur, saltpetre, charcoal, a little phosphorus and..."

Francois crawled over to the silent man. As he got closer, he saw blood trickling down the trellis that had broken his fall. He dabbed at the man's cut with his handkerchief, relieved to see that his injuries were not severe and even more relieved to see his chest still rise and fall.

"Gunpowder?"

"No. Gunpowder would make a loud noise. Did you hear a loud noise?"

Imogen stood, brushing down her dress and looked all around, focusing more on their location than either of the two men.

"I did not. Phosphorus? More theatrics, Imogen?"

"Perhaps, but I was forced to improvise with what I had in my pockets."

Francois could only imagine what she would have done had she had her bag with her.

"They will both recover soon, and it would be best if we are not here when they do. I have precious little left in my pockets, and neither of us is in the best condition to defend ourselves."

With Imogen's help, he stood, steadying himself on the back of a chair. The steward was making even more noise now and was clearly close to recovery. Francois was far from satisfied with either of their conditions, but he knew Imogen was right. She was already looking out of a window at the almost deserted promenade deck.

"Take off your apron, Francois. We must try and blend in with the other passengers, and the last thing we need is someone asking you for a plate of crumpets."

Francois untied his apron and laid it across the back of a chair. He pulled his waistcoat straight and retrieved his broken spectacles from the chest pocket. He tried to focus, then took them off again, squinting and looking around, finally settling his gaze on Imogen.

"What is the matter?"

"My spectacles...I cannot see clearly whether they are on or off."

He waved one hand in front of his face as Imogen grabbed the other, pulling him towards the sliding door, pushing one open and letting the cold air hit their faces. The aspirin had had little effect, and the pain still made his leg throb as Francois leaned on his friend. He couldn't remember pain like this since he was a boy, but he did his utmost to appear calm as they walked along the promenade.

They had only walked a short distance when Imogen stopped and looked at a small notice.

A Deck - First Class Staterooms & Main Staircase

"Stairs, Francois. We must get off this deck."

She opened the door, surprised by the grandeur of the ship's interior and the staircase in front of them. They had both travelled on passenger ships before - indeed, Francois had crossed the Atlantic years before on The Majestic, but this vessel was as grand as anything they had ever seen or heard of. They moved quickly down the stairs, paying little attention to the few other passengers they saw.

"We must conceal ourselves."

"We cannot just barge into a cabin and assume it to be empty, Imogen."

"I have no intention of opening every door, Francois. Also, I would remind you that Imogen DiRossi does not 'barge'."

Francois looked down the deserted, white-panelled corridor, then up at the small sign above their heads.

"These are First–class Staterooms."

"I see no reason to compromise civility and comfort as we hide, Francois."

"The distance between the doors does indeed suggest a certain opulence. Is it likely that one will be vacant on a vessel such as this?"

Imogen wasn't listening as she reached into her pocket and turned to face him, dropping the second of two red lenses into her spectacle frames.

"Watch and learn, Mr Meyer."

Francois spoke to her behind as she bent to study a door handle

"I have done little else since we met, Imogen. Why should today be any different?"

She leaned closer to the door and began to mumble, examining each one closely as she walked by.

"Occupied…occupied..."

Francois became impatient and worried that the recent events on the deck above would soon catch up with them.

"Imogen…"

She gave no indication of sharing his concern, merely stopping, standing up straight and removing her spectacles.

"This will do. It has been unoccupied for some time."

"It has?"

"Yes. There are no fingerprints on the handle, smeared or otherwise. It is, however, locked."

Francois immediately realised the purpose of the red lenses. One second later, prompted by the tilt of her head, he knew what she required of him and knelt next to the lock, putting his weight on the stronger leg. Imogen turned her back to him, nodding politely as an older woman passed by. Gifted and experienced as she was, her attempt to wander casually up and down, hands behind her back, would have fooled no one had they been the slightest bit bothered about their caper. Francois worked as quickly as his blurred vision would allow, relying on the feel of the lock against his pocketknife blade more than anything else.

"Imogen, please try and relax. I would remind you that this is not the first time we have committed a crime together..."

The lock clicked.

"...something which makes me rather glad that my father is long passed."

He removed the blade from the lock and stood, inviting her to enter the dark room with a sweep of his arm, all the time peering up and down the corridor. When they were both inside, he closed the door and plunged them into almost total darkness. Imogen remembered the approximate location of the light switch from the brief time the door was open and fumbled for it. It clicked, but there was no light.

"Imogen?"

"I am here," said Imogen.

There was a quiet scrape of metal, and then a tiny flame on her wrist lit her face.

"As am I," he replied, with a slight chuckle in his voice. What shall we do?"

He heard rustling and gentle clinking for a few moments, and then Imogen's face was lit by a small candle.

"We shall prevail, as always."

She placed it on the dresser, filling the room with dancing shadows and dim light. Only then did they fully take in the room and see the untidy reality of their situation. Most of the furniture was either broken or stacked against the wall. The double bed was undamaged, as was the dresser and wash basin. There were two chairs next to an upset table and many dark red stains on the carpet. When he opened the bathroom door, Francois was pleased to see that at least the bath and toilet were undamaged.

"I believe we have solved the mystery of Cabin B81's lack of occupancy, Francois. I can only guess what happened here, but whatever it was, it was to our advantage.

"Finally, events have turned in our favour."

"So it would appear."

Imogen put her foot on one chair, took a glass tube from a pocket on her shin, and emptied the contents onto the candle flame. The light flickered, then intensified, finally changing to a bright white light. It illuminated the room but exposed even more of the damage. Francois sat on the bed, taking the weight off his leg and sighing with relief.

"The Aspirin seems to be having a little effect, Imogen, but my leg has never hurt like this."

Monica had shared the details of Francois' childhood injury out of concern for him rather than as a subject of idle gossip, assuming that one day Francois would tell Imogen himself. In the meantime, Imogen decided that when that happened, she would feign surprise and concern, but for now, she would respect his privacy.

"Perhaps we will visit the Infirmary and obtain something stronger. In the meantime, I will do what I can. Now… tell me, what do you remember before you regained consciousness?"

Imogen put her palm to his forehead and left it there. He closed his eyes and concentrated.

"The clock. You were repairing the clock."

"Yes, and you were ill, but you seem…hmm…curious."

"Imogen?"

"I remember your temperature being significantly elevated, but now, it seems much less so. In fact, it is more or less normal for you."

"I have always been possessed of a sturdy constitution. What do you mean 'for me'?"

She continued, her mind engaged in matters far more pressing than Francois' question.

"I think it more likely that we have been unconscious for some considerable time, and your body has had time to heal."

"It does not feel as if we have been asleep long."

"I have been rendered unconscious more than once and was never aware of the passage of time when my senses returned, so I cannot be sure. Besides, we are clearly no longer in Paris, and this is an ocean-going vessel, so I can only conclude that we have been unconscious long enough for us to travel from Paris to LeHavre. However…"

She raised her arm and sniffed her armpit several times. Then, before he could stop her, she leaned closer and sniffed Francois' torso.

"…our clothes are clean, and we appear reasonably fragrant."

Imogen moved quickly to the window and peered out, cupping her hands around her eyes.

"The ocean is far from calm, and the glass is very cold, which would suggest that we are on The Atlantic, on a westerly heading, bound for The United States of America."

She stepped back from the window, took out her pocket watch, and studied it briefly.

"We are heading southwest, and judging by the size of this vessel, New York is the likely destination."

She turned to Francois, holding the watch in the flat of her palm and revealing that the face incorporated a compass on its outer edge. Behind the watch hands, an additional, tiny red hand clearly showed their course.

"The last time I looked at the clock on your bedroom wall at home, it was almost 10.00 am. As you can see, my watch now shows 10.46 am, and the clock in here does not agree."

Francois looked over Imogen's shoulder and saw that the clock showed almost 9.30 pm.

"As we travel west, we would lose time, not gain it."

Imogen snapped the watch closed, returned it to her pocket and sat on the bed beside him. She had known him long enough to see that he was doing his best to put a brave face on a moment of considerable worry. She patted his leg twice, then pointed at the cabin door.

"A simple barricade at the door should ensure our privacy as we sleep, Francois. Our presence would be hard to explain to a curious crew member or confused passenger."

He dragged one of the two chairs and leant it against the cabin door, wedging it under the handle and testing its sturdiness a few times. Once satisfied, he lifted the table and stood it back on four legs, dusting the top with his shirt sleeve. Satisfied with his efforts, he turned to face the bed and pondered rather obviously. Imogen turned to look at the bed and then back to her friend.

"Francois, the bed is large enough for us both to sleep comfortably. I understand your respectful hesitation, but we share a home and a certain amount of comfort in each other's presence. Undoubtedly, some would see things differently, but that is their business, not ours. The world will not end if we share a bed."

Imogen stood, turned her back to him and held her hair up, baring her neck and the top fastening of her dress.

"I can usually remove my dress unaided, but the top clasp is still troublesome despite Monica's recent attention. If you would be so kind…"

"Of course."

Even though he had seen Monica less than two hours ago, it felt like a long time ago and far away when he heard her name spoken out loud. He undid the clasp on Imogen's dress, and it opened to reveal her bare, pale skin and the light brown leather of whatever she was wearing underneath. She turned around and let her hair fall down her back again.

"Thank you."

"You are most welcome."

To give her a little privacy, he walked to the cabin window and stared out, cupping his hands around his face, much as Imogen had done. But it was now dark, and he could see little but the reflection of his best friend removing her dress, leather corset, and leggings. She laid them neatly on the table and padded towards the bed in her stockings and white undershirt, sitting on the edge and looking up at him.

"I think it would be best if you also undressed, Francois. You look like you are waiting for a tram."

"Yes, I…"

Despite his efforts to appear relaxed, he still struggled with the situation. Imogen sometimes struggled with the rules and impatience of polite society. Still, in a relatively short time, she had grown as comfortable with Francois as she had been with anyone she had ever met.

"Francois, I am somewhat familiar with the nature of your undergarments, as I am sure you have more than a passing familiarity with mine. Maria's laundry routine is hardly a secret, and I am sure our undergarments have spent many happy hours boiling in her copper pot before being dragged through her mangle together. In any case, you cannot sleep in your shirt, trousers, waistcoat and shoes."

He looked down at his shoes, now scuffed and dull from their recent adventure.

"No, I cannot."

She pulled down the blankets and climbed into bed with her customary care and modesty. When she was settled, Francois glanced across at the empty half of the bed, closest to the wall.

"I am, however, conscious of propriety, Imogen."

"An attitude that does you credit, but we are safely away from society's vulgar gaze, and I believe I know you well enough not to have to inquire about your intentions - amorous or otherwise."

Imogen rested her hands on her thighs and twiddled her fingers on top of the blankets, looking up at Francois, eager to puncture this tiny bubble of awkwardness.

"What you and I share, Francois, is a social contract. We walk together, dance together, and caper together. It has never been my intention to make you uncomfortable or overstep the boundaries of our friendship."

"You have never done so, Imogen. I have always found your behaviour quite proper and charming…if a little unconventional."

Imogen feigned a coy smile, wishing for a moment that she knew how to blush, feeling this would be the perfect moment.

"Why, Mr Meyer, is it any wonder that Monica pursues your affections with such single-minded veracity?"

"I am not sure how to answer that."

"You need not. Now, please remove your trousers and get into bed with me."

Francois watched as she reached behind and pulled her long hair forward, draping it over the front of her left shoulder. When satisfied, she looked up at him again and patted the space in the bed next to her.

"Hurry now; the hour is late."

"The view out of the window would seem to suggest it is, but my brain tells me something quite different."

Imogen glanced up at the clock.

"I agree, but we cannot exist separate from the world around us, and I would hate to miss breakfast."

"As would I."

Francois undid his waistcoat and laid it across the back of the chair. Turning his back to her, he removed his shirt, trousers and shoes to reveal long, white, woollen underwear that covered almost all of his body. He took longer than necessary to arrange his clothes in a neat pile on the chair, then climbed over Imogen with as much dignity as he could muster. She lifted her knees to allow him past and turned her head to watch him struggle.

"I have more Aspirin if you are still in pain."

"I will soldier on for now, thank you. I am confident that sleep will help."

With obvious discomfort, Francois tucked his feet under the blankets and fussed a little until he sat up with his hands in his lap. He briefly looked down at the gap between them, then up to see that she was watching him closely.

"I admire your resolve, Francois, but I would prefer it if you did not toss and turn all night."

"Please do not nag. I am making every effort to cope with an extraordinary day."

"Imogen DiRossi does not na…"

He tugged at the blankets gently, pulling more to his side of the bed.

"Occasionally, she does, and as with most things, she excels at it."

"Thank you."

"That was not a compliment."

Francois continued to adjust the blankets until he was satisfied, the whole time under Imogen's careful gaze.

"I am unable to recall a moment when I have nagged."

"The Louvre, last month. Twice, you asked me to walk more quickly in the hope that we would outpace the other visitors to the Mona Lisa and be the first to bathe in her noble gaze."

She glared at him in silence, recalling the moment differently.

"She has been a resident at the museum for 104 years, Imogen. She was unlikely to have moved by the time we arrived."

Imogen was about to reply when she noticed the wash basin mirror and the bickering married couple it reflected. She narrowed her eyes at their reflections, then looked slightly to the left and saw Francois' reflection, which seemed equally awkward. As the silence continued, Francois decided to say something—anything, in fact.

"I should visit the barber."

She answered his reflection.

"Yes."

He reached behind, fussing a little with the hair that

barely reached beyond where his shirt collar would be.

"It seems that as my hairline recedes, there is considerable and unnecessary compensation where it matters least."

"I find excessive vanity unflattering in a man, but if you continue down this Rapunzellian path, I would certainly be less willing to take your arm in public. I have no desire to share my morning stroll with someone who has the look of Lord Byron about them."

"I would make a poor fop, Imogen. You may rest assured that I shall deal with matters as soon as possible—unless you wish to…?"

"Thank you, no. Your tumbling locks are best left to Monica's skilled fingers and patient attention. Besides, I am not quite sure where I would even begin."

At the mention of Monica, Francois' expression dropped a little, something that Imogen picked up on quickly.

"We will be home soon, Francois; of that, I have no doubt."

"Yes, I know."

"I am aware that the nature of your relationship with Monica has changed recently. I assure you it is far from common gossip; however, I must report that Monsieur LeGrande has already chosen the suit I must buy him for the wedding ceremony, and Belle has almost finalised the floral arrangements, but all is discretion. Also, Boreas would very much like to carry the ring."

"You tease."

"A little, but if it is not overstepping the boundaries of our friendship, I have to say that I approve of your decision. You have both made an excellent choice."

"We are both far from the first flush of youth."

"Certainly, no one could accuse you of not walking the full length of the shop counter before making your selection, Mr Meyer."

"Pardon?"

"You possess a certain charm, Francois—one that the women of Paris seem to find most distracting. After three months, I am still no closer to understanding your appeal, but it clearly exists. The fact that you have not pursued a relationship with any of the fifty-four women who have smiled at you while we have been out walking suggests that your heart belonged to Monica long before I arrived."

"Fifty-four? You have kept count?"

"The lifting of your hat seems to bring a coy smile to the lips and a tremble to the knees of Paris' most desperate and available."

"Desperate?"

"Forgive me. Curious, perhaps."

"My ego is suitably crushed, Imogen."

"Excellent, but the matter is largely moot. Cupid's arrow

has finally split your chest wide open and plunged deep into your upper left ventricle."

Francois pulled a face.

"I feel suddenly sick."

"Pre-marital nerves, no doubt."

"In any case, I do not think we will marry. Monica does not wish to change the way we live our lives, and I agree. She is immensely proud of her life and business, and the café is..."

"Francois, whatever you decide, you will have my support."

"The Café is your home, Imogen, and it always will be."

"Of course it is. I have my study just how I want it to be, and I promise you that any attempt to evict me will be met with the sturdiest resistance."

Imogen smirked, slid under the blankets and lay flat with her head on the pillow. Francois followed suit, almost managing to hide the pain in his leg. Before laying his head down, he propped himself on his elbow and looked at the still-burning candle. Despite the hour or so they had been in the room, it hadn't grown any smaller.

"Perhaps I should have extinguished the flame before climbing over you."

"Perhaps."

Imogen turned her head towards it, blew, and extinguished the flickering flame from half away across the room. There was a moment's pause as their eyes got used to the dark.

"Imp."

"114."

"Incorrect."

"I am not."

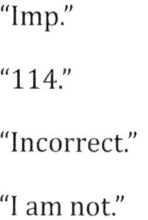

Cabin B81 - Tuesday, April 13th, 1912 - 1.05 am

Moonlight washed over the bed, coloured by the elaborate stained glass of the cabin windows. The sound of the wind had greatly lessened in the last hour, but the silence had not helped Francois fall asleep.

"You are very quiet, Francois. Could it be that we have exhausted all conversation?"

"It is the middle of the afternoon, Imogen—all evidence to the contrary. It will soon be time for dinner, and we will be missed."

They had climbed into bed almost four hours ago, and as Francois had predicted, sleep still eluded them. Imogen reached out, picked up her pocket watch from the bedside cabinet, and opened it. Feeling that it was somehow important, she had not yet adjusted it to local time.

"I suspect Maria was the first to notice when she arrived with our morning coffee and cake at eleven o'clock several hours ago. It is not unknown for us to leave the café when the mood takes us, so she would not have been overly concerned."

Francois looked over at Imogen's watch, but he still couldn't make out the numbers on the face.

"I would not want them to worry."

"We are quite the unpredictable pair, Francois. I am sure they are confident in our ability to visit the market without serious harm. It would not be the first time we let fancy and impulse lead the way. Let us not forget the Parmesan incident."

"None could be found at the market. We searched a little farther afield, that is all."

"Five trams, eleven shops and two markets."

"You exaggerate. It was a lovely afternoon."

"We were absent for almost seven hours and returned home with a small piece of Brie. Maria was so overjoyed at our safe return that she embraced me for almost three minutes."

"As always, I defer to your terrifyingly precise recall of events. Whatever would I do without you?"

"I endeavour to influence your life positively whenever possible, Francois."

"...as do I with yours."

Imogen frowned. Such a thing had never occurred to her.

"You do?"

"Certainly. The woman who arrived at my café three months ago was incapable of creating an edible Macaron, for instance."

"As I told you when I first donned your spare apron and you passed me the wooden spoon, it was something I had simply not attempted before."

"You tied the apron back to front, Imogen."

"It had been a long day."

"It was a quarter past eight in the morning."

"I rose early."

"You always rise early."

Imogen huffed.

"I can turn my hand to most things, given sufficient, patient instruction. Your directions were unclear, and as such, I struggled to meet your somewhat lofty expectations."

Francois smirked in the dark, remembering that first chaotic and mildly profane afternoon, which ended with them both sitting on the floor covered in flour and sugar, giggling like children. When she returned from the market and discovered them, the look on Maria's face was forever etched on his memory.

"You are a fine student, Imogen - quick to learn and slow to anger. Perhaps baking is simply not your forte."

"Oh, hush."

Francois closed his eyes for the nineteenth time and thought calm, relaxing thoughts. As before, it did not help.

"Imogen?"

"Yes?"

"Despite the late hour, I would very much like a cup of coffee and a Macaron."

"I do not usually carry Macarons about my person. However..."

She threw back the blankets and swung her legs over the side, stretching both arms high and then out to the side before standing up. For a few moments, she rummaged in her folded clothes, hidden in the shadows and darkness. Francois could hear the familiar sounds of glass and metal clinking together and the quiet mumble that usually accompanied his friend's endeavours.

"Caffeine at this hour is inadvisable, but considering our current situation, I believe we can make an exception. A little civility would not hurt."

The sudden relighting of the candle took Francois by surprise, filling his vision with large, white splotches.

Blinded for a moment, he heard the basin fill with water. When he could see clearly again, he saw a collection of vials and small pouches on the dresser. She turned around, brandishing two small metal cups that folded out from each other like Russian dolls.

"One must always be prepared, Francois. Visio nocturna!"

"What?"

There was a bright purple flash, a quiet hiss, and once again, Francois was blinded by his friend's exuberance and skill. The flash grew brighter and brighter until a sweet but pungent smell filled the cabin.

"Night vision, Francois!"

"This is hardly the time for a surprise test of my Latin vocabulary, Imogen. I am blinded. Again."

"It will pass."

"I certainly hope so. What was that, anyway?"

"Sugar, Potassium Chlorate and a little Sulphuric Acid. A simple, very hot fire."

Gradually, the sharp smell subsided, replaced by the robust and comforting aroma of coffee.

"Imogen, you carry Sulphuric Acid about your person?"

"You do not?" she replied with a smirk.

She was only half-listening as she dabbed her

handkerchief on the new, possibly permanent purple stain on the wood panelling behind the dresser. After a short while, she gave up, returned to the bed and passed him a steaming cup. She climbed in next to him as he took a sip and wrinkled his nose.

"Ewww..."

"Oh, forgive me."

Imogen dropped a sugar cube into his coffee and stirred it with her pencil.

"Imogen, you are extraordinary."

"Thank you. You are not the first to tell me, but you are certainly becoming the most frequent."

"Shall I stop?"

Imogen considered this for a few seconds, then replied in an entirely matter-of-fact fashion.

"It is not an unwelcome compliment."

"Too often?"

"A little, but I do not object. I am confident that you mean well. You, too, have your moments, Francois Meyer."

"Thank you."

"Biscotti?"

Imogen passed him a small nutty biscuit, taking a delicate bite of another.

"Where on earth did that come from?"

"Monsieur Borelli's stall in the market last Monday. I also tried something called a frosted doughnut, but I cannot recommend it."

"That was not quite what I meant."

"I know. Please try to keep crumbs out of the bed."

She put what remained of her biscotti on the bedside cabinet and picked up a small piece of paper.

"What is that?"

"I found it on the floor a few moments ago, just inside the door. It appears to have been pushed underneath at some point after we took up residence."

Francois leaned over, but his vision was still less than it once was.

"I cannot see well enough to read it."

"Well, firstly, it seems that we are aboard the RMS Titanic, a vessel of which I am unfamiliar, and secondly, it details the various shipboard facilities and attractions we may take advantage of. It seems there is a swimming pool, gymnasium and a barber, Francois."

She glanced briefly at the back of Francois' neck as he self-consciously put his hand to the back of his collar. Imogen turned over the paper to find a simplistic drawing of an Egyptian Pyramid and a selection of hieroglyphics surrounding more traditional lettering. Francois could just about make them out if he continued to squint.

"What do the symbols mean?"

"Nothing. It is utter gibberish. However…it seems that we have an opportunity to enjoy a display of Egyptian Artefacts from the collection of Professor Ahmed Sadek."

"You know him?"

"Only by reputation, but he himself is not on board. I am unaware of a mother or sister in the same field, so I must assume this woman is his wife."

Imogen held the paper closer to Francois, but even with a squint, he couldn't make out the words.

"Doctor Penelope Sadek. Noon tomorrow, in the Café on this very deck. I suspect it will be a productive and enjoyable way to pass an hour or so."

Her joy at such a distraction was obvious, and Francois was glad that she would have something to focus on other than keeping her friend calm.

"It sounds very much the sort of thing we will both enjoy", lied Francois.

"Quite so."

For a short while, they listened to the sounds of the ocean and dipped biscotti in their Espressos.

"Imogen, could we be dreaming?"

"It's certainly possible but unlikely. If you are dreaming, then your subconscious has crafted a facsimile of Imogen DiRossi convincing enough to engage in our current conversation. You have also decided to place me in my underthings, which I find more than a little troubling."

"I..."

"Oh hush, I am teasing, and now you are blushing. Forgive me."

"Of course, but there is a time and a place for teasing."

"A somewhat ironic use of language, Francois."

"Please continue, Imogen."

"Certainly. If I am dreaming, then..."

She put down her Espresso and reached for the itinerary and her pencil, scribbling in a space at the bottom. Francois watched, attentive as always. After a moment, she held the notebook up to his face. He moved it a little further away, squinting at an exquisitely described mathematical equation, which, finally, he could almost read.

$$e^{i\pi}+1=0$$

"What is that?"

"Euler's Identity. It is considered to be an exemplar of mathematical beauty as it shows a profound connection between the most fundamental numbers in mathematics. I will spare you a more fulsome explanation, but to put it in simple terms, it is considered a proof that implies the impossibility of squaring a circle."

"I see."

Francois didn't see.

Imogen frowned slightly, amused at Francois' attempt to engage with the subject. Although he sometimes struggled with more involved ideas of mathematics and science, he always made a valiant effort to keep up.

"It is unlikely that my subconscious would be capable of understanding such a hypothesis, so I am almost certainly not dreaming. Of course, you could be dreaming, and your mentally fabricated version of Imogen DiRossi could have just babbled a complete buffet of nonsense."

Once again, Francois was unsure where the compliment ended, and gentle criticism began. Imogen put the piece of paper between them and again placed her hands in her lap.

"Do I often participate in your dreams, Francois?"

"Oh yes," he said a little too quickly, "we have had several adventures, precious few of which have come close to the terrifying and dangerous reality of my waking life, but we have visited The Great Pyramids and been skiing on more than one occasion. Have I ever impinged on your subconscious?"

Imogen held her Espresso cup close to her mouth, thought for a second, and then took a sip.

"Yes, you have on occasion, played a small part. Several weeks ago, I dreamt we were both flying unaided high above some particularly barren moorland. We were hand in hand, but for reasons that are unclear, I released my grip, and you plummeted towards the ground as I laughed. I am still unclear about its significance or whether it has any. Freud believes a dream can represent a disguised fulfilment of a repressed wish, but I have never been one to take his nonsense seriously. Also, you were naked."

She calmly took another sip of coffee. Francois remained silent for far longer than she expected, his eyes wide and looking straight up at the ornate ceiling. There was a hint of worry on his face.

"You laughed?"

"Yes, but as neither of us is able to fly, I suspect the situation will not arise any time soon. You should not be overly concerned."

Francois was still not satisfied.

"But…you laughed?"

"I did. I must confess, Francois, considering our current unexplained presence on a large ocean-going vessel, with no memory of how we arrived, your sudden interest in my subconscious is somewhat odd."

"I am merely trying to distract myself. This is all very

troubling."

"Yes, it is, but we will gain little by the endless reiteration of what little facts we have. Consider this. For the most part, we are unharmed; we are safe, warm and dry. Most importantly of all, you are not alone, and neither am I. We shall attempt to learn more in the morning, but failing that, we will arrive in New York in a few days. Until then, we must do little more than stay out of harm's way and remain inconspicuous."

"You make it all seem very simple."

"I have lived a life of adventure and caper, Francois. Our current situation pales in comparison to my more colourful escapades. Do not worry."

"I cannot promise a total lack of worry."

Imogen put their empty cups on the bedside cabinet and, once more, lay down, pulling the blankets up to her chest. Francois did so a few moments later.

"Tomorrow, I shall send a telegram to Nikola and inform him of our intention to visit. We shall have dinner, over which my oldest friend will meet my newest. I will need to prepare you for such a meeting; of course, Nikola is a genius and a most particular one."

"Perhaps he will not take to me. I would hate to disappoint one you hold in such high regard."

"He is my friend, as are you, Francois. There is no need to compete for my approval."

"If you are certain, then I shall not worry any further."

She knew him well enough to know when he was less than honest, but three months in his company had also been long enough to understand much about what made Francois Meyer tick. Still looking up at the ceiling, she patted his leg.

"I have tasted Nikola Tesla's homemade Lemon Tart on three separate occasions, and each experience has been more regrettable than the last. He may well have been the first to transmit electricity through the air, but the man could not bake an acceptable dessert with a gun to his head. You bow to no one in your skill with the whisk, Mr Meyer."

Francois looked down at her hand and then at the side of her face, still troubled.

"I was naked?"

"Go to sleep, Mr Meyer."

Francois' eyes rolled back in his head, flopping slowly into Imogen's cupped hand, and he began to snore before she laid him flat on the pillow and slid her hand away. She disliked the use of hypnotic suggestions, but occasionally, his need for sleep gave it some justification; at least, that's what she told herself.

Imogen had slept in a surprising variety of places, both inside and out, and in all weathers, but the wheezing and sighing from the other side of the bed was something new. Out of arm's reach, in a small pouch, just above the knee of her leggings, lay an adequate answer to the nasal melody, but for now, she made do with a more direct intervention. Still looking up at the ceiling, she extended a single finger and placed it under his nostrils. Starved of air for a moment, he snorted, mumbled the word "bustle" and fell silent.

She turned her head and looked at Francois, wondering why he was dreaming of such a mundane item of ladies' apparel but grateful that his breathing was now quiet. Imogen had little idea of what tomorrow would bring, but more often than not, that was a good thing. Seldom had she experienced such a conflicting mess of unexplained happenings and contradictions, but one by one, she would explain them. Careful not to wake her partner's slumber, she turned onto her side and faced her friend, correcting the thought.

We will explain them. Sleep well, you ridiculous man.

A few moments later, she too was asleep.

CHAPTER FOUR - KIPPERS & KERFUFFLE
RMS Titanic, Cabin B81 - Saturday, April 13th, 1912 - 7.05 am

Francois' nostrils filled with the aroma of coffee, making him think for a moment that he was at home. Instead, he opened his eyes to find Imogen's face and an Espresso just inches from his own. She had not yet dressed but looked as tidy and presentable as when she had climbed into bed the night before.

"Good morning, Francois."

"Good morning, Imogen. Thank you."

He took the cup, sipped its hot, dark contents, and looked at her smooth, light-olive skin. His smile widened as he studied every line and pore.

"What is the matter? Why are you looking at me like that?" she asked.

Francois raised his free hand and rubbed one eye, then the other.

"Because I can see you. Clearly, Imogen. Every detail of your face..."

She glanced at his spectacles as they lay on the bedside cabinet, one lens missing and the other cracked and useless, then leaned in close. She lifted his left eyelid, staring intently at the eyeball. After a few moments, she rested her own spectacles on her nose and looked more closely through dark green lenses.

"If you could limit your protestations of my beauty to a minimum, I would be very grateful. On the last occasion, you had consumed a considerable amount of brandy, and I let the comment pass. This time, however..."

"That was not my intention; however, I have never appreciated your features from this distance unaided. Please do not deny me this new experience."

"Hush. Remain still."

She lifted his other eyelid, stared for a moment, then returned her spectacles from whence they came.

"I see nothing that would explain the improvement in your vision, but I am not particularly skilled in this area, and my tools are limited."

She held up three fingers and waved them slowly in front of his face. He followed them with his eyes.

"Unus et unus plus alio."

"One plus one and another? I have no idea why you find Latin grammar so difficult to grasp, Francois. Your troubling accent aside, you are as fluent in French as anyone I ever met. The two languages are surely not so different."

"It has only been three months, Imogen, and you are the only person I know on whom I can practice. I learnt French surrounded by French people."

Imogen counted on her fingers, a teasing smirk on her face. She was actually quite impressed with his gift for language, and she knew Latin was more difficult than most. Francois watched closely and nodded along, watching her count out loud.

"Unus, Duo, Tres…"

"I will do better."

"Of course you will."

She looked down at Francois' lower half, resting comfortably under the blankets.

"How is your leg this morning?"

"It hurts a little, but less so than yesterday, and my shoulder no longer aches at all. How are you feeling?"

"I have no pain, but…"

Unable to explain any other way, Imogen pulled one stocking down a little, revealing more of her thigh than Francois expected. She put a finger on a small white scar. He peered at it with as much propriety as he could muster.

"Three years ago, a bullet entered my thigh and exited on the opposite side. There being no Doctor at hand, I attended to my own wounds. The scars I have carried since then were a testament to my limited proficiency at the time. Now, this single mark is all that remains of either. I thought little of it until you mentioned your wound."

Francois put down his empty cup and pushed his undershirt aside. The bullet scar that had marked his shoulder since the event at the château was as pale and faint as Imogen's. He watched her curious face as she leaned over and touched it with the tip of her finger.

"Based on my own experience, wounds such as ours take many years to heal, and even then, a scar will always remain."

"You have been shot many times?"

"Twice. My thigh and, long ago, my chest. She put her hand on her breast and winced a little. That is a long and rather involved story that will have to wait for another time."

Imogen pulled his shirt across, covering what was left of the scar. Then, she moved her finger to his chin, lifting it slightly to examine his eyes.

"Whatever has happened to us, we seem mostly the better for it."

"I have needed spectacles to navigate the world since I was five years old. Three years ago, I began wearing a second pair to read the numbers in my ledger."

Francois held his fingers up in front of his face, a faint smile on his lips.

"This morning, I see old fingers and a face I am discouraged from complimenting, both with nothing but my own eyes."

Imogen pulled up her stocking, stood, and walked to her tidily folded clothes, taking them into the bathroom and closing the door. Francois threw back the blankets, stood and stretched his arms above his head. Outside the window, he could see calmer waters than the sounds of last night suggested. He washed in the cold water of the basin and dressed, looking as smart as he could manage and feeling all the better for the familiar reflection in the mirror. In the absence of his hair creme, he combed back his hair with a wet comb and was fussing with his collar when Imogen emerged from the bathroom. She moved next to him, sharing the mirror and then adjusting his collar.

"Whatever has happened, Imogen, I am grateful for now."

He blinked three times, still far from bored with his newfound visual acuity.

"I admire your optimism, Francois, but things are not as they should be. For now, however, there are more pressing matters to attend to. I suspect our Francs will not be welcome on board. We must exchange them, and then Violet & Montague can partake of breakfast."

"Is subterfuge really necessary?"

"Until we understand more of our situation, discretion may be the best course of action."

"That plan would have a better chance of success if I had a jacket."

Imogen looked him up and down.

"Hmm…yes."

His suit jacket still hung on the hook next to the café counter. He never wore it under his apron, as he felt it emphasised his tummy.

Imogen opened the cabin door and looked left and right as several passengers walked by. After a few minutes, she took a step forward and blocked the path of a short, round man. Somehow, Imogen had found a Frenchman, and the return of her soft, accentless French made Francois wish for home, and all that was familiar.

"Madame?"

"I wish to purchase your jacket."

The portly man was clearly baffled.

"I beg your pardon?"

"Your jacket. I wish to purchase it. If you were wearing a splendid hat, I would wish to purchase that too, but your jacket will do for now."

She held up five ten-Franc notes, and the man's face lit up. With each passing second, he became less confused and quickly removed his jacket, giving it to Imogen and taking the money.

"My wife owns such a hat."

Imogen looked down at her dress and then back up to him.

"It is of a similar style and colour, Madame. It is quite splendid."

"Then I shall wait. Hurry now…"

She waved him away, and he walked back the way he had come as quickly as politeness would allow. Imogen turned and passed the jacket to Francois, looking down at his trousers and back to his face.

"The style and colour are very much 'you', Francois."

Francois put on the jacket, admired himself in the full-length mirror on the wall, and sniffed the lapel.

"It smells of tobacco, and now I smell of tobacco."

Imogen sniffed Francois' arm and wrinkled her nose.

"I am sure a brief walk on deck will rid you of any residual odours."

She fussed with the jacket, then ran her hands down his arms. The sleeves were a little long, but he was his usual presentable self otherwise. She thought of the particular smile Monica kept for such moments and managed a close approximation as she brushed an imaginary piece of lint from his shoulder.

The heavy footsteps and wheezing behind them heralded the return of the portly man clutching a splendid hat. As he had promised, it was similar in style to Imogen's dress. She put it on, and Francois made room for her in front of the mirror.

"You are the picture of elegance, my dear."

Imogen raised an eyebrow, tutted and gave the man another five ten-Franc notes. The man felt slightly uncomfortable as he wondered what to do next.

"Our business is concluded, Monsieur. You will forget this moment, myself and my husband. Do I make myself clear?"

The man nodded quickly but remained rooted to the spot. Imogen once more waved him away, this time in the opposite direction.

"On your way now."

He scurried away as Imogen returned to the mirror. As she attempted to adjust the hat, Francois moved her hands away, seeing to the task himself. Once satisfied, he took a step back and admired his efforts.

"How on Earth did you find a Frenchman?"

"Observation, nothing more. He walked like a Frenchman, much as you do."

"I am not French."

Imogen narrowed her eyes and shook her head slowly, her French returning briefly.

"Oh, Monsieur Meyer, you are as French as anyone I have ever met. One need not adorn your neck with a string of onions and tuck a baguette under your arm to banish all doubt…"

Her English voice reappeared as if it had never been gone.

"…now, let us find the Purser and exchange what remains of our French currency."

She stood in the hallway while Francois closed the cabin door. It clicked shut, but without a key, it was still unlocked.

"Imogen, perhaps we could find a key?"

"Perhaps, if there is time. Although I suspect the busy crew will have more pressing matters to attend to than visiting an unoccupied cabin, they know to be in a state of disarray."

She slipped her arm into his, and together, they walked towards the stairs. Francois continued to sniff very obviously.

"I smell like Jacques."

"Yes, you do. However, I understand that some women enjoy the smell of stale tobacco."

"I am not married to such a woman, am I?"

"No, you are not."

"Imogen?"

"Violet."

Francois sighed.

"Violet?"

"Yes?"

"You paid fifty Francs for this stinking jacket."

"Yes, I did. Once again, Happy Birthday."

RMS Titanic, The Purser's Office, Saturday, April 13th, 1912 - 9.00 am

Chief Purser McElroy carefully counted out the notes on the counter. It was an unusually large amount, even allowing for the calibre of passengers onboard, but he remained professional and made no comment.

"Thirty-eight dollars and thirty-eight cents, less commission, Madam. Will that be all?"

The Purser passed the notes and coins across the counter to Imogen.

"Yes. Thank you."

He nodded, and she walked over to Francois, who had been patiently waiting to one side. She frowned as she handed him half of the money.

"Two-percent commission is extortionate, even for a vessel of this opulence. The Franc is strong, though, so this should be adequate for the remainder of the journey. I will be able to obtain more in New York," grumbled Imogen.

"Surely this will be enough?"

"It almost certainly will, but it is always best to be prepared. It is a vulgar truth that money greases the machinery of life, Francois. You would not have a jacket without it, and I would not be wearing this splendid hat."

Francois put the coins and notes into his wallet and then tucked them into his jacket pocket.

"He would have probably accepted a lot less."

"Perhaps, but we are not in a Moroccan Bazaar, and even if we were, Imogen DiRossi does not haggle."

At the top of the stairs, they met a steward walking in the opposite direction. He pointed them in the direction of the À la Carte Restaurant.

"À la Carte?"

"Yes, they will not ask for our cabin number or inquire as to our identity. Passengers on vessels such as this can purchase a less expensive ticket and pay for their meals as they go, so to speak."

"Do you think they will have Kippers? It is some time since I had Kippers for breakfast."

Imogen stopped walking, forcing Francois to do the same, and wrinkled her nose.

"Why on earth would you say such a thing? I have known you for some time and have never seen you eat Kippers."

"Maria will not allow them in her kitchen."

"My appreciation for Madame Dubois grows with every passing day."

Francois ignored her comment, clearly excited.

"However, we appear to be on a British vessel, which means there is a Chef who knows one end of a Kipper from another."

Imogen began walking again, causing Francois to stumble briefly before matching her step.

The restaurant was full of polite chatter and the gentle tinkle of cutlery against China. Imogen and Francois stood in the doorway as a steward approached and addressed Francois politely.

"A table for two, sir?"

Imogen looked around for a third person rather obviously and deliberately, then addressed the young man.

"Yes, unless you intend to join us?"

Her sarcastic wit was lost on all but Francois, who coughed to hide his amusement. A few moments later, the steward pulled a chair out for Francois, who sat down eagerly. Imogen saw to her own comfort before the steward could do so. Unsure of what else to do, he bowed and left.

"The menu is mostly French, Imogen."

Imogen tried and failed to hide her relief.

"Yes, so it appears. I fear your hunt for Kippers will be fruitless."

"We shall see. Based on the size and luxury of the cabin, if we had paid for a ticket, it would have been reassuringly expensive and, I believe, entitle us to make a fuss."

"Your logic is faultless, Francois. Your ability to caper is improving more quickly than I could have possibly hoped."

Francois raised his hand, and the steward returned.

"I would like Kippers and two poached eggs."

"Sir?"

"Smoked Herring or Mackerel served with two lightly poached eggs. I believe your chef will be familiar with the dish."

"Yes sir, I am aware of Kippers; it is just that our menu is…"

Francois regarded the young man with his best 'Imogen' stare. Had he been wearing his spectacles, he would have looked over them. The steward stopped talking for a moment, then continued.

"…and for your wife?"

Imogen coughed, very obviously. The steward looked up, meeting her stern gaze.

"His wife is perfectly capable of deciding for herself."

"Of course, Madame. What would…"

"Baked apple, oatmeal porridge, four slices of light toast,

strawberry preserve and some cheese."

Imogen quickly scanned the menu card.

"Cheese, Madame?"

"I see no cheese listed, but I am confident you will secure me a small selection. No Gorgonzola or any other blue variety, though; I have no desire to spend tonight bent over the lavatory."

Francois lifted his menu card higher, hiding almost all of his face. To his credit, the steward remained calm despite Imogen's polite and slightly unnecessary pomposity.

"Certainly, Madame. A pot of tea for two?"

"No. From where do your coffee beans hail?"

"Madame?"

"Kenya? Columbia? Vladivostok, perhaps?"

"Vlad..."

"Eastern Russia - a cold and barren place, first settled by the Chinese in the early 7th century. Now a thriving Pacific seaport."

"I shall enquire as to the source of our coffee, Madame."

"Never mind; you may bring us a pot of coffee made from the finest beans on board, regardless of their source."

"Yes, Madame."

"…and in future, you will address me as my husband's equal. I possess a brain, numerous valid opinions, as well as a gaze-worthy bosom. Perhaps you could focus more on the former and slightly less on the latter…Dario."

Francois glanced at the young man's small name badge, again appreciating one of Imogen's more charming habits. What happened next surprised them both. The young man leant in closer, lowering his voice and dropping his slightly high-pitched attempt at a French accent.

"Please accept my apologies, Madame. I meant no offence and will endeavour to do what you ask. This is only my third day in Signor Gatti's employ, and I still have much to learn."

The corners of Imogen's mouth curled slightly as Dario's native Italian accent returned momentarily.

"One never stops learning, Dario. Tell me, where is your home?"

At the sound of her soft Italian voice, his eyes lit up.

"Anzio, Signora. My family have had a fruit stall in the market for three generations. I am the first of my family to seek a life elsewhere."

Francois saw Imogen's eyes twinkle for a moment and heard her voice crack slightly as she replied. He had learned a few words of Italian, a language Imogen used too rarely for him to absorb, but the tone of their conversation was as bright as the light that shone through the windows and across their table.

"I am familiar with Anzio Market. I visited it often as a child."

The young man bowed his head and put his hand on his heart as he did so.

"I am far from my family, and I know they worry about me, Signora, but you have lifted my morning with memories of my home."

"And you have lifted mine, Dario."

Dario Lombardi smiled and hurried off as Imogen unfurled her napkin and laid it across her lap.

"You are smirking, husband."

Francois leant around the large vase of flowers in the centre of the table.

"I am anticipating my Kippers, Violet, nothing more. In times of stress and excitement, I find it best to rely on the simple pleasures. I enjoy Kippers, and you enjoy dismantling the patriarchy one poor boy at a time. What are you doing?"

Imogen opened a small jar and smeared a familiar, clear gel around her nostrils.

"Peppermint gel, along with a brisk post-breakfast walk on deck, should banish the odour of your breakfast from my nasal passages. Should that not be enough, I shall perhaps find my own cabin for the remainder of the voyage."

"...and deny me the pleasure of your company and riveting conversation? Let us not allow a little smoked fish to come between us, my dear."

"Oh, hush."

Dario returned ten minutes later with their breakfast on a silver trolley that rattled gently as he made his way across the carpet. Everything was as they had asked, but he had saved the best for last.

"...and for Madame."

He laid a small cheese plate on the table with an elegant flourish. Francois regarded it curiously, seeing several he could not identify despite his years of experience.

"What is the green one, Dario?" asked Francois.

"I do not know, sir, but I was told it was the finest we have."

Imogen bent her head until her nose almost touched the cheese. After a few sniffs, she straightened.

"Excellent."

"Violet?"

"Schabziger, husband. I have never been served it outside of its native Switzerland. The green colour stems from the use of Blue Fenugreek in its preparation."

Dario bowed his head and pushed the trolley away as Francois watched Imogen stare happily at some cheese, unsure of where to lead the conversation.

"When I was a small boy, my father told me that The Moon was made of green cheese."

The fork, with which Imogen had recently stabbed a large piece of Schabziger, stopped before it reached her mouth as she leaned around the flowers.

"Why would he say such a thing?"

"I was six years old, and it made me laugh. He was so often busy, but sometimes we sat on the steps at the front of the shop and looked up at the stars and Moon together. He would put his arm around my shoulder if it were cold, and I felt very safe."

Imogen ate her cheese, watching Francois remember something she had never known or could possibly miss. He noticed Imogen watching him, smiled and lowered his voice in a close approximation of Harold Meyer.

"One day, Frankie, a man will visit the stars and look down upon us, and we shall seem as small to him as he will to us."

"Frankie?"

"Yes. To my mother, I was Francois, and to my father and friends, I was Frankie. When she passed away, I was Francois once more, and I never asked why. Even at nine years old, I understood.

Imogen had no idea how to handle her friend's latest information, so she continued in the only way she felt comfortable.

"Your father was a man of vision and imagination, albeit with a fanciful grasp of science and astronomy."

She swallowed her cheese, a little unprepared for the full-bodied flavour, but hid it well.

"Yes. He was not quite what you'd expect of a policeman, but aside from carrying crates about the docks, there were few occupations suited to a man of his stature and temperament. He carried a pistol but never fired it once. From the moment it was issued until he was injured in the Tompkins Square Park Riots and was forcibly retired, it sat snug in its holster. My mother had always wanted to own a shop, so when he retired, he invested what little they had and purchased 117 Widow Hill."

"Widow Hill?"

"Yes, I never found out why the street was so named. Despite its name, I remember a happy, busy place with many kind people. Their business was not as profitable as they'd hoped, but I knew little of this. I was a young man before they were free of debt. Only after my mother died and I became more involved in shop matters did I realise how hard it was."

"I suspect that your proficiency today is in no small measure down to what you learnt as a young man."

"I have nothing but love and happy memories of them both, but I did not want to live a life of debt and worry."

Imogen smiled and began to speak, but he cut her off.

"Not as much, anyway."

"That is the way of business, Francois. Neither of us is perfect, and we both have our worries, but our business is in profit, and the one thing I am confident of above all else is my café manager. I am sure that they would both be very proud of you."

She leaned forward, squeezed his hand, and then popped another piece of cheese in her mouth. Francois finished the last of his Kippers and looked around.

"I must say that The RMS Majestic was nowhere near as palatial and grand as this."

Imogen took a sip of her coffee.

"I suspect you could not have afforded First Class passage on a vessel like this. It seems no expense has been spared."

"I'm not sure we could even now, Imogen. Second class on The Majestic was expensive enough, but it was a one-way trip, and my parents' shop sold for more than I expected, so I indulged in what I expected to be a once-in-a-lifetime experience."

"You had no intention of returning to New York?"

"No, there are too many memories. It is a chapter closed, I feel."

"I am sorry if re-opening it will cause you pain."

"Thank you, Imogen, but it is hardly your fault. New York is not a small city, and I suspect Mr Nikola Tesla lives far from anywhere I am familiar with. I had one friend when I was a boy, but she was much older than me and will now be in her late fifties. She may well have moved on or even have died."

"Was it not unusual for a boy to have a female friend so much older?"

"As you know, I have never been afraid of society's judgemental gaze, Imogen, as our friendship proves. There are those who look at you and me and find much to ponder."

"Yes. Do you find that…difficult?"

"Not in the slightest. Their opinions are their own and of no matter to me."

Imogen lifted her napkin from her lap, dabbed her lips, and then favoured her friend with a kind smile.

"Nor to me."

Dario had been watching from a distance and was soon at their table; this time, he knew to whom he should address his question.

"Will there be anything else, Madame?"

"No, thank you. Tell me, Dario, do I see Mr John Jacob Astor across the room?"

"Yes, Madame, he has sat in here twice so far. It seems he

enjoys the relative quiet. You are acquainted with him?"

"Only by association; he is a great supporter of my friend, Mr Nikola Tesla. I have never actually met him in person."

"He is alone, Madame, and he does not seem busy. Perhaps I could make an introduction?"

"Oh no, I do not think that would be appropriate at this time. Perhaps later."

Dario nodded and left. Imogen continued to discretely watch Astor over Francois' shoulder, keeping her eyes fixed on him as she sipped her coffee.

"You look puzzled, Imogen."

"Observant as always, Francois. Nikola has what could be described as a fractious relationship with Mr Astor, but as of Nikola's last letter, things seemed to be on a more even keel."

"Fractious?"

"Several years ago, Astor invested $100,000 in Nikola's idea for a new lighting system. Unfortunately, as he had done several times before, he took the money and used it for something else entirely. Astor was not pleased, but they have recently reconciled."

"That is good."

"Yes. The phrase 'I may have discovered the secret to powered flight' seemed key."

Francois laughed into his napkin.

"...and Astor seriously believed him?"

"Nikola can be quite persuasive when the need arises."

Imogen flattened her hand on the table, exposing a small, golden object no bigger than a broad bean in her palm. Francois leaned forward, seeing an intricate and finely detailed design.

"Most attractive."

Imogen winked at him and tapped the top of it. The object sprouted wings as delicate as those found on an insect, and when she tapped again, they flapped so rapidly that Francois saw nothing but a blur. A third tap saw it rise a few inches into the air.

Francois moved back in surprise.

"What the...?!"

Imogen leaned down and blew on it, which sent it slowly across the table towards her surprised friend.

"What is it?" he said, lowering his face and squinting.

"Nikola calls it a Bumble, but when he first presented it to me, I was only nine years old, and I suspect he was attempting to appeal to my childish sensibilities."

Francois leaned a little closer, reaching out with a curious finger but not quite touching the device.

"How does it…"

"How does it work? Beyond the fact that it has a power source far more efficient than the one that powered my glove, I have very little idea. The mechanism is clearly gyroscopic, but at Nikola's insistence, I have never let my curiosity get the better of me. It simply is what it is."

"Imogen, it is flying."

"Yes. Yes, it is. Inglenook finds it most entertaining."

"So, I am not the first to be taken into your confidence?"

She slipped a ring over her index finger and held it up. The sphere returned to her smartly, stopping with a soft tap against the ring. The wings ceased flapping, vanishing as quickly as they had appeared, and Imogen returned the Bumble to a small pocket in her dress.

She looked up at her best friend to find him staring at her in astonished silence.

"Yes?" said Imogen in the manner of one who had just answered her front door.

"I believe Mr Orville Wright was the first to achieve powered flight on December 17th, 1903. In what year were you nine years old, Imogen?"

Considering this, Imogen began to explain in what Francois had always considered her well-meaning but long-winded teacher voice.

"Well, as you know, I am not entirely certain. My mother

was never…".

"Imogen!"

She jumped back a little at the sudden volume of Francois' voice.

"1885 or thereabouts.", she said quietly, conscious of the number of heads that had turned following Francois' outburst.

Francois lowered his voice and leaned across the table. Imogen did the same.

"You possessed the secret to powered flight eighteen years before the rest of the world?"

"Eighteen years and four months, actually. Powered flight indeed, but I do not believe Nikola has yet been able to construct a device capable of lifting a human being."

"I am surprised Mr Astor did not offer Nikola his very soul in exchange for such a device."

"Nikola may be eccentric, but he is not an idiot. I understand that he dazzled Mr Jacob Astor with a prototype that hovered for a few minutes, then fell to the floor with a puff of smoke and a somewhat flatulent retort."

"He sold the sizzle rather than the sausage."

"I beg your pardon?" said Imogen curiously.

"A phrase my father used often – a comment on the value

of showmanship."

"Ah, yes. It has the ring of Barnum about it."

"Yes. Are you an admirer of PT Barnum?"

"No. I find him…very obvious."

"As do I, Imogen, as do I." Francois said as he stood, "Now, if you will excuse me, I am in dire need of a haircut. I will be no more than an hour and shall return to meet you in plenty of time for Doctor Sadek's presentation."

CHAPTER FIVE - COFFEE, CAKE & PENELOPE T
B Deck - Saturday, April 13th, 1912 - 11.30 am

Imogen and Francois stood outside the café a little over an hour later, looking up at the small sign above the door. Imogen hid her surprise and amusement well, but not completely.

Cafe Parisien

For the third time, Francois spoke the name aloud.

"One could suspect a guiding hand in our lives, Imogen."

"I am sure one could, assuming they had abandoned all reason and good sense. It is a coincidence, nothing more."

"A remarkable one, Imogen, you must admit."

"The human brain looks for the familiar everywhere, Francois; it is how it makes sense of the world. Your mind ignores the irrelevant and focuses on that which makes sense and gives comfort."

Before Francois could interject, she leaned closer, straightening his jacket lapels and brushing his shoulders like a fussy but proud mother.

"However, I will defer to your fanciful interpretation on this one occasion."

Imogen turned away from her friend and walked ahead through the door. Only then did Francois notice the second sign, featuring a comical caricature of a tweed-suited French Café owner whose round face smiled warmly from beneath a reddish-brown moustache as his outstretched arm beckoned them inside.

Francois frowned at his comical doppelgänger for a moment, then hurried to catch up with Imogen, who was now standing halfway between the door and the cleared space at the far end of the room. She heard him approach but did not turn around as she critiqued her surroundings.

"There is a little too much wicker for my taste."

Francois also looked around at the lightweight furniture, shaking his head slowly.

"Furniture should not wheeze as you sit on it."

Imogen looked over her shoulder at him, lifting her eyebrow and a chuckle in her voice.

"No, it should not."

Francois took in more of the café, admiring the vine-covered trellis and simple but elegant decor.

"Perhaps weight was a factor in its selection; we are aboard a boat, after all."

"Quite so, but still…it is quite awful…and we are aboard a ship, not a boat."

Silently, Francois added wicker furniture to the small but growing list of things that caused Lady Imogen DiRossi's blood to boil. By the time he had done so, she had selected a nearby table and hovered cautiously above the seat for several seconds before she allowed it to take her weight. He joined her just as a waitress appeared with her notebook and pencil, smiling at them both but speaking only to Francois."

"How may I help you, sir?"

Imogen tensed rather obviously and interrupted before Francois could open his mouth. Her English was faultless as usual, but her sudden East European accent surprised both him and the waitress.

"A pot of coffee and two slices of your finest chocolate cake, if you please..."

Imogen glanced up at the small label attached to the girl's chest.

"...Elsie."

"You are aboard The Titanic, madam; everything we have is most certainly the finest available."

Imogen's chair squeaked and bent slightly as she shifted her weight, forcing her to grip the arms.

"Except perhaps my chair?"

Francois hid a smirk behind a menu card as the girl smiled and walked away out of earshot.

"Imogen, was that really necessary?"

"Perhaps not, but considering the price of a ticket on this

vessel, I think the comment is more than justified."

"We have not paid."

"A fact of which she is not aware."

"True. You must forgive me, Imogen; this is my first foray into nautical crime. I have only recently added 'stowaway' to the list of things I intend to omit from my memoirs."

The waitress returned with a surprising suddenness and placed a pot of coffee, a sugar bowl and two cups and saucers on the table. Perhaps in response to her recent dealings with Imogen, she didn't dawdle and was soon on her way. Neither Imogen nor Francois spoke during her brief visit; instead, letting their eyes follow her slightly nervous, rapid movements.

Francois lifted the coffee pot.

"Shall I be Mother?"

"Pardon?"

Imogen would have continued her enquiry, but the familiar and enticing aroma of coffee once more filled her nostrils. She sipped, wrinkled her nose, and returned the cup to the saucer. Using the exquisite tongs provided, she dropped two sugar cubes into the cup, lifted the china teaspoon from her saucer as if poised to stir, and then used it to stab the air, emphasising her point.

"Also, if I were one to wager, which I am not, I would confidently risk five Francs on the assertion that their cake is no better than your own."

Although he knew better than to ask, Francois wondered why she felt the need to maintain the accent when only he could hear.

"Perhaps. Russian, Imogen?"

"Hungarian. I see no reason why subterfuge should be dull; as you know, I am always prepared to add colour and texture to our endeavours."

"Of course."

The teaspoon continued to wave in his general direction.

"I perhaps fancy Montague to be a diplomat of sorts, wooing a naive young girl with his sophisticated ways, lifting her out of Carpathian poverty and whisking her to the altar with his typical, self-serving, but well-intentioned enthusiasm."

"You make me…him sound quite the cad."

"Not at all. A few rough edges, that is all. I am sure Marika will be the making of him."

"Marika?"

"Marika Kovacs, a name that you obviously found awkward and unpronounceable. In what will no doubt be the first of many such compromises on her part, she has recently deferred to your oral deficiencies and settled on the name Violet."

"She has?"

"Yes. I suspect she is still smitten with your sophisticated ways and…"

"Charm?"

"I was going to suggest wealth, but as you wish, your 'charm'. Furthermore, it is a recent marriage, and you must tread carefully. There is still ample time for her to come to her senses and return to her loving family, heartbroken but wiser for the experience."

"I will certainly make every effort to satisfy."

"I am pleased to hear it."

Imogen stirred her coffee, allowing the teaspoon to clink in her fine china cup. She then favoured Francois with a gentle, mocking frown.

"Imogen, could you please stop referring to us in the third person? If there is one thing our current predicament does not need, it is another layer of complication."

She gently tapped the spoon on the cup's rim and returned it to the saucer with a few well-chosen Hungarian words. Francois needed no translation. Imogen's "hush, you ridiculous man" face was already seared onto the fleshy tablets of his brain. The face he pulled in reply was just as familiar to Imogen and, judging by her face, just as unwelcome. Thankfully, the breathless waitress returned with two enormous slices of chocolate cake, each on a fine piece of White Star Line crockery. She placed them on the table, curtseyed and eyed Imogen nervously.

"Sir…Madam, please enjoy."

Imogen and Francois spoke at the same time, Francois in English and Imogen in the native tongue of her latest and possibly finest creation.

"Thank you."

"Köszönöm"

Elsie Figgins once more curtseyed and left Violet and Montague to enjoy coffee and two slices of excellent chocolate cake.

The Café Parisien - Saturday, April 13th, 1912 - 11.58 am

As they ate, activity in the cleared space at the far end of the café increased. A young woman with a natural air of authority was directing a group of stewards in what seemed to be a complex operation. Her voice was educated and clear, easily carrying down the length of the café.

"No, no, no. Here! I must have room to move between the exhibits and explain their importance. What must I do? Crawl underneath the table on my hands and knees?"

She slapped an awkward young man about the head with a presumably antique scroll, causing it to shatter and cover the young lad in dusty confetti. This seemed to anger her more than his ineptitude, but it distracted her long enough for him to quickly make his escape. A few minutes later, under her strict guidance, four tables stood in a neat semi-circular arrangement, each covered in a crisp, white tablecloth. As the stewards left, two very large, dark-skinned men entered, each with a large crate. They were impeccably dressed in smart, white suits and red bowties and appeared entirely mute. Whether this was out of deference, or some physical impairment wasn't clear.

Francois drained his third cup of coffee, tutting as he lifted the pot lid to find it empty. Imogen had been watching events at the far end for a while, but this was the first time she had commented aloud.

"It seems that Mrs Sadek has little patience for the inept."

Francois looked over his shoulder, watching the men lay the contents of the many crates on the tables according to Sadek's precise directions.

"Indeed. She seems quite particular and more than a little impatient. No doubt you approve."

"To a degree, but beating up those in your employ is usually counterproductive and a last resort at best."

Sadek shouted.

"That is almost 3,000 years old, Mahmoud! It is irreplaceable. You are not!"

Francois turned his head again, seeing the big man walking backwards and bowing as he went.

"I must confess, Imogen, I am grateful you are with me. I am not all that keen to talk to her alone. She seems frightful."

Imogen was already on her feet, brushing cake crumbs from her dress, when he turned around again.

"Perhaps a little eccentric, nothing more. Strong emotion often walks hand in hand with a brilliant mind, Francois. I am sure you are quite safe. All I ask is that you try not to break anything."

Francois stood up, far from convinced and a little offended. He knew she was teasing and, as usual, was happy to play along.

"I shall endeavour not to embarrass, Imogen."

"Thank you."

Doctor Sadek was making the final adjustments to her display when she noticed Imogen's booted toes and looked up. Her smile was very much at odds with the recent scene, but it was genuine and quite disarming. Doctor Sadek's long brown hair, tipped with blonde, fell past her pretty face, making her look no more than twenty years old, but her qualifications and reputation would suggest that she was at least twenty-five.

"I am not quite ready," she said indignantly, gesturing at the display behind her.

Imogen took out her pocket watch, looked at it, and then allowed the lid to close slowly before returning it to her pocket. Doctor Sadek looked over at the clock on the wall, stood up straight, smiled at them both, and held out her hand to Imogen.

"Penelope Sadek."

Gently taking her hand, Imogen gave it the politest of shakes.

"Violet Smith, and this is my dear husband, Montague."

Penelope raised an eyebrow on hearing the uncommon name, sending a cold shiver of familiarity down Francois' spine. He bowed his head politely.

"Delighted, Madame."

"Doctor."

"Pardon?"

"I am Doctor Penelope T. Sadek. You may call me Doctor Sadek."

Imogen interjected, growing slightly frustrated with the excessive formality.

"T?"

"Tallulah. My mother was a dancer of sorts."

"...of sorts?"

Penelope ignored the question and gently shook Francois' hand.

"An American, sir? New York, perhaps?"

"Yes, but our home is in Paris."

"Four years ago, I interned at The Louvre under Professor Pierre Maloné. It was there that I met my husband. Paris is a most beautiful city."

Faultless French dripped from her lips as she caught Francois's twinkle in the eye, replying in the language of his home.

"I have been to the museum many times, Doctor. Perhaps this is not our first meeting, but it is merely the first time we have conversed - very much my loss, I feel."

Imogen's sigh was loud and obvious, but Penelope nodded politely, quite deliberately ignoring her and smiled back at the charming Café owner.

"...also, mine, Monsieur, but one must not waste a moment regretting what could have been when the present offers so much."

In the months he had known Imogen, he had met few people who were not intimidated by her to some degree, and none were as young as Doctor Sadek. Francois could feel Imogen's disapproving gaze stab at him like the point of a furled umbrella.

"...and you, Violet? I cannot quite place your accent?"

Imogen opened her mouth, but Francois quickly interjected, lightly putting his arm around her waist in a loose approximation of marital affection. He couldn't be sure what sharp and unforgiving item he had grasped beneath her dress, but its sharp edge dug into his fingers.

"Violet was born in Hungary but left when she was a small child."

Sadek's eyes widened slightly as she smiled at Imogen.

"Yet your accent remains."

Imogen's reply was sharp, rapid and almost entirely incomprehensible.

"One may take the girl out of Hungary, but not Hungary from the girl."

She made a mental note to discuss the finer points of convincing backstories with Francois at a later moment.

"Well, quite," said Doctor Sadek, somewhat taken aback.

Francois' chest swelled a little at Imogen's reply; he was not entirely sure if he was prouder of Imogen or his fictional wife. He had no idea what she had said, but it was clear from Doctor Sadek's face that she had no idea either.

Imogen leaned forward quickly, slipping easily from her husband's awkward embrace. She put her hands behind her back and looked more closely at a small clay figure on the table.

"Osiris. 22nd Dynasty. Quite splendid."

"Why yes, but I have seen better examples. You have some knowledge of the period, Violet?"

"A little. Egyptian history fascinates me, and recent events have reawakened my interest. Your collection is impressive, Doctor Sadek, but I am curious to know why you chose to display it here."

Sadek picked up the piece and handed it to Imogen, who carefully turned it over in her hand. Francois had already noticed the nearby statue of Aset and knew Imogen had seen it, too. Although it was smaller than the one they had found inside the fountain in Place St Genevieve, it was very similar.

"I am escorting this small part of my husband's collection to New York, where it will be on loan to The Metropolitan Museum of Art. I grew bored watching the view from my cabin window, so I offered to display my artefacts and perhaps educate those interested in such things."

As they talked, a dozen or so other passengers had begun to browse the collection under Sadek's aides' watchful eyes.

"My husband would very much like a position on the museum board, and he feels the loan of these items will open that door a little wider, so to speak. The board members are pompous and deathly dull, but I recognise his wish to advance his career. As always, I shall bathe in his wake."

There was a slight bitterness in her voice. Imogen frowned, recognising a kindred spirit and someone who had encountered the same barriers as she had.

"You are hampered by an outdated system that values

gender above talent and experience. I am confident that it will not always be the way, but for now, it seems we must be content with being difficult and causing somewhat of a nuisance whenever possible."

"Why, Violet, you should not speak so. What if Montague was to hear of such attitudes?"

Imogen looked at Francois, who was charming a small group across the room and enthusiastically waving his arms around.

"My husband is a rare man, Doctor Sadek, blessed with patience, kindness, and an ability to embrace the most radical of ideas. He does so with good humour, an open mind, and an almost complete lack of worry about what others may think. I am most fortunate to have found him."

Sadek followed Imogen's gaze but said nothing. Imogen seemed lost in thought as she watched Francois.

"Of course, if you repeat what I have just said to his face, I will have to kill you. It will be quick and almost painless, so do not be overly concerned. We Hungarians are a proud but violent people."

She smiled at Sadek, who smiled back, not entirely convinced of Imogen's seriousness.

"Aset," pointed Imogen matter-of-factly.

Sadek shook the worry from her face and focused on the statue now inches from Imogen's nose.

"Yes, Violet, a particular interest of mine."

"Really? May I?"

Sadek nodded, and Imogen picked up the statue. It was smooth, cool and a little more than half the size of the one in her study. Sadek cleared her throat.

"My first thesis, and, I think, my finest, concerned the myths and legends of Aset. I was mocked for what many consider the more fanciful and unlikely aspects of her life. Are you familiar?"

"Somewhat."

Sadek continued, happy to have found an equal in such matters.

"I am convinced there is some substance to the legends of The Risen Dead, but I am often mocked for it. My husband tolerates my interest, but only out of duty and affection. Aset was said to have brought her dead armies back to life, and much contemporary evidence adds weight to the idea - almost too much to ignore but ignore it they do."

"Resurrection of the dead seems unlikely. I understand that the prevailing opinion is that Aset was a gifted physician, nothing more, and the fanciful aspects of her story are merely a mistranslation."

"I am fluent in seven languages of the era and have a working knowledge of five more. I rely on no one else for my translations, Violet. I stand by my own interpretation even if no one else does."

"I meant no offence, Doctor Sadek."

Sadek sighed. Her frustration was not with the present company.

"... and I took none. I am sometimes too quick to respond defensively, and perhaps I should apologise. They do not listen to me because I am young and pretty, Violet."

There was sadness in her voice, telling of frustrations all too familiar to Imogen as she contemplated the statue and what they had seen that night in the café, which was still unexplained. She looked into the wise young face before her and smiled.

"It is our cross to bear, but we will prevail, although our path may be longer and strewn with obstacles. Promise me that you will persist. There are wonders yet to be explained, and people like you and I will ensure that they will be one day."

Sadek thought for a moment.

"I believe I shall, Violet."

"Excellent, Doctor Sadek."

"Please call me Penny. Despite my years of study and research, my doctorate owes more to my husband's influence. My name and reputation are my own."

She turned to one of her aides and gave him instructions in rapid Arabic. He nodded politely and left.

"I promised my husband that I would not display this; it is somewhat valuable and not for the public's gaze."

A few moments later, the man returned with a small wooden box and handed it to the Doctor. She opened it, took out a leather pouch, and laid it on the table before Imogen. The pouch was roughly twelve inches long and fastened with faded suede laces that she began to untie.

"The bindings are not original, I'm afraid. They are an acceptable approximation fashioned by an old man in a Cairo backstreet last year. However, they are as close to the original as I could manage."

She moved the laces to one side, only then realising the aide was looking over her shoulder. She barked at him in Arabic, and he stepped back a few paces.

"Your companions seem most attentive."

"My husband's most loyal aides, sent here to spy on me as much as to ensure my welfare. Last month, Mahmoud threw a young man into The Nile for winking at me. He takes his responsibilities very seriously, and it seems he can lift and throw a man a considerable distance when the need arises."

She turned around again, this time addressing him more calmly, and he moved further away. Then, she turned to Imogen and reverently opened the leather pouch.

"This, Violet, is The Serpent's Grasp."

The bracelet sparkled in the sunlight that shone through the café windows. It was simple but beautiful: a gold and silver banded snake that wrapped around the lower arm from wrist to elbow.

"I have no substantive evidence that Aset wore this, other than a few carvings and a brief, incomplete reference on a small tablet, but..."

She placed it loosely around her slim wrist, then ran her fingertip from her elbow to her wrist. As it moved downwards, the snake gently coiled tighter against her skin until it was snug. She lifted her arm and turned it about in the sunlight.

"...who else would wear such a thing?"

"Indeed."

Doctor Sadek lowered her wrist, twisting her arm nearer to Imogen and wincing slightly.

"What is the matter?"

"It is growing tighter on my arm, and I don't seem to be able to..."

Suddenly, her arm jerked towards Imogen, who quickly stepped back. The bracelet on Doctor Sadek's arm was becoming increasingly uncomfortable, and she clenched her other hand on the table for support.

"Mahmoud, quickly, assist me!"

Rapidly, her aide moved towards her, clearly concerned but unsure as to how he could help.

"The bracelet is growing tighter; help me get it off!"

He fumbled for the clasp, but his fingers were too large.

The bracelet continued to constrict the girl's arm, bulging her flesh in the gaps. She cried out again, panic in her voice.

"Mahmoud!"

Imogen pushed his hand away, her smaller fingers finding the clasp and pulling at it. The bracelet immediately opened with a satisfying snap and fell onto the table. Sadek relaxed, stumbling into Mahmoud's arms. She was grateful for his support and concerned, soft words for a few moments, but when she became aware that so many were staring, she pulled away.

"Thank you, Mahmoud…Violet."

Imogen smiled, nodding at Mahmoud, who returned the gesture. Retrieving her spectacles from her dress pocket, she leaned a little closer and looked closely at the artefact through clear, thick lenses.

"You are quite welcome. My efforts required little skill, merely smaller fingers. Has that ever happened before?"

"No. I have worn it several times and, no, never."

"Intriguing. I see no mechanism other than a simple clasp."

Imogen leaned closer still, keeping her hands behind her back, unwilling to touch the bracelet again. Doctor Sadek's arm was red where it had tightened, but she seemed unharmed as Mahmoud applied a lotion to it. As Imogen looked down again, the bracelet seemed to move towards her. Investigating this further, she stepped sideways slightly, and it moved in her direction once more. It was now at the table's edge and in danger of falling off, so she retrieved a pencil from her pocket and tried to push it back. To her surprise, it resisted with just enough force to remain in place.

"Oh my."

She put the pencil down and pushed the bracelet with two fingers. The Serpent's Grasp instantly flipped over on its axis, wrapped around her wrist and closed. Across the room, a sudden tingling caused Francois to forget his current conversation; he mouthed Imogen's name and looked over to see her raise her arm in surprise. The gold and silver bracelet twinkled in the sunlight, distracting him momentarily.

"Francois..."

He saw Imogen's lips move from across the room, too far for him to hear, but somehow, he did hear her. Ignoring all politeness and civility, he pushed past his small, attentive audience and rushed to her side.

"Violet..."

"I am...quite well...I think, but I cannot be sure..."

Imogen realised that Sadek was staring at them both.

"...my love."

Francois put his arm on Imogen's shoulder, just as she lost consciousness and collapsed to the floor.

Imogen opened her eyes and took a deep, surprised breath, realising she was now upright and standing in the dark. It was a deep, inky blackness, and the only sound was her own breathing.

"Francois?"

Imogen put her hand to her shoulder, resting it where her friend's hand had been moments ago. Francois was no longer next to her, and she was entirely alone. Clearly, she was dreaming - perhaps hallucinating, but her mind seemed unusually aware.

"2, 3, 5, 7, 11, 13…"

She stopped reciting prime numbers, satisfied that her mind was active. Only then did she hear something familiar and comforting.

"Boreas?"

The flap of his wings grew louder, but she couldn't see him until he was almost upon her and slowing to land on her wrist. As she raised her arm, she felt the grip of his claws and the surprising lightness of his weight. He cawed, adjusting his position and tilting his head at his friend. He had brought a strange blue glow with him that lit a small area around them.

"Where are we, Boreas?"

The crow tilted his head the other way, cawed again and flew off, leaving Imogen alone and once more in the dark. She turned around slowly, talking to no one in particular and raising her voice.

"Why am I here? I presume there is a purpose to this?"

There was no reply, so Imogen sat on the floor, lifting her dress to the thighs and crossing her leather-covered legs. She took a deep breath and closed her eyes.

"Very well. I shall wait."

"Imogen."

She had been so relaxed and close to meditation that she didn't reply or open her eyes.

"Imogen?"

The smell of coffee and the sound of a crackling fire were enough to make her open her eyes. She was at her usual table in the Café, in front of the fire, but she was no longer alone.

"Imogen?"

A familiar black kitten was sitting on the table, staring up at her. Imogen closed one eye and peered down at her.

"Inglenook?"

The kitten's mouth moved.

"Hello, Imogen."

Imogen moved back a little in surprise.

"Cats do not talk."

"Do they not?"

"No. They do not possess a sufficiently complex larynx."

Inglenook meowed twice and then once more very loudly, opening her mouth wide as she did so. Imogen moved back a little more to avoid the unexpected, fishy-breathed intimacy.

"I shall have to take your word for it. I seem in fine voice today."

"Also, your thought processes are not sufficiently developed to allow conversation."

The kitten was no longer looking at her. Instead, it looked around at the deserted café.

"This is a nice place. I like it here."

"I…"

"Please do not worry, Imogen. You are quite alright, and your mind is as sharp and clear as ever."

"I take it you are not Inglenook."

"I am, but also, I am not. It is difficult to explain in a way that even you could grasp, Imogen. Suffice to say that I am far away, and this place and Inglenook are both very close to you - hooks on which to hang my tale if you prefer."

Imogen's eyes grew wider, surprised at the articulate feline in front of her, whose eyes now looked deeply into hers.

"I must say that I find your command of language fascinating, Imogen DiRossi. As you may have surmised, I am making use of it. Inglenook is a bright little thing, but I would stumble at the simplest crossword puzzle, whatever that is. Incidentally, she does not like to be lifted by the scruff of her neck. It does not hurt, but it robs her of dignity."

"Oh…"

"I am sorry, but Inglenook's thought processes are a little muddled. A book with pages in the wrong order, if you like."

Inglenook stretched her front legs, yawning and pushing her bottom and pointy tail into the air before settling down again.

"She very much likes it when you tickle her stomach."

"Yes, I know. There is purring."

"She is very fond of you and also of Francois, but she enjoys him thinking otherwise."

Imogen very slowly moved closer to the table, her fascination for the moment overriding her confusion. She bent low until her nose was closer to Inglenook's face.

"What is happening to me?"

"You are currently unconscious on the floor of the Café Parisien aboard the RMS Titanic and have been for almost four seconds now. What you have yet to realise, despite my best efforts to help, is when you are."

"When? I do not understand. Explain!"

"I would prefer to let events unfold naturally. You will soon wake up, and hopefully, you will remember at least some of what I am about to show you. However, you are not The Other, so I cannot be certain."

"The Other?"

"Yes, The Other. She is different."

It was clear that there would be no further explanation.

"You must go now."

"Where?"

"Home, eventually, but on the way, I need you to do something for me."

"What would you have me do?"

"Take it, Imogen. She should not have it. Take it to The Other."

"Take what? Why must you be so imprecise?"

"I am a cat. Considering that fact, I might suggest that I am doing quite well. In any case, I have only done this once before, and I am not sure how much you will remember. She must not have it, Imogen. Take it."

Imogen nodded slowly, as confused as she ever had been.

"Now...pick a card, Imogen, any card."

Francois' pack of cards hadn't been on the table when she had arrived, but it was there now, just to the side of Inglenook and fanned out, much as it had been when she had sat here this morning. She reached out for one, but Inglenook's paw was tapping another, her claws making a gentle scratching noise. Imogen pulled it out, and Inglenook looked up at her.

"Splendid."

The brightest white flash forced Imogen to close her eyes. The sounds and smells of The Café faded, replaced by a gentle breeze and a distant hum that she couldn't identify.

"Open your eyes, Imogen. All is quite well."

As she opened her eyes, Imogen felt the warmth of summer on her face. Sky, clouds, metal…Paris. Dizzy for a moment, she put both hands on a nearby railing and saw the city a thousand feet below. The railing was as it had been the last time she had visited Eiffel's Tower, but now a wire mesh stretched over her head. The strong breeze lifted Imogen's hat, and she turned around, reaching out, but someone else had caught it.

"You really must learn to hold onto that hat of yours, Imogen."

Elizabeth walked towards Imogen and held out the hat, her own hair in a long, red ponytail down her back.

"I grow tired of this," said Imogen as she took the hat and threw it behind her.

"I know. I must confess that I expected this to be a little more straightforward. Your mind is not what I expected."

"Is that an attempt to flatter?"

"No. You despise flattery."

Elizabeth tapped the side of her head a few times with her finger, then smirked.

"…also mime artists, wicker furniture, iced doughnuts and the works of Sir Arthur Conan Doyle."

"Where am I?"

"You are in Paris, Imogen, as well you know."

"I am not."

Imogen turned and looked out past the fine mesh that rose over their heads and across a vast, unfamiliar city.

"Actually, this is not strictly your Paris, but that isn't quite the point for now."

Imogen turned quickly and grabbed Elizabeth's hand with a firmness that surprised them both.

"Are you even real? Is any of this real?"

Elizabeth smiled. It felt familiar and safe, but Imogen had no idea why.

"I am confused, and I do not like confusion."

"Something has happened to you and also to Francois,

Imogen. It happened to me a long time ago, and soon you will understand quite what it is; until then, I need you to concentrate."

"No."

Imogen hated this loss of control, and refusal seemed to be her only option.

"Please, Imogen. Current events have a purpose and an important one. I promise you and Francois will return home once matters have been resolved."

Elizabeth leaned close enough to Imogen to see herself reflected in her eyes and planted a small kiss on the tip of her nose.

"I shall see you again soon."

With that, Elizabeth and The Eiffel Tower blurred from existence. The world spun around Imogen, seemingly only to slow down when there was a need to highlight an event.

Now, she stood in a forest clearing, watching a little girl pick flowers and sing to herself. Imogen smiled as she watched the happy child pat her horse and speak to it as if it were a friend. Then she felt the sting of regret as her mother's face appeared through the ragged curtains at the back of their cart. The little girl laughed and climbed in again as the cart disappeared down the dusty road.

The years rushed by, and images of her marriage and her husband reminded Imogen of a life forced upon her and her eventual escape across the sea. Then, years alone—

the forests, the towns, and the few people she trusted with her life—a time of learning and experience but little else.

The edges of her mouth curled in a smile as she saw Place St Genevieve, The Café, Francois and all her new friends, human and not. Boreas flew close, and she reached out her hand, but then he was gone, squawking as he passed over her head. She could hear Belle and Jacques arguing and see Monica sweeping the cobbles outside her shop, but as with little Iris, none of them seemed to be aware of Imogen's fleeting presence.

More memories rushed past until things were no longer familiar. She saw Nikola Tesla standing on a bridge lit only by gas lamps. He leant on the stonework with one hand as blue sparks fell from his other hand into the fog that wrapped around his feet. But he was crying and mouthing words she couldn't hear. As she reached out, he looked to his side, so disturbed by what he saw that he ran, disappearing into the darkness and out of sight.

"Nikola…"

Now, it was Place St Genevieve again, but it was dark and cold. There was a scream and manic laughter, followed by fire and the sound of people shouting. Francois suddenly stood before her, his smile brief before it was replaced with anger.

"You were wrong, Imogen. You did not listen to me, and now he is dead."

Imogen felt a surge of emotion and reached out for her friend, but he stepped back, out of reach, and his voice faded.

"You were wrong, Imogen…"

Then, the sea, a lighthouse, grass, unfamiliar voices and cold, damp air. A girl ran with a dog, calling his name as she hurried to catch him. Elizabeth, her hair and face aflame, pointed and smiled.

Images flashing by more quickly now. Imogen felt small, looking up at the towering figure of The Statue of Liberty and the skyline of New York; wind, rain and intense cold spun around her. She covered her eyes, unable to stand the rush of information.

"Stop this!" she screamed.

Suddenly, all was quiet and still. Imogen felt a hand on her shoulder, squeezing gently.

"Francois?"

She opened her eyes to see soft green grass, trees and the ruins of a castle. confused, she tried to take it all in as Elizabeth's arm dropped away from her.

"I am sorry, Imogen, but this is your life and your purpose. You will remember at least some of this, which must suffice."

"Who are you?"

"I am far away. The Other will explain. Listen to her."

"Who is The Other you keep mentioning?"

"You are safe now, both of you. Imogen…remember, she must not have it."

Slowly, darkness enveloped Imogen, and she fell to the ground.

Long before she opened her eyes, she smelt Francois' cologne and immediately felt safe and calm, knowing he was nearby.

"Imogen?"

As her surroundings came into focus, she felt a second gentle tap on her cheek and his whispering voice.

"Francois?"

He smiled down at her, almost uncomfortably close, but she noticed the others nearby and realised why he was being so quiet.

"You fainted."

"I did not."

"You certainly gave that impression."

"Hush."

Imogen raised her voice as she sat up, once more confidently Hungarian.

"Thank you, Montague, I am quite well."

Francois helped her to her feet, brushing her behind with almost inappropriate enthusiasm, but she allowed it, somewhat impressed with his dedication to the role she had forced upon him.

"That will do, husband. We have an audience, after all."

"Of course."

Standing to the side, Doctor Sadek had been watching the exchange.

"I am glad you are well, Violet. May I have my bracelet?"

"Yes, of course."

Mahmoud took The Serpent's Grasp from Imogen with exaggerated politeness and wrapped it up slowly and carefully in its suede wallet. He nodded and muttered in his native tongue as he took it.

"You are most welcome, Mahmoud."

Sadek, Mahmoud, and Francois all looked at Imogen in surprise, but it was Sadek who spoke.

"Violet?"

"Yes?"

"I did not realise that you spoke Arabic."

"I do not, certainly not with any fluency. I am acquainted with a retired soldier who travelled the world in his youth, and I have learned what I can. Why are you all looking at me in that manner?"

Francois watched Imogen's lips move, hearing the

unfamiliar, soft and often guttural words interspersed with more familiar nouns. Unsure what else he could do, he once more touched her shoulder. Intrigued, Doctor Sadek kept her voice calm as she tilted her head to one side.

"You most certainly are speaking Arabic, Violet, as am I."

Imogen paused, disorientated momentarily, wondering why Francois gripped her shoulder. In the space of a minute, she had recited at least seven different languages until Hungarian-accented English returned. How her brain coped with it all was a mystery that Francois would never solve. She looked up at him, clearly still puzzled.

"I am not sure how that is possible."

Francois felt relief as he patted Imogen's shoulder twice. Just before he had time to remove it, she lifted her hand and patted his in return.

"I would very much like to return to our cabin, Montague. I do not feel at all well."

"Yes, of course."

Imogen nodded at Sadek, who showed genuine concern.

"Are you sure that you are quite well, Violet?"

"Yes, thank you, Penny. It was a pleasure to meet you. I hope we can talk again before New York."

"Yes, I would like that very much. Perhaps dinner at some point? I dine alone in my cabin under the watchful eyes of

Mahmoud and Ammon. Quite when they eat, I have no idea."

As if on cue, Francois took Imogen's arm and led her from the café. When they were out of sight, Imogen straightened, obviously not as damaged as her audience had thought.

"Thank you, Francois. I am, in fact, quite well, but I have just had the most inexplicable experience, and I needed to be away from that room."

"You were unconscious for less than a minute, but I was quite concerned to see you...out of sorts."

"Worry not, Francois; I am in fine fettle and as constant as The Northern Star."

With that, Imogen walked into a large Yucca Plant.

"Oops..." she giggled.

The Café Parisien - Saturday, April 13th, 1912 - 12.45 pm

Penelope Sadek watched Violet and Montague leave, confused and frustrated at recent events. Behind her, Mahmoud and Ammon continued to supervise the few remaining visitors, but her interest had only one focus. Not one for frivolous entertainment or the company of crowds, she had found the trip a bore and had spent most of the time reading in her cabin. Now, she wandered up and down the tables, nodding politely and answering the mostly uninformed but well-meaning questions. The afternoon had provided more distraction than she had planned, but it had undoubtedly passed a few hours, which was good.

Almost an hour later, the last of the passengers had left. Once her aides had safely removed the artefacts, the three stewards reappeared to help clear the empty tables.

Mahmoud bowed his head and spoke with his usual deep, concerned voice.

"You seem distracted, Doctor."

"It has been quite the afternoon, Mahmoud, has it not?"

He nodded, wary of his place and the privacy of his employer.

"Mahmoud, I would like to know more about Violet Smith. Her husband is clearly a harmless, if charming, buffoon, but she intrigues me. Be discrete, as I know you can be."

"Yes, Doctor."

Sadek smiled as he nodded and walked away, leaving her alone to watch the ocean from the café window. She had lied to Imogen. The Serpent's Grasp had reacted like that once before, but it had only moved a few inches, and the girl who touched it screamed in pain and ran off. That was in The Louvre several years ago, and the girl had any number of directions to run. Even if Mahmoud or Ammon had pursued her, she would have vanished into the crowds of Paris.

This was different, though; for the next few days, Violet Smith had nowhere to go.

Cabin B81, Saturday, April 13th, 1912 - 12.55 pm

Francois hung Imogen's hat on the hook behind the door as she lifted her legs onto the bed and rested against the pillows.

"Can I get you anything, Imogen?"

"Some water, please."

As he disappeared into the bathroom, Imogen pulled up her dress. The pockets in her leggings were mostly empty now, making her feel vulnerable. Francois returned with a glass of water.

"Francois, I have six Aspirin, some coffee, some powdered milk, five sugar cubes, and a few trinkets. Of course, if we need to make someone vomit uncontrollably, I have three vials of ground Devil's Ivy, but otherwise, I have never felt so unprepared."

She lifted her bare wrist, twisting it in the light through the ornate windows. Francois sat on the bed and took her hand, pulling it down gently until it rested on her leg.

"Imogen DiRossi, you are the most prepared and

resourceful person I have ever met. Your continued presence is possibly the only thing keeping me sane and calm."

"Oh, hush."

"Your intellect and experience are what keeps us safe, not what you hide in your skirts."

Francois blushed in the brief, awkward silence and patted Imogen's leg as he wondered what to say next.

"I believe you have just soured a rather genuine and touching moment, Francois."

"Yes. That was not my intention."

"It is of no matter; as usual, we shall be uncomfortable for a moment and then move on."

"Agreed."

Imogen took out her watch, unnecessarily checked it against the wall clock, and then returned it to her pocket as Francois glanced around the room. Several seconds passed.

"You strange man."

"Yes."

Francois smiled as she crossed her booted feet. He could tell she was preoccupied. Unusually, she seemed to struggle to vocalise what she was thinking.

"During my brief period of unconsciousness, I experienced something that I cannot explain. It was neither a dream nor a hallucination - I have experienced both before, and this was quite different."

"It was? What did you see?"

"Boreas, The Café and many other familiar things, but also…"

"Imogen?"

"…the past and many things I have not experienced. I cannot remember it all, which frustrates me no end."

"You remembered your home and your family, Imogen. Perhaps your mind merely sought to comfort you."

"Perhaps, but the experience lingers, and I struggle to settle my thoughts. I cannot shake the feeling that there are things I must do. Inglenook was most insistent."

Before Francois could comment on her intriguing statement, Imogen swung her legs over the side of the bed, forcing him to stand. She took her hat from the hook and adjusted it in the mirror.

"I require fresh air and a walk! How is your leg? Are you fit to accompany me?"

"Of course," said Francois, standing up straight and only stumbling slightly. He looked out of the window at the white-tipped waves and wished he had the scarf Monica had given him on his last birthday.

"It looks chilly."

"Faint heart never won fair maid, Francois."

A few moments later, as they climbed the staircase, Francois gave a young man from Iowa two dollars in exchange for a bright red woollen scarf. The eager man hurried away down the stairs with his unexpected windfall, worried that Francois would examine the ragged item too closely and change his mind.

Francois didn't change his mind. Instead, he threw the long, warm scarf around his neck, forcing Imogen to lean out of the way to avoid the flying, tasselled end. She regarded his snug, beaming face for several seconds, rolled her eyes and then walked on ahead.

"You look like a snowman."

"Thank you."

"It was not a compliment."

"I know."

CHAPTER SIX - SEA BREEZES & OLD FRIENDS
RMS Titanic, Promenade Deck, Saturday, April 13th - 1.15 pm

The moment they opened the door to the promenade, the wind hit their faces, having stopped briefly to grasp a good deal of The Atlantic Ocean. Francois gasped, leaning back against the door as the wind whipped spray into his face. His aching limbs were of little help as he clung to the door frame with one hand and pulled his new scarf over his mouth with the other.

"Hell's teeth!"

Imogen walked boldly onto the deck, put one hand on her hat, and took a deep breath. She closed her eyes and spun around to face Francois, beaming in the face of nature. The wind gusted, lifting her hat under her hand.

"Oh, my!"

"Imogen, I am cold."

Imogen raised her voice to be heard over the freezing gusts of wind.

"Well, of course you are; we are sailing on The Atlantic Ocean! And clearly, far enough North for us to feel it!"

"I can certainly feel it, I promise you!"

"Oh, hush. Come here."

Imogen encouraged him away from the door, supporting him with her arm and making it look like the reverse was true. He straightened as best he could, and together, they walked with as much dignity as they could muster.

"Did you not walk on deck on your voyage from New York?"

"Just the once, and that was quite enough. My brief foray on deck and the subsequent tumble caused me to lose both my hat and considerable dignity, so I chose instead to retire to the calm of the saloon and its well-stocked bar. It was there that I made the acquaintance of one Albert Maison, a young man who taught me how to play Backgammon. The weather was foul for almost the entire journey, so I spent much time playing Backgammon and drinking fine Whiskey with a new friend. I discovered quite quickly that doing so almost completely cured my seasickness."

"A judicious course of action."

"Yes, and had I foolishly wandered on deck instead, I may not have met Albert, he may not have mentioned his uncle in Paris, and I would not have met that Uncle and inherited his café."

Imogen held on firmly as another gust pushed them back slightly, misting them with more spray.

"How fragile the binds that tie us together, Mr Meyer."

"Fragile indeed."

There was a pause as Francois wondered who would state the obvious first. After a few moments, he could no longer wait.

"We would not have met."

"No..."

Imogen turned her head to face him, still gripping his arm.

"No, we would not."

"That is not a happy thought, Imogen."

"It is a thought, Francois, nothing more. As you can clearly see, we are together, and you cling to me both physically and metaphorically. I suspect it will take more than an ocean breeze to tear us asunder."

"Breeze?"

She leaned against him briefly, her elbow nudging him in the ribs. Before he could respond, Imogen caught sight of the stern, let go of his arm and marched ahead with single-minded determination. Francois stumbled forward awkwardly, the chill of the wind numbing his legs enough for him to make good time.

Ahead of him, Imogen was climbing a short ladder onto the raised deck at the stern. She ignored the two small children who sat above her on the docking bridge, swinging their legs and watching the world go by, but a few moments later, as Francois walked beneath them, he looked up and they waved back.

Much as she did at the top of Eiffel's tower, and with the same sense of abandonment, Imogen ran the last few steps and leapt onto the second bar of the railings, leaning over to watch the ship's propellors churn the waters below.

"Imogen, please take care."

"I am quite well, Francois, I promise you. Look at it! Power! Science! Human ingenuity at its finest!

Francois carefully did as she asked, keeping his feet firmly on the deck and gripping the railing in the absence of Imogen's steadying arm.

"It is most impressive, Imogen. Also, it is terrifying and dangerous. Please step down and…"

"Three propellers, I believe. The pattern is quite distinctive. Perhaps we can find a steward or possibly an engineer to tell us more."

She leaned over even further, forcing Francois to grasp the back of her dress as she shouted above the chaos from below. She slipped a few inches, laughing excitedly.

"Please do not fuss, Francois; I am quite safe."

"Francois Meyer does not fuss; he worries when his friend indulges her habit of dangling recklessly from yet another of the world's engineering marvels."

Francois clung to her dress and what he knew to be her concealed undergarments, peering down at the churning waters far below.

"If you were to fall in, Imogen, it would be the end of you. This ship would take a considerable distance to come to a full stop, by which time you would be gone. Then what would I do?"

The noise of the propellors almost completely drowned out Imogen's voice.

"... cluck like a mother hen."

Francois only heard the end of her playfully critical response and neither heard the young man approach from behind.

"Sir! Madam! Please…I must ask you to take more care and step away from the railing. Please…"

The eager voice got closer and louder, initially muffled by everything around them. Francois straightened, turned around, and met the gaze of Steward 3rd Class Berni Rosseau, standing straight and eager in a crisp white uniform and smart cap. The moment he recognised Francois, the colour drained from his face until it almost matched his jacket.

"Ahhhhh!"

Berni jumped back almost two feet, then steadied himself on a bollard. He felt his heart beat loud enough in his chest to be heard over the waves.

"Monsieur?"

Berni's eyes darted to Francois' right, and the figure bent inelegantly over the railings. Francois' eyes widened, and his grip tightened on the railing. Imogen chose this moment to straighten and turn around, one hand still on her hat as she continued her narration.

"...two driven by the engines and a third usually by steam from the boilers..."

Berni's memories of the events at Château Porticcio were still fresh in his mind despite his best efforts to forget. However, the sight of Violet and Montague brought it all rushing back. Imogen looked the young man up and down, failing to hide her surprise completely.

"Monsieur Rosseau! What a pleasure and a surprise it is to see you again."

Berni's mouth hung open as he sat on the bollard, undid one button of his jacket and put his hand on his chest, replying in trembling but precise English.

"Good afternoon, Madame...you may speak to me in English. I must speak to all passengers in English."

Imogen allowed herself a little smile and nodded, noting Berni's almost complete lack of French accent.

"You seem most proficient, Berni, and in such a short time."

"Madame?"

Francois reached out and offered his hand to Berni.

"It is very nice to meet you again, Berni; I trust you are well? I assumed you were on a path to a position of some importance under Monsieur Peretti at The Château, and yet here you are - a long way from home and wearing a smart uniform."

As the conversation continued, Berni began to relax.

"I remained in my post for some time, but I grew restless and sought out opportunity elsewhere. Monsieur Peretti was kind enough to provide a letter of recommendation. The offices of The White Star Line much appreciated both his name and the letter."

Imogen took a step closer and also offered her hand.

"It seems The Wolf's influence spreads far and wide, Berni. One must take every opportunity to improve one's circumstances."

Only when she got closer did she notice the lines of experience in the young man's face and the merest shadow of a moustache on his top lip.

"Had I not, I would have spent the last three years carrying a silver tray about his private rooms in the château, and as you can see, there is a wide world outside Paris."

Imogen's head tilted sharply.

"I beg your pardon?"

"Madame?"

Francois turned to Imogen, then Berni, coming to the same conclusion seconds after Imogen.

"You said three years."

"Yes, sir. It has been almost three years. I left the château some three months after we first met, shortly after my mother's birthday. Five months later, on Wednesday, 29th October, I took up service on RMS Titanic when my training was complete. It is all in my logbook—every moment, event, and…misstep."

Imogen's head was spinning - an infrequent and uncomfortable experience in her case. She took out her watch, opened it and thought of the clock on the cabin wall. Francois was hurrying to catch up with her thought processes, worried at his friend's brief loss of composure. She looked down, forcing herself to concentrate, then spoke calmly and quietly.

"Berni, what is the date?"

"Madame?"

She took a step closer, raising her voice.

"The date. What is today's date?"

"The 13th of April, Madame."

Francois also took a step forward and gripped Berni's arm.

"What year is it?"

"Sir?"

"What year is it, Berni?"

"1912. You do not know the year?

Francois let go of Berni's arm and stepped back.

"Shit!"

Imogen turned to her friend and quickly slapped his arm with enough force to make him stumble against the railing.

"Ow! I feel the moment justifies profanity."

She turned back to Berni, who looked as confused as ever. Imogen frowned, trying to regain her composure, but her mind was whirling.

"I am sorry, Madame Violet. Today is the 13th day of April 1912. I am not sure what else I should say. I meant no offence."

"You did not cause any, Berni; it was merely a surprise, that is all."

Imogen leaned her back against the railings and closed her eyes briefly, trying to organise her thoughts. Then, she let out a sigh, opened her eyes, and folded her arms.

"...and my name is not Violet. I am Imogen DiRossi, and this is Mr Francois Meyer."

Berni looked from Imogen to Francois and back again. Eager to calm the poor young man, Francois tried to explain.

"Violet and Montague are a fiction, Berni. We required a

certain amount of anonymity to affect an entrance to the château. Forgive us."

"…and you are not married?"

They briefly looked at one other and then returned to Berni, replying together.

"No. We are not."

"Forgive me, Sir, Madame…it is just that…"

Imogen was already pacing up and down. Neither Francois nor Berni felt the need to interrupt her mumbling.

"1912, 1912, 1912…three years, ten months, two days…"

She stopped, looked at her watch briefly, and then looked up at Francois.

"…twenty-two hours…and nine minutes. Francois!"

"What?"

"We have…"

Berni looked at them both, unsure whether to stay or leave. Fortunately, Imogen decided for him.

"Thank you for your assistance, Berni; we hope to see you again during the voyage."

The young man stood and bowed at the neck.

"It would also give me great pleasure. If you could tell me

your cabin number, I will call on you when I have a moment."

Imogen had wandered down a rare conversational cul-de-sac, and only Francois knew the way out.

"Tell him, Imogen. I cannot bear another layer of deception. He is a good man and more than capable of discretion."

She took a few seconds to consider her friend's idea and quickly agreed.

"Berni, I realise this may put you in a difficult position, but we are forced to rely on our previous association with you and possibly take advantage of it."

"Madame?"

Imogen took a deep breath.

"We do not know how we came to be on board and do not have tickets. We have been concealing ourselves in Stateroom B81, and we would be very grateful if you would allow this to continue until we arrive at our destination. We found the cabin empty and in considerable disrepair, and we have inconvenienced no one apart from The White Star Line Company. I believe they can bear the cost of our passage easily."

Francois smiled at Berni, his gentle shrug adding little to the conversation. Imogen briefly considered a small financial inducement, but the young man's smile told her all she needed to know.

"Twice now, you have added a little colour and excitement to my life. I enjoy my job, but there is precious little adventure. I shall keep your confidence and offer what service I can."

Imogen nodded and shook his hand.

"Thank you, Berni. We are in a somewhat mysterious situation, and it is comforting to know that we have your confidence and discretion."

"You are very welcome, Madame. My responsibilities include B Deck, and my name is known to all on board. Please ask for me if you require anything."

"A key to lock our door would be an excellent start," chuckled Francois.

"Of course. Is there anything else?"

Imogen made another quick decision. Although imposing on this young man felt wrong, she saw little alternative under the current circumstances.

"Berni, I would not ask this if we were not in such a dire situation, but we require medications and other items usually found in an infirmary. It would be more prudent to visit when there are few witnesses."

Berni's tone was eager and more light-hearted than either Imogen or Francois expected.

"Infirmary? You are aboard The Titanic, Madame, and we have a well-staffed hospital, although only two beds were occupied when I took morning tea to the nurse earlier.

The quietest time would be between 10.30 pm and 4.00 am. Even then, a nurse is on duty, and two doctors will be asleep in their cabins nearby. Nurse Jacobs is a fine woman who takes her duties very seriously. In any case, I believe you will find what you seek in the surgery on the C deck. Nurse Jacobs usually watches the patients below in the hospital on D deck, but I cannot promise she will not climb the stairs at the sound of intruders."

"It is unlikely that she will allow us to take what we wish and leave without many questions?"

"Most unlikely. Perhaps I could distract and lead her elsewhere for a short time?"

Already, a plan was forming in Imogen's mind, giving her something to focus on.

"Yes, Berni. We would need no more than ten minutes. Also, could you provide a simple drawing of the layout? You have my word that we will not take anything that will in any way limit the medical services onboard."

"Of course, Madame. Now, I must return to my duties, but I will visit your cabin as soon as possible. Do not worry, my friends. Berni Rosseau is at your service."

He bowed at the neck.

"The adventure and the caper," said Francois as he patted Berni's arm.

"Monsieur?"

"We are very grateful for your assistance, Berni. We are in

a bit of a bind, and it is no small comfort to find a familiar face and one who is willing to help."

"Not at all."

As he straightened, the wind lifted and carried his cap far behind. They all heard a playful scream and turned to see a young girl running after it as it tumbled along the deck. Francois recognised her as one of the children he'd seen high on the docking bridge when they'd first arrived at the stern. Full of determination, she ran this way and that, laughing happily until there was a brief drop in the breeze, and she fell on the hat. She was too far away for any of them to hear clearly, but she hit the deck with a thump, letting out one final, almost glorious expletive.

"Son of a bitch!"

Her long blonde hair blew in the ocean breeze as she got to her feet, holding Berni's squashed cap. She walked towards them, wiping the dirt from the peak and doing what she could to straighten it as she got closer. Offering the briefest curtsey, she held it out, clearly proud of her achievement. Berni saluted and smiled.

"Thank you, Miss."

"You are most welcome, sir. Could you please direct me to the second-class lounge? I have been trying to find my Mama for some time, with no success."

She glanced briefly at Imogen and Francois and smiled, but she reserved her attention for the young man as he put his cap back on.

"Certainly, Miss."

He nodded to Imogen and Francois as the girl looped her arm in his and led him away, already chatting happily. Francois and Imogen watched the couple walk away until they were out of earshot. Just as Imogen was about to speak, the girl briefly looked back and winked at them both.

RMS Titanic - The Stern, Saturday, April 13th, 1908 - 1.45 pm

Imogen and Francois held onto the railings, watching the ship's wake and trying to comprehend what they had just heard. Together, they stared at the horizon, letting the wind blow onto their faces. Francois could see that Imogen was deep in thought, so he waited. Finally, the moment arrived. Speaking to the churning foam of the ship's wake, she uttered one word.

"Shit."

Francois turned and smiled at the side of her face. A few tiny wisps of hair had escaped the brim of her hat and now blew loosely in the wind, which had finally dropped a little.

"Once again, we are of one mind, Imogen. Is it possible that none of what he said is true?"

"It is certainly possible, but why would he lie? We have very little evidence to contradict what he said and much that supports it."

"Then we have journeyed in time?"

"As ridiculous as it seems, I find it harder to believe that we have slept for almost four years only to wake up far from home. I am quite prepared to ask others what year it is, but I suspect their answer will be the same."

"But how, Imogen, and why?"

"How? I have not discounted the idea that it is a natural phenomenon. I find it harder to believe that it is within the wit of man to bend the laws of physics in such a manner. As for the why, I have no idea at all."

"Based on your experience with the bracelet, it is unlikely the two events are unrelated. One inexplicable event is usually enough for one day."

"I have come to the same conclusion. Now, let us walk."

They left the raised stern deck and made their way back down the promenade. Francois loosened his scarf and let it hang, the two ends hanging before him.

"What is happening to us? I can see without my spectacles; our scars have faded and…"

Francois stomped his leg on the deck twice, staring at his shoe as it thumped against the wood. Then he stopped and looked up at Imogen before twirling around on the spot until he was dizzy.

"My leg aches still, but it is now dull and…"

He stomped again, almost falling over with excitement. Several passengers were watching now, making Imogen feel quite uncomfortable. She steadied Francois and led him away, whispering.

"Yes, it is quite wonderful, but we still have no idea what has restored us to such rude health. I do not doubt that these mysterious events are all connected somehow, but until we know more, we must be discrete and return to our cabin."

RMS Titanic, Stateroom B81, Saturday, April 13th - 2:14 pm

Francois closed the cabin door behind them as Imogen sat on the bed. He removed his jacket, hanging it over the back of one of the chairs, and sat beside her. She was very quiet, her head full of ideas and questions.

"What are you thinking, Imogen? Now would not be the best time to retreat into yourself."

Imogen smiled and patted his hand.

"Do not worry. I am still here. In the excitement and confusion, we have not considered those who are not with us. We have been missing for a considerable time. From their point of view, we vanished from the face of the earth and presumably left no trace."

Francois felt a great sadness well up inside him, and his mind filled with the faces of his friends and his home.

"We must send word, Imogen. A telegram…we must send a telegram!"

This time, she grabbed his hand and held on. Her voice was quiet but insistent.

"…and what would we say? How would we explain what has happened in so few words? We could send a dozen telegrams and still not express ourselves and our situation clearly. We have been gone long enough for them to move on, Francois. The Café, our friends and life in Place St Genevieve would have continued without us."

Imogen thought of Boreas flying high above the square and Inglenook, now older and plump from years of Maria's indulgence, both safe and quite well but out of the reach of her caring hands. She wiped her face, failing to stop a single tear from falling down her cheek.

"Our return will need careful thought, my friend. I know it is difficult, but they are as sad or happy today as they were yesterday. A few more days will make little difference."

Francois wiped his arm across his face and sniffed. Imogen didn't need to look at him to know precisely to whom Francois' thoughts had turned.

"I promise you, she will be fine, and her joy at our return will eventually wipe away the pain of our disappearance."

They sat silently for almost ten minutes, remembering their home and family, drawing strength from each other. Weak from it all, Francois wiped his face again.

"I have never cried in front of you before, Imogen."

"Not since you trapped your hand in the cellar door, no."

He blew his nose on his handkerchief and chuckled through his tears.

"I had forgotten that moment. An hour of almost exquisite agony."

"You whimpered for almost three. I made less of a fuss when I was shot. Actually, so did you."

"You are my rock, Imogen DiRossi."

"Thank you."

"...and you are sure that are you quite alright?"

"Yes, I believe I am."

Imogen stood up, clasped her hands in front of her, and looked down at him.

"I think it is time for us to take a more direct role in our current situation. We have wasted too much time letting events wash over us. I have been unable to dismiss my... hallucination, and I am certain that it is central to matters. My memory of it is fractured and clouded, but one phrase lingers... "Take it, Imogen. She should not have it. Give it to The Other.""

"You believe it was something beyond a hallucination?"

"When a hallucination is the second most remarkable

occurrence on any given day, I would suggest it is worthy of note."

"I agree, so…take what from whom?"

"We have only met two women, and whilst Miss Elsie Figgins carries herself with a charming innocence, I suspect Doctor Sadek is more deserving of our attention, as is the bracelet."

"The bracelet?"

"Yes."

"…and who is The Other?"

"I have no idea, but Inglenook and Elizabeth were quite insistent."

Imogen disappeared into the bathroom before Francois had completely digested her parting comment. Following in her footsteps, he tapped on the bathroom door.

"Imogen?"

"Francois, I am in the bathroom."

"Of course you are; I saw you close the door. Where else could you possibly be?"

There was a short pause as Imogen considered her reply.

"As comfortable we are in each other's company, Francois, I believe this to be something of a first."

"Nonsense. Only last week, you explained the intricacies of

something or other to me through the bathroom door. I was taking a bath, and you barely paused to breathe. Surely, you can spare me a moment as you wash your hands."

"But I am not washing my hands, Francois…"

Francois' face drained of all colour as he took half a step back, wondering what to do. He briefly considered running up on deck and leaping to a watery death, but fortunately, Imogen replied before he could hide his embarrassment in so drastic a manner. Her usual balanced and calm tone seemed only slightly distracted.

"What can I do for you?"

"I…was wondering…"

"Yes?"

"Is it still your intention to break into the hospital later tonight? We both seem well enough."

"To obtain The Serpent's Grasp from Doctor Sadek, we may need to distract or even subdue her aides. I cannot be confident in our ability to do that until I know what materials are available to me."

"What of the good doctor herself?"

Francois heard the unmistakable sound of a lavatory flush and hurried to sit down at the dresser, almost falling off the stool as he did so. Imogen emerged, drying her hands on a small towel and briefly taking in the scene before her. She turned and hung the towel over the brass bar on the inside of the door and closed it, ignoring Francois' obvious embarrassment.

"Doctor Sadek is an admirable woman, and I take no pleasure in what we must do, Francois."

"Must?"

"What I saw felt far more than a hallucination. I have hallucinated on several occasions, and it has never stayed with me like this. A power that could leave such an impression on me should be listened to, should it not?"

"As usual, your interpretation of events is reasoned and convincing. You have a plan?"

"Berni will distract the nurse. We will enter, take what we need, and be gone within minutes."

"Not your most elaborate scheme."

"The chances of being discovered are small. Provided Berni can be relied upon, I am confident of success. Would you prefer something more elaborate?"

"No, but I would appreciate the company of Imogen DiRossi and not High Priestess Zotti of Bulgaria on this particular caper. Do you think you could manage that?"

Imogen frowned, briefly filling the room with her second Eastern European language of the day.

"Quite so," said Francois, not knowing what she had said but more than familiar with her tone.

"Taking The Serpent's Grasp is another matter entirely," she continued.

"Doctor Sadek is young, Imogen, but quite formidable. Even without her aides to help, she will not give it up easily."

"No, she will not. Depending on what we find in the hospital, I may be able to ensure she is not even aware that we have taken it. That would probably be for the best."

"For us, certainly."

"Yes, but even if we take the artefact without being seen by either Doctor Sadek or her aides, we will certainly be at the top of her list of suspects, considering what happened earlier. The only thing in our favour is that no one knows we are in here, apart from Berni Rosseau."

"...and what of 'The Other'?"

"One problem at a time, Francois, one problem at a time. Perhaps this 'Other' will find us. After all, I was told to give it to them, not that I must seek them out."

"So, we take it, then wait in here for a knock at the door?"

"That is certainly one option. I have yet to think of another."

There was a knock at the door. They glanced at the door and then back at each other. Again, a quiet, polite knock was heard, followed by Berni Rosseau's loud attempt at a whispering voice.

"It is Berni, my friends."

Francois opened the door, and Berni hurried in, placing a small laundry sack on the dresser. He straightened his jacket and retrieved a small key from his top pocket.

"For your door, my friends."

"It is most fortunate that there was a spare, Berni," said Imogen as she took the key.

"Actually, Madame, the keys are not unique, a fact known only to the stewards of a certain grade and above. This key will open more than one stateroom, but my professionalism will not allow me to divulge which," said Berni with a slight chuckle.

Imogen turned the key in the lock, heard a satisfying click, and then unlocked it again. Francois was already examining the sack and removing several items. Berni turned his attention to it and began to help.

"There are some items for your bathroom - fresh towels, soap and some food. Considering your circumstances, I thought it might be better if you avoided the dining rooms."

Francois lifted out a wicker hamper and opened it to reveal an assortment of fine food and drink. He removed the lid from a chutney jar and tasted some with his finger.

"Berni! This is quite splendid. You have stolen it?"

"There was a small reception in the first-class Lounge earlier and far more food than was necessary. One hamper will not be missed."

In a surprising moment of physical affection, Imogen patted Berni's arm and smiled warmly.

"It is fortunate that we found you here, if a little surprising. I hope we are in a position to repay your kindness at some point in the future."

"Please, think nothing of it. However, there is something else you should be aware of, Madame. On my way to your cabin, I was detained by a very large man with a very deep voice who asked about Violet and Montague Smith.

Francois frowned.

"White suit? Odd red hat?"

Berni nodded.

"Yes. He was polite but quite insistent. I have spoken to other crew members, and it seems I am not the first he has spoken to. Also, he said you were Hungarian."

Francois smirked.

"What exactly did he ask?" enquired Imogen.

"He asked if I knew of you and the location of your cabin. I said that I did not and then took a circuitous route here via D deck and two areas not accessible by passengers. I can assure you that I was not followed. Why does he wish to meet you, Madame Imogen?"

Imogen sat down on the dresser stool and sighed.

"The man is an aide to Doctor Penelope Sadek. There was an incident at the exhibition, and it seems we have piqued her interest. I cannot say I blame her for her curiosity."

"Ahh…in The Café Parisien. My duties took me elsewhere, but I am aware of Doctor Sadek. She has taken three staterooms."

"Three?" exclaimed Francois, surprised.

"For herself, her aides and a considerable amount of luggage."

"Which staterooms, Berni?" asked Imogen.

The young man frowned, considering her question.

"So, you do wish to meet her again? I am a little confused."

Imogen glanced at Francois, who was now sitting on the edge of the bed. He shrugged and smiled.

"He deserves to know it all, Imogen. He has shown us trust and deserves the same in return."

She knew Francois didn't mean everything, but he was correct. Berni looked at Francois and then at Imogen.

"You can rely on Berni Rosseau, my friends; I can promise you that."

"Yes, we know, Berni…" said Imogen as she sat on the dresser stool, "but it would be difficult to explain."

"As difficult to understand as you not knowing how you

came to be on board or that you did not know today's date?"

Imogen opened her mouth to speak, but Berni continued.

"...or how you twice took my breath with a wave of your hand and a puff of smoke? Yes, Madame Imogen, I remember, but I have told no one. As I said, you may trust Berni Rosseau."

Francois laughed.

"A courageous man of integrity, Imogen."

"Indeed. I am sorry for any discomfort I caused in the château."

"I had a most persistent cough for a week or two and several strange dreams, but otherwise, I am undamaged. Now, please tell me how I may help you."

Francois had grown tired of sitting and letting his friend bear the responsibility of explaining everything. Abruptly, he stood, rubbing his hands together, placing them behind his back and paced up and down slowly. Imogen watched, wondering why his actions seemed so familiar.

"Everything we have told you so far is true, Berni. We have no idea how we came to be on board. We took residence here but have not been as discrete as we should have. As we are both unharmed, we thought it best to accept our fate and travel to New York, where Imogen has friends. After a brief stay, we would return home, hopefully putting the whole matter behind us."

Thinking it best to avoid the subject of time travel for the moment, Francois continued.

"We did, however, decide to make the most of our situation, and this morning, following an excellent breakfast, we attended Doctor Sadek's exhibition, during which we became aware of a certain artefact in her possession. We know for a fact that this artefact was recently stolen from an acquaintance of ours, and we intend to...steal it back."

Francois stopped pacing and raised his eyebrow at Imogen, who favoured him with a teasing frown. His Sherlockian pastiche was no better than hers had been in her bedroom previously, but it had lightened the moment.

"Elementary, my dear Francois."

He bowed his head politely.

"Quite so."

Berni looked confused.

"Normally, I would insist that we inform the captain of such a thing. He would send a telegram and have the authorities waiting when we dock."

Pondering this, Imogen added, "Obviously, we would prefer a more discrete solution, Berni, and one that does not require us to explain our presence on board."

He took a pencil and notepad from his pocket, sketching a surprisingly detailed floor plan.

"Doctor Sadek has taken Staterooms on the port side, almost adjacent to yours - B98, B96 and B94. She has complained several times about the smell of the nearby fish store but insisted on three adjoining cabins, and those were the only ones available."

He laid the sketch flat on the table. Imogen and Francois looked at each other and then at Berni, who traced a finger along several corridors, one after another.

"As you can see, there are several ways to approach and an equal number by which to make your escape."

Imogen was genuinely impressed with the young man's detailed sketch and resourcefulness.

"...and the hospital, Berni?"

Berni unfolded another piece of paper from his pocket and laid it next to the first. It was similarly detailed.

"I have found a passenger willing to assist in our endeavour for only a small financial consideration. Nurse Jacobs will be elsewhere at around 10.40 pm. I cannot be sure for how long, but it will be at least fifteen minutes."

"Remarkable work, Berni," said Francois as he looked over the sketches.

"Thank you, my friends. If you will excuse me, I shall return to my duties."

With that, Berni straightened his jacket and left. Francois closed the door behind him and locked it.

"What an extraordinary young man."

Imogen nodded, her mouth already full of cheese and chutney. She mumbled something unintelligible and waved a small bottle of Bordeaux at Francois. He stabbed the cork with his pocketknife, pulling it out and putting his long years of café ownership to good use.

"1866. Imogen, this wine is older than me."

Imogen swallowed the cheese, wiped her mouth with a crisp White Star Line napkin and took the bottle from him.

"Thank you."

"Imogen, are you sure alcohol is wise? Will it not dull your reflexes?"

She had already removed two small wine glasses from inside the hamper lid, filling them both by the time Francois had finished his question. She took a small sip, swilled it around her mouth appreciatively, and emptied her glass. As Francois watched quietly, her eyebrows wiggled, and the glass vanished in a bewildering flourish of her hands. Francois frowned as she held up both hands, showing him the front and back.

"No, it will not."

Turning her back to him, she took the small selection of toiletries to the bathroom, fully aware that he was still staring at her and wondering precisely what he had just witnessed.

"On the dresser, Francois."

Francois looked down to see her empty glass next to where she stood moments ago and muttered quietly before taking a sip of the best wine he had ever tasted.

"Imp."

CHAPTER SEVEN – CAPER & CONFUSION
B Deck - Saturday, April 13th, 1912 - 4.00 pm

Mahmoud knocked on Doctor Sadek's cabin door and waited patiently for an answer. As always, her voice was clear and full of purpose - something he approved of in no small measure.

"Enter."

Penny recognised Mahmoud's gentle knock and the respectful pause that followed. He thrived on politeness and ceremony, bowing his head as he entered and closed the door behind him.

"I am unable to locate Violet or Montague Smith, Doctor. Indeed, I can find no evidence that they are on board. They do not appear on the passenger manifest, and no crew member knows of them."

"Then I am correct in my suspicion that they are not who they appear to be. More is happening here than it seems, and I suspect our meeting was not an accident. Continue your investigations, Mahmoud. Perhaps find a crew member in need of financial incentive. Whatever it takes. Do I make myself clear?"

"Always, Doctor."

Sadek nodded, as did her aide. He turned and left, leaving her alone with her thoughts. On the table next to her lay the leather pouch, and inside, wrapped safely, was The Serpent's Grasp. Since she came to possess it, there had been more than one unexplained occurrence, but this latest one intrigued her to the point of distraction.

The Promenade Deck - Saturday, April 13th, 1912 – 9.40 pm

Francois pulled his jacket collar up and shivered.

"We are sailing south; why is it getting colder?"

"The Gulf Stream. Warm water currents travel North from The Gulf of Mexico towards Europe. Our current northerly position puts us at the mercy of stronger, colder winds from the Arctic. First observed in the early 16th century by Juan Ponce de León but not studied extensively until the late 19th century by your own Benjamin Franklin."

"Ah," said Francois in the manner of someone who did not understand as quickly or as entirely as Imogen would have hoped.

"Why do we sail so far North?"

"Vessels crossing The Atlantic sail as far North as is considered safe to take advantage of The Earth's curvature. It shortens the distance travelled. It is a fascinating topic worthy of study, Francois."

"Whatever would I do without you?"

"I have no idea; perhaps stumble on blindly, feeling your way through a life free of exciting and distracting incident?"

"No doubt. Imogen, as time passes, I find it increasingly difficult to know when you are teasing and when you are not."

"Oh, I am not teasing. The more time I spend in your company, the more impressed I am with your knowledge of the world and even more so with your eagerness to add to it. When we return home, I suggest we purchase a large, comprehensive map and display it prominently. Perhaps on the wall outside our bedrooms? Adding to our knowledge of the world around us would be an excellent way to start the day, would it not?"

They continued their slow walk, silent at the mention of the café and home, until something in the distance caught his attention, glistening in the few rays of moonlight.

"What is that?"

Imogen's small telescope slipped from her right cuff into her hand. She put it to her eye and peered out across the calm sea.

"Ice. Perhaps a dozen floes and at least one more significant berg. They are not an unusual sight this far North, Francois. You need not be concerned."

She passed the telescope to her friend, who put it to his eye.

"I have just never seen such a thing before," said Francois.

"They present no danger to a vessel of this size, I promise you. We are on a well-chosen course with an experienced crew. Perhaps you should focus more on our immediate caper."

"Yes. A little petty theft is just the thing to shake me out of my malaise."

Imogen ignored his comment and checked her watch.

"10.15. We must go."

"Imogen, your watch is glowing."

"Yes," said Imogen, holding it closer to Francois' face.

"The case is relatively new, and the compass ring is an addition of my own, but the watch itself was a gift from a kind man I met while travelling with my mother as a child. I had no idea of its true wonder until I lay in my bed that first night, by which time Signor Panerai was long gone.

"Panerai? Giovanni Panerai? THE Giovani Panerai? You have a Panerai watch?"

"Yes, but I was unaware of his notoriety or the value of his gift until many years later. I toured Florence with my late husband and visited his shop. Surprisingly, he still remembered me, but I suspect it was my mother's skill and kindness rather than an inquisitive child he remembered."

"Kindness?"

"You need not pull that face, Francois. His bowels were a little uncooperative, that is all - too much strong coffee and fine food, according to my mother. A few herbs, some hot water and a moment of privacy in the bushes, and he was soon on his way."

"…and in return, he gave you his watch?"

"Yes, and he gave my mother enough money to feed us both for a month."

"How very generous."

"He had been constipated for some time; I understand. His relief was considerable and vocal."

Imogen dissolved into childlike giggles, putting her hand to her mouth. Francois was not far behind, the tension of the last few days momentarily disappearing.

"He…he woke up all the bats. The sky was dark for almost half an hour!"

Imogen put the palm of her hand flat against Francois' chest, leaning on him as she tried to catch her breath. She had begun the tale to distract him but had lost herself entirely in the recollection.

"Forgive me, Francois. I am still not used to having someone to share memories with. That one took me a little by surprise."

"Please do not apologise. I have had you listen to enough of my past."

"Quite so, but still…"

Francois opened the door to the inside corridor and held

it open until they were inside, both grateful for a bit of warmth.

"You may put your collar down now, Francois. You look quite dashing and mysterious but also very furtive."

"I do?"

"Yes. I would rather people were distracted by my exquisite features than my suspicious-looking companion."

Imogen took out Berni's sketch as Francois adjusted his collar. She pressed it to the wall, studied it carefully for the third time, folded it and put it back in her dress pocket. Then, she made a few final adjustments to Francois' collar, finishing with a pat on his arm and a mischievous wiggle of her eyebrows.

"If you are quite ready, it is time for us to be somewhat of a nuisance."

"A discrete one, I hope."

"Naturally. We shall be as a leaf on the wind in our shenanigans."

Imogen stepped out and along the corridor, with Francois following close behind, ready with a question, as always.

"I have always wondered what a shenanigan is."

"A small, brown hamster-like creature, hunted to extinction early in the 18th century. Notable for its ability to ask one too many questions."

"Very funny."

"I thought so."

Imogen's pace was quick and determined as she followed the route she had memorised that afternoon. As she disappeared around a corner, Francois hurried to catch up, but he almost collided with her when she suddenly stopped and turned to face him.

"If we do not find the hospital empty, you may need to fabricate an injury. A limp, perhaps?" said Imogen distractedly.

"I'm not sure I remember how, but I'll do my best."

"Of course you will," she smirked.

With that, she turned around and set off down the long corridor.

The Poop Deck - Saturday, April 13th, 1912 - 9.50 pm

Berni Rosseau wrapped his arms tightly around his torso, trying to fight off the cold night air. His coat would have helped, but he'd felt sorry for his newest friend and had wrapped it around her shoulders.

"Are you warm enough, Miss?"

"Yes, thank you, but I was quite warm enough before you smothered me in your coat, and now you are cold. You are a silly man, Berni Rosseau, but a nice one. I like you."

"Being nice is my job," said Berni, as he cupped his hands around his mouth and breathed heavily into them.

The girl swung her legs under the bench and looked about, seemingly unaffected by the chilly night air.

"I think it is far more than your job, Berni. I am a very good judge of character, and if I was not certain of your niceness, I would not be sitting here with you and would not have agreed to participate in your daring scheme."

"Then I am flattered, Miss, but what of your parents? Do they not worry about you wandering the deck at this hour?"

"My Mama is asleep in cabin B47, and even if she were not, I would still be here. I am very sensible and quite capable of taking care of myself. Besides, you promised me a dollar for my trouble, and I would very much like to buy myself a new dress and bonnet when we arrive in New York."

"Oh yes, of course," said Berni, taking a dollar out of his chest pocket. The girl took it and tucked it into the small chest pocket of her dress.

"Thank you, Berni. Now, how shall we proceed?"

Berni wondered at his new friend, torn between the importance of helping Imogen and Francois and endangering a child he had known for less than a day.

"At 10.30, Nurse Jacobs must be called away from her post

for at least fifteen minutes, so we must create a diversion of sorts. Perhaps you could faint, and I would need to rush for assistance?"

"I am sure I can do a little better than that, but first, we shall move inside where it is warmer. You are trembling, you poor man."

She climbed down from the bench, took Berni's coat from her shoulders, and returned it to him. He bowed and clicked his heels together playfully.

"Thank you, Miss."

"You are very welcome, Mr Rosseau, but we are friends now, and you must call me Jayne."

D Deck, The Hospital - Saturday, April 13th, 1912 - 10.05 pm

Nurse Jacobs put down her pen and drank what remained of her peppermint tea. Now that Doctor Simpson had assured Stanley Able that he had nothing more than a touch of gastroenteritis and not cholera, he had finally fallen asleep, leaving her to finish her daily report. It had been an unusually quiet voyage for the hospital, with only two patients requiring a bed. There were the usual bumps and bruises, trips and falls, but Doctor Simpson and Doctor O'Loughlin had visited those passengers in their cabins, leaving her to watch over the bedridden.

She finished the document with a flourish of her pen and

sat back in her chair, rubbing her eyes and stretching. Her son smiled up from the photograph on her desk—far away and safe with her sister, back in Southampton. She knew Joe loved his Aunt May but that he would have wanted to be with his mum more.

"Your dear mum needs some more tea, Joe." She whispered.

She would miss his sixth birthday, just as she had missed his fourth, but her work paid well. In two more years, she would have saved enough to make her home ashore, take a senior position at Southampton Union Infirmary and never miss another birthday. Absent-mindedly stroking her fingers on the photograph, she smiled and took her teapot to the hot water boiler.

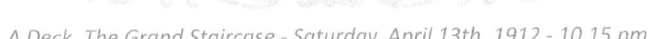

A Deck, The Grand Staircase - Saturday, April 13th, 1912 - 10.15 pm

Berni and Jayne leaned on the high bannister and looked up at the dome over the grand staircase. The ship was quiet at this hour, but an occasional crew member still wandered about, busy and efficient.

"It is quite magnificent, Berni - such elegance. Every time you turn a corner on this ship, there is another wonder to behold."

"I still cannot quite believe I am part of it all, Jayne. My mother and I grew up in a house not much bigger than your cabin."

Lost in happy memories, Berni hadn't noticed Jayne climbing onto the bannister rail, now steadying herself with one hand on the vertical beam. Berni took a step back, looking up at her.

"What are you doing? Climb down…please!"

She looked down and smiled, seemingly without a care in the world.

"Do you trust me, Berni Rosseau?"

Berni straightened and looked up at her.

"I think so, but I have only known you a day, Jayne. At this very moment, I feel more worry than trust. Please…do not cause a scene."

She looked over her shoulder, wobbling a little.

"We are alone; do not fuss."

She moved her arm from the beam and shuffled her feet sideways, almost perfectly balanced and steady. Berni reached out with both arms.

"Come down, please…"

"Trust and do not worry, Berni."

With that, she winked, stretched her arms wide and let herself fall backwards as Berni watched in disbelief.

"Jayne!"

He leaned over the bannister and screamed as her body

slammed into the floor below. He never took his eyes off her as he ran around and down the steps, then kneeled next to her twisted, unmoving body.

"Jayne!!"

Passengers and crew began to gather, curious at the noise but too disturbed by what they had witnessed to come any closer. Berni looked around for someone familiar, finding a short, tidy girl in a cabin maid's uniform.

"Gladys! A doctor! Run, girl!"

Gladys Jones pushed through the crowd and disappeared down the hallway as Berni took Jayne's hand and cupped her cheek.

"Oh, what have you done, you silly girl? What have I made you do?"

Her little body sighed quietly, and then one eye half-opened.

"Ouch."

She spoke too quietly for anyone but Berni to hear.

Startled, he made the same noise as when he had first seen Imogen and Francois earlier.

"Ah!"

Jayne tensed a little at his sudden cry.

"Shhh, Berni."

Bernie leaned closer and whispered in Jayne's ear.

"What have you done? You are injured; Are you in pain?"

"Of course, I am in pain. Did you not see how far I fell?" she whispered through the discomfort.

"We cannot wait for the Doctor; I must carry you to the hospital."

"No, no...that is not the plan. Wait for the Doctor!"

Berni was no longer listening.

"Dear God! Look at your foot!"

Jayne sat up slowly, the cracking of bones audible in every movement, whispering a rapid, unladylike profanity.

"Son of a bitch...son of a bitch...son of a bitch..."

When she could reach it, she put her arms around Berni's neck.

"If you must carry me, please do it carefully, at least for now. I would gladly have made my own way to the hospital, but I believe my foot is broken, and it might take several hours to get there."

Berni carefully lifted her into his arms and politely pushed his way through the crowd. She buried her face in his shoulder and held on.

"Try not to drop me."

"I will not. You are not heavy."

Safely away from the crowd, she lifted her head and chuckled.

"Why thank you, kind sir. I make every effort to maintain my figure."

Berni's head was a muddle. He expected so little of today when he woke this morning.

"I do not understand."

"No, you do not, but that is alright for now."

Nurse Jacobs came running down the corridor towards them, with Gladys not far behind. Berni felt Jayne's body go limp, and her head fell back against his arm.

"Mr Rosseau! What have you done!?"

"She fell."

"So I am told, but you should not have moved her so soon afterwards."

"I did not think it would be safe to wait."

Nurse Jacobs pressed two fingers to Jayne's neck, tutted and started to walk backwards.

"Slowly and carefully, Berni. Her pulse is very weak."

As the nurse turned away, Jayne opened one eye and winked. Berni leaned his head closer and whispered loudly.

"How are you doing that?"

Her voice bounced as Berni ran along, adding an amusing vibrato to her reply.

"I am happy and content, with few pressing concerns. I highly recommend such a lifestyle."

"Happy and content? I may never relax again. You have broken your foot, Jayne."

"...and I have given my right knee quite a bash too."

She lifted her left arm slightly, displaying a thumb bent almost entirely backwards.

"Oh my!"

Berni grimaced at the sight of it, regretting his overindulgence at lunchtime.

"Oh, for heaven's sake, child, whatever will I tell your mother?"

"Bumps and scrapes are not uncommon in the life of an active and inquisitive child. She will understand."

Jayne giggled and quickly shut her eyes again as they reached the hospital. Nurse Jacobs patted one of the empty beds just inside the door.

"Here, Mr Rosseau. Carefully, now...carefully."

Berni laid Jayne down on the bed, seeing the full extent of her injuries - her left foot twisted and limp and her right leg swollen at the knee.

"Stay with her, Mr Rosseau. I must wake Doctor Simpson."

She lifted Jayne's hand.

"Hold her hand, Berni. If she wakes, she will be in great pain, and you will need to comfort her."

He watched her go but was suddenly distracted by a tug on his hand. Jayne had pulled herself into a sitting position, and her face was very close to his.

"The Doctor must not find anything serious. Straighten my foot."

"What?"

"Straighten it. Please put your hands on it and point it in the correct direction."

"The pain."

"It will hurt like the devil, but you must. I cannot do it myself. I will pass out. I always do."

"I cannot do it either…you what?"

From the stairs above, they could now hear hurried footsteps.

"You must do this, Berni. I will scream very loudly, but you must not worry.

C Deck, Near the Hospital - Saturday, April 13th, 1912 - 10.25 pm

Imogen and Francois sat on a bench outside the second-class library on C Deck. One was a picture of calm, and the other, slightly less so, as they regarded the sign on the door opposite.

Hospital & Surgery

"A Hospital. I am breaking into a hospital."

Imogen leaned against him, lowering her voice and straightening her skirts, just as she would if they had interrupted a walk in the park to rest Francois' leg.

"Yes, Francois. One more entry in your journal of shame."

"I would be grateful if you could not enjoy this quite so much; besides, I do not keep a journal."

Imogen took out her pocket watch, checked it against the clock on the wall and then put it away again.

"Perhaps you should. These last few months have most definitely been worthy of the written word."

"Yes, Imogen. I suspect a permanent record of our crimes will greatly assist the police when we are finally brought to justice.

"April 13th, 1912: A bright, cold day on which Imogen and I stole miscellaneous items from a hospital to aid in the later theft of a precious Egyptian artefact. Also, I had kippers for breakfast, and my leg, which has crippled me since childhood, is completely healed."

"Completely?" said Imogen, ignoring his sarcasm.

"Yes, it would appear so."

Francois gripped his thigh firmly and lifted his leg, shaking his foot about.

"Unless the efficacy of Aspirin has improved immeasurably since my last headache, it would seem that something quite remarkable has happened."

Imogen watched Francois' foot, equally puzzled yet strangely mesmerised.

"I am at a loss to…"

The scream of a child interrupted Imogen's reply, startling them both.

D Deck, The Hospital - Saturday, April 13th, 1912 - 10.25 pm

As predicted, Jayne fell limply against the pillow. Berni loosened his grip on her stockinged foot, still feeling the bones shift and move slowly. This made him feel sick to the stomach, which, combined with his concern for Jayne, was almost too much to bear. At that moment, Doctor Simpson burst into the hospital ward.

"Move!"

Doctor Simpson shoved Berni to one side and sat on the bed.

"She fell? How far?" he said quickly.

"From the bannister above the grand staircase on A deck to the floor below, sir."

"She fell down the stairs?"

The truth would sound absurd and not help matters, so Berni improvised.

"Yes…yes, sir. It was quite the tumble."

Nurse Jacobs looked at Jayne's body, unable to make sense of the story compared to what she had first seen when Berni had carried her into the hospital. She looked again at the child's foot, sure of her memory when she met Berni's eyes, confirming that everything was not as it should have been. To her credit, Nurse Jacobs stayed silent. Doctor Simpson continued to examine Jayne for almost ten minutes, muttering to himself.

"Aside from a nasty thumb fracture and a few bruises, I see no serious injury. She may be slightly concussed, but her pulse is steady, if a little…slow. Keep her here until she wakes, and we will consider further treatment. In the meantime, please see to her thumb, Nurse. A little Morphine for the pain if needed, but tread carefully; she is very young."

"Yes, Doctor."

Simpson glanced at the clock, then retook Jayne's pulse.

"Remarkable. Please wake me if her condition worsens, Nurse; I will be on duty at six and must sleep. Have her parents been informed?"

"I will notify her mother immediately," said Berni.

"Excellent, Mr Rosseau. See that you do. Considering the lack of patients, I have no issue with her spending the night here with her daughter if she wishes."

Doctor Simpson nodded politely and left. Berni followed shortly after, climbing the stairs and pushing the surgery key into the lock as he passed. In the rush of activity downstairs, it had been the work of a moment to retrieve it from the hook in Nurse Jacobs' office.

C Deck, The Surgery - Saturday, April 13th, 1912 - 10.35 pm

Berni hurriedly opened the door at the top of the stairs, next to the surgery.

"You have perhaps ten minutes, my friends."

"The scream?" said Francois, his voice full of worry.

"A patient. Her care will occupy Nurse Jacobs for a short time, but you must still hurry. The key is in the surgery lock; please leave it there when you have taken what you need. Hopefully, one of the doctors will believe they left it there and will be in no hurry to make any theft public if their own carelessness is to blame."

"Thank you, Berni."

"It is no trouble, Madame Imogen. Events did not unfold as planned, but Nurse Jacobs is occupied for now. If you will excuse me, I must inform the child's parent of her injuries."

"Is it serious?" said Francois.

"For reasons that I cannot fathom, it seems not. Good night, my friends."

Berni bowed at the neck, then hurried off down the corridor.

"He capers with some efficiency for one so young, Imogen."

"Perhaps, but he lacks many of your finer qualities, Francois. Your position at my side is in no danger."

Imogen opened the hospital door carefully and peered around it before opening it wide. All seemed quiet downstairs as she turned the key in the surgery lock.

"Quickly now."

She ushered Francois into the surgery, closing the door behind her. The room smelled of soap, disinfectant, and a dozen other chemicals. Imogen was already browsing a large cabinet of flasks and bottles, mumbling and lost in her thoughts.

Reaching inside his jacket, Francois took out the sack Berni had delivered their hamper in earlier. He laid it on the glass examination bed and looked around the room.

"Perhaps I will start a journal if we return home."

"When we return home, Francois. I think that would be an excellent idea. You have a small gift for storytelling."

She took two bottles from the shelf and put them on the examination table. Francois read each label, pulled a face, and then carefully put both in the sack.

"I do?"

"Yes, you have conjured a most compelling narrative on more than one occasion. I would happily edit your initial drafts into a more polished form before publication. Wrap those in a towel, Francois; the bottles are strong, but the contents are quite corrosive."

Francois took two towels from a small pile next to a wash basin and wrapped them carefully.

"Edit?"

Imogen turned her attention to the drawers beneath the glass cabinets, throwing small bags and packets into the sack as Francois held it open.

"Yes, you have a tendency to lose yourself in irrelevance and float off on wings of fancy. It is not a criticism, but any reputable publisher will have little time for such fluff."

"Oh, I am to publish my work?"

"Of course. I would very much enjoy seeing my name in

print."

"Our names, Imogen."

"Yes, of course."

Francois glanced up at the clock and shook the sack gently, helping the contents settle.

"Imogen…eight minutes."

"Yes", said Imogen, glancing around the room with her hands on her hips, "I believe I have enough."

Before closing the cabinet, she pushed some of the flasks closer together in a futile effort to hide their theft. Francois picked up the sack and stumbled a little, unprepared for the weight.

"The perfect crime."

"Oh, hush. Caper is no excuse for untidiness."

"Surely you are not serious."

"Not entirely; now come, Mr Meyer, we must be on our way."

Francois opened the door, leaning against it almost clumsily. If Imogen was aware of his struggle with their loot, she hid it extremely well.

"No, after you, Lady DiRossi. I insist." he puffed.

Imogen nodded and locked the door, leaving the key behind as instructed. After much huffing from Francois, she also took hold of the sack, and together, they made their way back to their cabin. The few people they encountered on the way were far too polite to question the curious pair and their tinkling bag."

Outside their door, Francois sank to the floor and sighed loudly, resting his tired behind on the plush carpet as Imogen retrieved the key from somewhere inside her dress.

"You will be the death of me, Imogen."

"Probably, but not tonight. Now, get up off the floor, you ridiculous man; we have a priceless Egyptian artefact to steal and much to prepare."

Imogen offered her hand and pulled Francois to his feet.

"However, we do have time for cheese and some more of that excellent chutney. Also, another glass of wine. Do you think Mr Rosseau could find us some more?"

"I am confident the resourceful Mr Berni Rosseau could obtain almost anything at this point. I have half a mind to offer him a job."

They dragged the sack inside, and Francois sat on the dresser stool. Imogen bent down to check her face and hair in the mirror.

"But when would you offer Mr Rosseau a job?" said Imogen as she tucked a stray hair behind her ear.

"At the earliest opportunity. I am sure we could match his current salary, and combined with the café's proximity to his family, I am sure he would accept."

"That is not quite what I meant. As I see it, our immediate future could unfold in one of two ways. Firstly, when we next meet him, you will present Berni with our more than generous offer. Then, we complete our strange, unexpected journey and arrive in New York. We visit with Nikola and eventually make our way home. In a few weeks, we would happily reunite with our surprised but overjoyed friends. Shortly after, Berni would become part of the Merle family, as you are pleased to call it, and we would be left to ponder the four years we have lost."

"That would be a more than acceptable conclusion to this current mess."

"Yes. I agree, but what if we were to return to 1908?"

"Is that likely?"

"We have travelled to the future, Francois. Is it any less likely that we may return to the past?"

"I have no idea, but at this point, I am happy to believe anything is possible."

"I propose that it is at least equally possible. If that were to happen, you could offer Berni Rosseau a job before he takes up employment with The White Star Line."

"Yes...yes, we would," said Francois slowly. Imogen could tell she was losing him in confusion.

"However, that would present a problem. If we had offered him a position in 1908, he would not have been on board this vessel in 1912 to assist us now."

Francois' brow furrowed.

"Pour me some wine, Imogen."

She passed him a full glass and sat down on the bed.

"The fact Mr Rosseau is here now could mean that we do not return and you do not offer him a position, but that will not stop us from trying."

Francois took a large gulp of wine and then sighed.

"Are we the first?"

"The first?"

"The first to travel in time. Outside the work of HG Wells and Jules Verne, that is."

Imogen mumbled inaudibly, then put her hand to her mouth until she swallowed her cheese and chutney.

"I certainly hope so. I would be especially pleased if we were the first to do so twice."

Outside Cabin B47 - Saturday, April 13th, 1912 - 10.45 pm

Berni straightened his jacket, took several deep breaths and stared at Jayne and her mother's cabin door. He had yet to decide what he would tell Jayne's mother, but it was his duty, and there was little that he took more seriously.

He knocked and waited, knowing Jayne's mother would be asleep. After a few minutes, he leaned closer and knocked again.

"Mrs Brewer, I have news of your daughter. There has been an accident. I must speak to you."

There was still no answer, and after a further few minutes of silence, Berni reached into his pocket for his master keys. What he was about to do was unusual but not forbidden, especially in such circumstances. He unlocked the door and opened it to darkness.

"Hello? Mrs Brewer? Madam? I am Berni Rosseau, your steward. I have distressing news about your daughter. There has been an accident. It is serious, but she will be well. She is in the hospital."

He found the light switch. The room was tidy and quite empty. If not for a parasol, some shoes and three small dresses hanging in the wardrobe, one could be convinced that it was unoccupied. Berni opened a drawer to find some stockings, handkerchiefs and undergarments, then sat on the stool with a heavy sigh.

"What on earth is going on?" said Berni to the empty room.

D Deck, The Hospital - Saturday, April 13th, 1912 - 11.15 pm

Nurse Jacobs wiped Jayne's brow and put her hand on the little girl's chest to feel the gentle beat of the child's heart as she slept.

"Thank you, Nurse; I am quite well, I think."

She jumped at the voice, quickly recovering her composure.

"I did not mean to startle you," said Jayne, giggling quietly as she opened her eyes.

"You did not."

"You are an excellent nurse but a poor liar, Heather Jacobs."

"Why thank you, Miss. I am more than content to be both. Lying is not a skill to be admired."

"It has its uses, but I mostly agree. Thank you for taking care of me."

"It is my duty, but you are most welcome. Are you still in pain?"

"A little, but it is of no matter. You have given me Morphine, and you should not have done that. It makes me too happy and too talkative."

"I only gave you a small amount. You have taken Morphine before?"

Jayne lifted her hand to look at her splinted thumb.

"Yes, I have taken a tumble on more than one occasion. You did this while I slept, which is most impressive. I am a very light sleeper."

"You are quite the mystery, young Miss, and your soft and surprisingly resilient thumb is the least of it."

She put her hand on Jayne's foot, confident that it would not hurt her, having done so several times while she slept.

"Your foot was twisted when you were carried in here by Mr Rosseau - twisted in a way that would suggest a break, but now…"

"I am quite well, Heather. There are things I do not understand either, but I do not waste time worrying about them. Life is short."

"That does not answer any of the many questions in my head, but for now, I will do as you ask. Also, how do you know my name, Miss?"

"I am Jayne, and your name is written on your pencil box - on your desk next to the photograph."

Heather looked over at her desk and nodded, wondering when Jayne had time to notice such a thing.

"Is that your son? In the photograph?"

"Yes, that is Joseph, but only my mother calls him that. Since he was old enough to talk back to his mum, he has insisted on Joe."

"Your only child?"

"Yes, he is now. He had a sister, Sarah, but she died."

"I am sorry. How did she die?"

"Diphtheria. She was almost three. Soon, I will be able to afford a home for Joe and me near my dear sister and work in a hospital that does not move about as this one does."

"You are a nice lady, Heather. I like you."

"You know nothing about me other than I have a son and that I know how to treat a broken finger."

"That is enough for now."

"Perhaps. Now you must rest, and I must prepare the surgery for the morning. Even a senior nurse must dust and sweep on occasion. Sleep well, Jayne."

Nurse Jacobs tidied the blankets, patting Jayne's tummy, and climbed the stairs. Jayne closed her eyes and asked a question that had been on her mind since she first saw the photograph on Heather's desk. As she asked it, she made no sound and lay perfectly still.

"Does she die, Ma'at?"

The reply was soft and familiar but, as always, tinged with sadness.

"Yes."

"I do not want her to."

The reply to that question took a little longer.

"She must."

"I do not often ask."

"You do not."

"But I am asking now. Would it matter so much?"

"It may or it may not. I do not see everything or understand everything."

"My whole life, I have done as you have asked."

A hint of amusement now.

"Almost all of your life and almost all that I have asked."

"That is true, but sometimes you ask too much."

"Have I not been grateful? Have I not helped you make your way in life? You are special, little one."

"Please save her; I know you can."

"No. I cannot, and we will not speak of it again."

After almost ten minutes of silence, Jayne opened her eyes, stared at the ceiling and listened to the hum of the engines until she fell asleep.

CHAPTER EIGHT – PLYMOUTH HARBOUR
The Hospital - Sunday, April 14th, 1912 – 9.15 am

"How are you feeling, Jayne?" Berni asked as he removed his cap and sat on her bed.

Holding up her bandaged and splinted thumb, she pulled a mocking, sad face.

"I am feeling much better. Thank you for coming to see me; I know you are very busy."

"I visited your cabin to tell your mother what happened, but she was not there. She was not there this morning and is still not there now."

"My mother is somewhat elusive and fond of deck games. I am sure she will be back soon."

Berni was growing tired of Jayne's misdirection and riddles but found it hard to be angry at this charming child.

"I have been inside your cabin, Jayne. I saw only your things and no one else's. I have checked the passenger manifest, and while there is a passenger named Christine Brewer, I cannot find anyone who has seen her."

Jayne shrugged and wiggled her thumb beneath the bandage, avoiding Berni's gaze for a moment. Her voice seemed to have lost a little of its usual confidence.

"It seems that I have grown careless and far too relaxed in your company, Berni. What will you do now?"

"I am not certain. I believed us to be friends, yet it seems you have lied to me."

"Not without good reason, Berni and with regret. I will explain almost everything if you allow me more time."

"Almost?"

She sat up and began to unwrap the bandage. It fell away, and the splints dropped onto the bed, revealing a pale but healthy thumb. Jayne pulled at it gently until it clicked loudly, wiggled it, and then stretched her fingers. Berni frowned, but the longer he spent in her company, the less surprised he became.

Jayne lifted the blanket, looking under and down at her half-dressed body.

"Please pass me my clothes and avert your stern gaze for a moment, Berni."

He picked up her neatly folded clothes, passed them to her and stood facing the wall. As he listened, she climbed out of bed, dressed, and then slipped her hand into his.

"Come with me."

"You should not have lied to me. I would have helped you, whatever your situation", Berni said as they walked to her cabin.

"I did not lie when I said you were nice or when I said that we were friends. It is simply a fact that there are things I cannot explain, and I am sorry about that. Please trust me a little longer."

Jayne squeezed his hand and smiled at him disarmingly. Her tone of voice felt genuine, and she seemed to leave him no choice.

"Very well, Jayne Brewer. For now, I will trust you."

"Thank you. She was right about you." Said Jayne as she opened her cabin door. Berni stopped when he realised what she had said.

"Who was?"

Jayne ignored the question as she took her clothes from the wardrobe and began to pack a small suitcase.

"Nurse Jacobs may wonder why I have left my hospital bed and come to ask why. It may be best if I move to another cabin. Is there one empty?"

"If it will not be too distressing, a passenger passed away in the night, and cabin C38 is now vacant. It smelled very strongly of tobacco when we took the body below, but the windows have been open most of the day."

"Do not concern yourself, Berni; I am not easily distressed…and I am rather fond of the smell of tobacco."

She passed him her parasol and turned to adjust her hat in the wardrobe mirror. When she was quite satisfied, she picked up the suitcase and retrieved her parasol.

"There. All ready."

"I cannot be seen walking the corridors of my ship while you carry your own case, Jayne. It would not be proper."

"No, I suppose not. Please be careful, it is quite hea…"

Berni lifted the case and stumbled, totally unprepared for its weight.

"What on earth is in here?"

"Oh, just a rather splendid clock. Berni?"

"Yes?"

"I am sorry to further impose on your time, but would it be asking too much if we made a brief detour on the way to my new cabin?"

Cabin B81 - Sunday, April 14th, 1912 – 1.20 pm

Francois rummaged in the hamper, examining what remained of its contents. He was already growing tired of the finest food that RMS Titanic could offer and held up a jar of a thick, dark substance to the light of the cabin window. Imogen was busying herself with a mortar and pestle recently provided by the ever-resourceful Berni Rosseau.

"I have been in the café business for many years, Imogen, but have honestly no idea what Maritatu is."

"Veal spleen and lung, boiled and sautéed in oil. If we had some bread, you could add a little grated cheese and enjoy a rather excellent sandwich, much enjoyed in the tavernas of Sicily. However, the odour is perhaps second only to your kippers in its impertinence."

"Then it is most fortunate that we have no bread."

"Yes."

A puff of red smoke rose from Imogen's bowl, narrowly missing her hair as she quickly leaned away. Francois knew better than to interrupt his friend when she was working, but he was bored almost to the limits of tolerance.

"How are you getting on?"

She looked up and turned to face him briefly, her hair askew and a blue smudge on the tip of her nose.

"Please read your novel, Francois."

"I have finished it."

"Please read it again," she said a little impatiently, returning to her work.

Francois continued to explore the hamper, holding up another jar and reading the label aloud.

"Kibreo?"

Imogen huffed quite obviously but didn't turn around.

"Cibero. The C is soft. Soup. From Tuscany."

She mumbled to herself in Italian, for once struggling to translate.

"Creste Di Gallo Pollo…the insides of the chicken. Tradition varies from region to region, but there is every chance you may find at least one rooster testicle. By all means, try some and report your findings."

Francois grimaced, returning the jar to the hamper and sitting on the bed. He picked up his copy of Peter Pan and thumbed through the pages quickly, looking up at the sound of Imogen's gentle celebration.

"Huzzah!"

Heavy blue smoke was now pouring from Imogen's bowl onto the carpet. It swirled around her feet, spreading outwards to a depth of a few inches. Quick as a flash, Francois grabbed the top blanket and lay it across the bottom of the door, containing the surprisingly pleasant-smelling fog.

"Thank you, Francois."

He returned to the bed and climbed onto it, standing awkwardly to evade the fog.

"Shoes, Francois."

"My apologies," he said as he kicked off one shoe and then the other. They vanished beneath whatever it was that Imogen had created, causing Francois to fear for his Brogues.

"Did you enjoy it?" she asked.

"Pardon?"

"Your novel. Did you enjoy it?" she replied quickly.

"Oh. Yes, there was much flying about."

"Birds?"

"Children. Also, there were pirates and a crocodile that swallowed a clock."

"...and the lead character? Mr Pan. Which is he?"

"Neither. He is a boy who never grows up. Honestly, Imogen, it is a curious but compelling tale."

Francois steadied himself on the mattress, moving his stocking feet about the soft bed and resting a hand on the wall as the fog rose. Seemingly oblivious to his actions, Imogen took a large gulp of her expensive wine and continued working, keeping her back to him.

"I am unfamiliar with the book, but based on your succinct review, I am minded to give it a wide berth. It sounds ridiculous."

With an irony lost on Imogen, Francois' eyes were drawn to the Bumble as it hummed and moved in a small circle over the bedside cabinet, making two small whirlpools of fog as it did so.

"It...it was not published until 1911, so your unfamiliarity is understandable. Imogen, what is it doing?"

"What is what doing?"

Imogen finally turned around in her chair, blowing stray

hairs from her face and pushing up her glasses.

"I am not entirely sure. Bumbling, perhaps? Its repertoire is limited, but in addition to a power source that has lasted more than two decades, it seems to possess a certain independence of thought."

"You joke, surely."

"Not at all."

the Bumble stopped and floated towards Francois, who waved Peter Pan at it in an effort to discourage its attention.

"Exactly how many flying creatures do you intend to befriend, Imogen? Has Boreas met this intriguing contraption?"

"Yes, but he was not particularly enamoured of it. Francois, why are you standing on the bed?"

She raised her hand, and the Bumble flew across the room, creating a small wake in the fog as it did so. As before, it came to rest against her ring with a tap.

"Imogen, you have a…"

Francois pointed to the tip of his nose.

"Oh, thank you," she muttered, wiping away the blue smudge.

"Far be it for me to question your efforts, Imogen, but we seem to be knee-deep in rose-scented, blue fog."

"Yes, and I am pleased that you noticed the scent. Technically, this concoction will serve its purpose without it. However, I was feeling a little frivolous."

Imogen stood, drank what remained of her wine and playfully kicked at the fog, making ripples and eddies around her knees.

"This wine is really rather good," she tittered.

"Yes, it is. Imogen, I have been thinking."

"Excellent. What about?"

"The clock."

She picked up a small vial of bright yellow fluid, opened it and emptied the contents into the fog. Immediately, a golden iridescence radiated outwards from her, the fog vanishing as it did so. In less than five seconds, all that remained was the delicate scent of roses.

"The cabin clock?" Imogen asked as she turned her head to look at it.

Francois climbed off the bed and picked up his shoes, relieved to see them undamaged.

"No. Our clock, at home. You were repairing our clock moments before we arrived here, and there was a similar clock on the mantlepiece in the smoking room when we arrived. I cannot remember the exact details, but do you think it is relevant?"

"I did notice the clock, but we left the smoking room in

such a hurry, and…"

Francois interrupted quickly.

"I remember that in my room, you said - 'Francois, please hold the small hand in place while I remove the faceplate'. I am not sure why I remember it so precisely, but I am certain that is what you said. The next thing I recall with any clarity is waking up with a sore head and your face extremely close to mine. Could it be that the clocks are important?"

"I have no idea, but it would be foolish not to consider it. However, we have other matters to attend to first."

"Do we? Does it matter so much? We did not ask for this, Imogen. Indeed, events have been forced upon us, and I have never enjoyed playing the pawn in another's game."

"Nor I, but too much has happened since we arrived onboard. I cannot simply leave and forget it all. No. We shall continue as planned for now."

Sitting down on the bed, Francois put his shoes back on.

"I understand, but I also want to go home," he replied, sighing heavily. Imogen sat down next to him, both hands in her lap.

"…and so we shall, Francois. Soon."

"You seem very certain."

Imogen leaned against Francois, gently touching his shoulder.

"We are together. How could we possibly fail?"

The Promenade Deck - Sunday, April 14th, 1912 — 2.15 pm

Imogen peered through the smoking-room window at the fireplace where they had first woken from whatever had caused them to arrive in the year 1912. Francois sat on the deck floor, looking up at her, occasionally looking left and right.

"So, now we are stealing a clock. This is becoming something of a habit, Imogen."

"We are not stealing it. I merely wish to examine it in the privacy of our cabin. If my theory is correct, it will remain in the cabin when we return to 1908. Our clock did not accompany us, and I have no reason to believe that this one will do either."

"We will be recognised and thrown out. On the occasion of our first visit, we made quite the impression. You will have noticed that your silent gunpowder broke three windows."

"One would perhaps think that such damage would have been repaired by now."

"I shall complain to the captain at the earliest opportunity."

Straining her neck, Imogen replied in a clipped tone.

"Oh, hush. Two passengers are seated at the far end of the room, and a single steward, whom I do not recognise, is attending to their needs. One might say the coast is clear."

"But you are still a woman, Imogen and as you were told, most forcibly, you are not permitted in the smoking room."

"I have a plan. Now, please get up before you ruin your only pair of trousers."

Imogen opened the sliding door through which they had escaped only a few days before. Although the furniture had been tidied, the small café still smelled of sulphur.

"There is a painting over the mantlepiece, Francois. It depicts Plymouth Harbour in the Southwest of England. I am familiar with the city, which is why it drew my attention during our brief time beneath it. Explain to the steward that your wife is a native of Plymouth and would very much like to appreciate the painting more fully. If he is unmoved by your request, offer him money."

Francois couldn't deny that it was a clever plan.

"Is there anywhere on Earth you have not visited, Imogen?"

She slipped into a Devonian accent with ease.

"Many such places, kind sir, but none so fair as the fine city of Plymouth."

For the second time in as many days, Imogen's accent startled Francois quite considerably.

"Oh, for heaven's sake, woman."

"Maid."

"What?"

"Were we wandering the cobbled streets of Plymouth's Barbican, you would address me as 'maid'."

"I would?"

"Yes, and were you also a resident of that fine city, you would likely offer an additional lascivious remark regarding my person."

"Ah."

"Possibly my shapely calves. The crudity of your outburst would depend on the quantity of cider you had recently imbibed."

Imogen had moved to the revolving door separating the small café from the smoking room and was now peering through it.

"Cider gives me wind," said Francois, putting a hand on his stomach.

"Yes, I know. Also, you are possibly the least lascivious man I have ever met."

"Thank you."

"That was hardly a compliment, Francois. You have also never run about our café in your underthings whistling a merry tune, and I have never felt the need to thank you for not doing so."

"I make every effort to please."

"Oh hush, you ridiculous, slightly charming man. Now, please initiate our plan. I shall wait here."

Imogen straightened Francois' collar, then pulled out a chair and sat on it, resting her hands in her lap.

"Charm is no effort, Imogen. One only needs to be sincere. I sometimes wonder if you think me shallow."

Imogen looked up at him, the edges of her mouth curling up slightly.

"There was a time when I might have done so, but that time has long passed."

"I am pleased to hear it. When I next wear my hat, I shall lift it in gratitude."

"Yes, I am sure you will, now, if only the steward were female, Francois, your success would be almost guaranteed. On this occasion, however, you have a steeper hill to climb."

Francois also peered through the glass door and saw a balding man many years his senior moving unsteadily between the smoking room's occupants with a worryingly full silver tray.

"I have fifteen dollars left. Do you think that will be enough?"

"Let us hope so."

The First-Class Smoking Room - Sunday, April 14th, 1912 – 2.30 pm

It was an excellent plan, but unfortunately, Steward First-Class Angus Merriman had decided to earn his ten dollars by sharing what little he knew of the painting.

"Norman Wilkinson's painting depicts a view of Plymouth that will greet our First-Class Passengers when we briefly drop anchor there on our return journey. It is a striking image, but I am not overly fond of it, sir – it is a little fussy, and the vantage point is too far from the city. Were Smeaton's Tower not visible, it could be almost anywhere."

Francois nodded, glancing at Imogen nervously as he did so. Unlike her pitch-perfect accent, her patience was beginning to wane, and the steward had no idea of the impending storm.

"Yes, I know. Thank you. I believe my husband mentioned that I was born in Plymouth. I would much rather study the painting without your incessant babbling."

Angus seemed determined to continue; however, almost as if she had said nothing at all.

"It is a matter of much speculation as to why he named his work so. Plymouth Sound is not often referred to as Plymouth Harbour."

"Please be quiet.", said Imogen pointedly.

He stopped briefly but, once again, completely ignored her.

"Oh dear, Sir, I fear your wife has little interest in the acquisition of knowledge. It was ever thus, I'm afraid.", said Angus with a dismissive, patronising laugh.

"Go away!" Imogen said bluntly.

Francois turned away, smirking into his sleeve as Imogen's patience evaporated.

"Madam?"

"Go away, or I will hurt you."

Angus laughed.

"Oh, sir, she has such spirit! Perhaps, when you return to the privacy of your cabin, you will teach her…"

The plush green cushion hit the side of the old man's face with enough force to knock him to the floor.

"Holy Christ!"

The carpet cushioned some, but not all, of his fall. He would never know how close Imogen had come to using the silver tray that lay on the table, inches from the cushion.

Francois quickly offered his hand to Angus as the old man tried and failed to stand on his own.

"Up you get…"

Standing nearby, Imogen still brandished the cushion, betraying not an ounce of regret in her eyes.

"The last few days have been quite stressful, I'm afraid, and my wife is overwhelmed by memories of her former home and…here you are."

Francois tucked his remaining five dollars in Angus' waistcoat pocket as Imogen continued to glare at the old man. With Francois' help, Angus got to his feet and hurried off as fast as his aged and now sore legs could carry him.

Imogen returned her attention to the painting as Francois watched him limp quickly towards a door at the far end of the room before also turning around to face the painting.

"He was extraordinarily irritating, Francois. Please do not look at me in that way."

"You briefly considered the silver tray, did you not?"

"Briefly."

"I am sure he will be fine. It is a very plush carpet."

Imogen took a step closer, rubbing the tip of her finger along the bottom of the frame.

"I lodged with a pleasant woman in Devonport, not part of Plymouth exactly, but treated as such by most."

Imogen's eyes wandered over the painting, wishing she

could make out more detail than there was.

"Ah. How did you come to be in Plymouth?"

"As you know, I travelled for several years when I left my husband and Italy behind. I had no particular destination or purpose other than to improve my mind and see as much of the world as I could. In late 1906, I had travelled almost as far west as it was possible to go without getting my feet wet. Plymouth is quite a pleasant place if you are fond of the smell of fish."

"You are not fond of the smell of fish, Imogen."

"No, I am not, but I had my peppermint gel."

Francois turned his head to see no sign of Angus Merriman and only two gentleman passengers whose acrid pipe smoke rose from behind their newspapers.

"We are not being watched," Francois whispered.

Imogen lowered her gaze to the clock, confirming something that she had suspected since Angus had first let them in.

"Francois, this is not the same clock that sat on the mantlepiece when we arrived."

He regarded her, a little confused.

"Are you sure?"

"Yes. It is similar, but it is most definitely not the same."

Cabin C38 - Sunday, April 14th, 1912 – 3.15 pm

Berni sat on the bed and watched Jayne jam her pocketknife blade into the clock faceplate.

"If you prefer, I could probably locate the key, Jayne. You may damage it if you continue to…"

"Voila!" exclaimed Jayne as the front of the clock sprung open, and she sat back in the chair. As Berni moved closer to look at the elegant piece on the table, Jayne grabbed his wrist.

"Please, do not come any closer. It is very important that you do not touch this clock."

"Would there be any point in asking you why?"

"None. Please give it a wide berth if you will excuse the pun."

"Could you perhaps tell me WHY you have taken it?"

"This is a very special clock, at least in the here and now. Soon, it will not be so. Indeed, it may already not be so. There is so much I still do not understand."

Berni blinked as he organised her words in his head. His English was not as fluent as people believed, and he still struggled occasionally. Jayne and Madame DiRossi, in particular, tested his understanding.

"Who are you, Jayne Brewer?"

"I am a little girl from Plymouth in England, and I am not all I appear to be.", said Jayne, shrugging happily.

"Both of those things, I already know."

"If I were to tell you more, your head would bubble and boil until it exploded, I promise you."

"That would be unfortunate."

"I have already told you more than I should and far more than I tell most."

"Are you in danger?"

"No, but there may come a time soon when others will be, including you. You must promise to do exactly as I say when that time comes."

"What is this danger?"

"You are a good person, Berni Rosseau, and if I told you, you would do your very best to prevent it, and that would not do at all."

"Very well, I promise to do as you say when your unspecified danger is upon me. Will I have to be very brave?"

Jayne opened her suitcase and put on a pair of black leather gloves. They were a striking contrast to her dress, something Berni couldn't help but notice. She smiled at him encouragingly,

"Yes, but I am confident you will not disappoint when the time comes."

His look made it clear that he was becoming more confused with every passing minute."

"I do not blame you for being frustrated, Berni."

"I am frustrated, but not with you. I saw you fall, Jayne, and here you sit, fit and well. I felt your heart slow, merely because you wished it, and…your foot, and your thumb…"

"I am sorry, but I have an irresistible flair for the dramatic on occasion. My left foot still aches a little, if that is any consolation."

"No, it is not," said Berni with a wry smile.

Jayne moved her hand closer to the clock face, and a tiny blue spark jumped to her finger, taking her by surprise and making her giggle.

"Oh!"

"What on Earth was that?"

"The answer to my question. This clock has not yet completed its business here, but fortunately, there are two clock hands, and I only require one of them."

Cabin B81 - Sunday, April 14th, 1912 – 6.20 pm

Francois lay on the bed, shuffling his playing cards. For the seventeenth time, he threw one at the empty wash basin and missed. Imogen had been busy at the table since they had returned from the smoking room, and he had seen little point in interrupting her work.

"Francois?"

"Yes?"

"That is quite distracting."

"My apologies."

Francois climbed off the bed and picked up the small pile of cards, returning them to the pack. As he sat on the chair beside her, he could see she was examining a small vial through her thickest spectacle lenses. Two more vials lay on the table, both full of blue powder.

"I have almost forgotten how I used to spend Sundays before I met you, Imogen. We were always busy, but Anton and Maria left me to my accounts for the most part. There was precious little excitement."

She smiled, filling the third vial from the bowl.

"We shall have many more Sundays, Francois, and plenty of time to read our newspaper and enjoy coffee by the fire. It just so happens that today we caper."

She put the cap on the last vial, pulled up her left sleeve and slipped the vials into three small pockets.

"We will not know precisely how to proceed until we have seen the location of Doctor Sadek and her two aides. However, I am confident of success."

"Of course you are."

Imogen sensed a lack of confidence in his voice.

"How do you think we should proceed? As always, I value your contributions."

"I am not certain, Imogen. I would prefer to avoid violence or confrontation of any sort, if possible."

"I agree. Distraction and diversion are infinitely preferable in a situation such as this.

"The fog?"

"As always, I have several ideas up my sleeve."

CHAPTER NINE – SNAKE & DAGGER
B Deck – Sunday, April 14th, 1912 – 10.45 pm

Imogen and Francois crouched outside the door of The Gentleman's Lavatory. She took out her telescope, peering down to the far end of the corridor, towards Doctor Sadek's cabins. Imogen had lent Francois a small mirror, and he was doing his best to imitate her actions.

Grumbling, he muttered, "This is less than ideal. I can see the edge of my left ear, a porthole and the top of a potted palm. I trust you are having more success?"

"I see one of her aides, presumably Ammon, smoking and clearly on guard. The cabin door is open, but I cannot see inside. Berni was certain that Doctor Sadek had taken the far cabin; the artefacts and other luggage were in the centre one, and her two aides were occupying the third one, which is closest to us."

Imogen lowered the telescope.

"It would be best to draw Ammon away in this direction."

"How do you propose that we...?"

Before Francois could stop her, Imogen stood, straightened her attire, and boldly walked into the corridor in full view of Ammon, who looked up as she leaned on the wall with one hand.

"What are you doing?" hissed Francois, still cowering behind the wall at her feet.

"I am loitering solicitously. I have seen it done many times but seldom had an opportunity to try it."

"...and?"

"Well, he has noticed me and is now walking in this direction. I have clearly piqued his interest."

"You are an attractive woman, Imogen, but I suspect he will soon realise you are not a harlot."

"I think that moment is already past. Stand ready, Francois!"

"Ready for what?" he said with an edge of panic.

Without another word, she turned around and hurried off in the opposite direction, leaving him alone. Angling the mirror around the corner, he saw Ammon hurrying after Imogen. When he was just a few feet away from Francois' hiding place, he stuck out his foot, and the aide tripped over it, flying forward and slamming into the wall opposite. Francois waited several seconds until he was sure Ammon presented no further threat, then crawled over to him.

Hearing the fracas, Imogen hurried back.

"Excellent," she said as she bent down, lifting Ammon's eyelids.

Francois leaned closer, glancing quickly at the small dent in the wall.

"Will he live?"

"Of course he will. There is almost certainly no permanent damage."

"Perhaps next time, we could discuss your plans in more detail before putting them into effect?"

"Carpe diem, Francois! I was confident in your ability to improvise, and you did not disappoint."

"You flatter me, but I did little more than panic."

Imogen poked gently at the large bruise on Ammon's forehead and wrinkled her nose.

"Oh, hush. Now, help me hide him in the lavatory."

"I do love a Sunday."

"Pardon?"

"Never mind."

Ammon moaned groggily as Imogen grabbed one of his feet and Francois took the other. Together, they dragged him into one of the grandest and thankfully vacant lavatories Francois had ever seen. Kicking the centre cubicle door open, he put the toilet seat down, and they sat Ammon on it, taking a few moments to steady him as he mumbled incoherently.

"What is he saying?"

"I have no idea. My fluency in Arabic seems to have vanished as quickly as it arrived," said Imogen, emptying the contents of a small paper bag into her hand.

"What is that?"

"Something that I wish I had more of. This man is quite large, and I am not sure…"

As she paused, Imogen pulled Ammon's mouth open, slapped her palm against his lips, closed his mouth and pinched his nostrils.

"Swallow," she whispered in his ear, and he did so. Almost immediately, Ammon lost consciousness, and they left him in the cubicle.

"How long will he be immobile?"

"I do not know for sure. As I said, he is a large man. Possibly fifteen minutes. My resources were limited."

Imogen backed up, closing the cubicle door behind her.

"Do not punish yourself, Imogen. It will have to do. Luckily, thanks to young Mr Rosseau, we have a second level of defence."

Outside in the corridor, Francois closed The Gentleman's Lavatory door and took out a handful of keys, all attached to a long chain. He tried three before finding one that fit snugly in the lock, turning it with a satisfying click. After trying the handle to be sure, he put the keys back in his pocket, sighed and smiled at Imogen.

"One down, one to go."

Cabin B98 – Sunday, April 14th, 1908 – 11.00 pm

Penny Sadek stood with her arms folded, looking up at Mahmoud. He was a foot taller than her and intimidatingly broad across the shoulders, but at this moment, his manner was deferential in the extreme.

"My apologies, Doctor. Violet and Montague Smith have vanished like sand in the desert wind."

Penny frowned.

"Despite your eloquent excuse, Mahmoud, I am still disappointed in you. I have come to rely on your efficiency and your..."

She looked up, suddenly distracted by a flash of gold in the open doorway.

"What is that?"

"I do not know, Doctor. An insect?"

Penny walked toward the door, and the Bumble backed off a little.

"Ammon! Are you asleep?" she shouted as she looked around the doorframe and watched the Bumble fly off down the corridor."

"Mahmoud! Ammon is gone. Find him!"

Mahmoud's brisk walk turned into a run as he hurried to catch up with the golden object, cursing it in his native tongue and searching around every corner for his friend.

"Ammon! Where are you?"

With Mahmoud still some distance away, the Bumble turned the last corner and stopped, hovering a few inches from Imogen's raised palm.

With her other hand, she threw the small blue vials toward the sound of Mahmoud's heavy footsteps. In an instant, the corridor filled from floor to ceiling with thick, blue fog. Imogen and Francois backed away as the fog engulfed Mahmoud, and his coughing and spluttering grew louder.

"Wait here, Francois. The fog may be enough, but if he emerges, I suspect he will not be in the best of moods and keen to unleash his displeasure on the first person he sees."

"So I should wait here and ensure I am the first person he sees? All things considered; I would prefer to be somewhere else."

Imogen passed Francois a small, round bottle of dark red liquid. It was twice the size of the blue vials and much heavier than he expected.

"A last resort, Francois. It lacks finesse but will do what needs to be done. Drop it and move as far away as you can, quickly."

Francois closed his fist around the bottle.

"Quickly. Far away. Yes."

Sensing his slight loss of confidence, Imogen grasped his shoulder and squeezed.

"All will be well. I have every confidence in you."

Imogen walked backwards a few paces, then took the long way around to Penny's cabin, avoiding the fog. The Bumble moved a little closer to Francois, hovering in his eye-line.

"Do not look at me like that. She has every confidence in me."

In the fog, Mahmoud's coughing and swearing grew louder as he approached Francois. Twice, he walked into something, and it crashed to the floor, making Francois jump each time.

Cabin B96 – Sunday, April 14th, 1908 – 11.10 pm

Imogen crouched at the door of cabin B96 and turned the knob. Inside, the room was dark as she quietly closed the door behind her. She knew from Berni's sketched plans that there were no connecting doors to the cabins on either side, so she felt confident she would not be disturbed when she turned on the light.

The cabin had been emptied of furniture and was now filled with packing crates. In the corner, on top of a small one, sat Doctor Penelope T. Sadek.

"Good evening, Violet. I must say, it would have been a lot easier for all concerned if you had made an appointment."

Imogen stood up straight, clasping her hands in front of her.

"My name is not Violet."

"No, of course it isn't, and neither are you Hungarian. Your accent was exquisite - almost perfect, in fact, but I have been studying languages for almost as long as I could read, and not only dead ones. I do wonder why you disguised both your name and your language. Such arrogance to dangle a tissue of lies in front of someone as intelligent as me."

"Perhaps." Imogen said as she nodded politely, "I am the Lady Imogen DiRossi."

"Lady? My, my...and your husband?"

"He is not my husband. His name is Francois Meyer, and he is my friend."

"He seems very charming, but his French accent is truly appalling, and his story was even less convincing than yours."

Imogen raised an eyebrow and allowed herself a little smile.

"He has lived in Paris for many years. Almost all of what he told you is true."

"Really?"

Penny's stern face relaxed for a moment, a trace of amusement in her eyes, but it passed quickly. Casually, she raised her arm to show Imogen The Serpent's Grasp fastened tightly on her wrist and a dazzling jewelled dagger in her hand.

"You will tell me why you want the bracelet so badly, Imogen DiRossi."

"I wish you would stop being so melodramatic, Penny. It is quite tedious."

Failing to hide her offence, Penny got up from the crate and took a step closer to Imogen.

"You may consider my previous offer of informality withdrawn."

"Very well, Doctor Sadek."

"I say again - why do you want this?"

"Unfortunately, I am at a loss as to how to explain."

Penny took another step forward.

"Please try. I saw how it reacted to you and what it did to you. I must know why. Twice now, I have seen it react in such a way. The other screamed in pain and ran, but you did not."

Imogen raised an eyebrow.

"There was someone else?"

"A few years ago, at The Louvre. I had not seen her before and have not seen her since. Perhaps an accomplice of yours?"

Imogen took a step forward.

"I have no idea what you are talking about. Before yesterday, I had never even heard of The Serpent's Grasp."

"I do not believe you."

"That is of no matter. I will take it and not damage it. I am more than capable of the former and will give you my word on the latter."

Penny raised the dagger and twirled it around her fingers. Imogen stepped back, twitching the fingers of her right hand and wishing, yet again, that Tesla's glove wasn't in pieces hundreds of miles away.

"I may not know who you are, but I know what you are, Imogen DiRossi. I have waited a long time to meet someone like you."

"I am both baffled and flattered, Doctor Sadek, but the hour is late, and it has been a long day."

Penny lunged at Imogen, who stepped aside easily. She twisted around, watching the young woman run clumsily into the cabin door. Raising her eyebrow at the sudden show of aggression, Imogen spread her palms in a gesture of reconciliation.

"I have no desire to injure you, Doctor Sadek."

"In that, we differ."

Penny deftly spun the dagger in her hand, keeping her eyes focused on Imogen.

"This dagger is older than the bracelet, but it sparkles like it was made yesterday. I consider it my duty to ensure that they stay together."

Imogen shrugged calmly as she tilted her head to one side.

"Then I will take them both. Tell me, have you ever used a dagger in anger, Doctor Sadek?"

At that moment, Penny's face told Imogen all she needed to know.

"You need not answer. It is clear to me that you have not."

"…and you have?" retorted Penny angrily.

"Yes, and as you can see, I am still very much alive. For many years, I possessed several impressive scars, but for reasons I cannot explain, they are now gone. Suffice to say they told of a life lived dangerously."

"Gone?"

Imogen saw something new in Penny's face – a moment of clarity and triumph, which quickly turned into a sneer.

"I have you, Imogen DiRossi! After all this time, the very thing I wanted more than anything else has come to my door, and I am starting to believe that you really do have no idea what I am talking about!"

The young woman leapt forward, forcing Imogen to grab the hand holding the dagger and twist it, losing her balance as she did so. Penny screamed in pain as they both fell to the floor.

Cabin B96 – Sunday, April 14th, 1908 – 11.25 pm

Farther down the corridor, Francois backed away from the large shape moving towards him, but not quickly enough. Covered in blue dust, coughing and angry, Mahmoud emerged from the fog. He leant on the wall with one hand, trying to catch his breath, sending puffs of blue from his mouth and nostrils.

"Are you quite well?" said Francois, taking another half-step back.

Mahmoud's reply was quiet but filled with rage. It was also in Arabic, but Francois needed no translation. For a moment, he feared immediate and violent retribution.

"Sawf 'aqtae 'atrafak wa'aksir raqabatak 'ayuha al'ahmaq alghamghama!"

Francois stepped back again, but Mahmoud's outburst seemed to drain the last of his strength, and he slid down the wall onto his behind. Francois waited almost a minute before getting closer and knelt next to him. He looked into the Egyptian's glazed eyes and smiled, confident of his safety for now at least.

"This is turning into quite the day, is it not?"

Mahmoud grunted again, lifting his hand slightly and then letting it drop heavily.

"We have much in common, you and I, Mahmoud. We have both chosen a life of adventure in the company of extraordinary women. I have a café. Well…we have a café, Imogen and I, but it is very much my domain. She is more of a silent partner. Most of the time, anyway."

Francois relaxed, sitting down next to Mahmoud, placing his hands in his lap and resting his shoulder against Mahmoud.

"All this nonsense is more of a hobby, as is this, in fact…"

Francois took out a pack of cards from his jacket pocket, shuffled them casually and then fanned them out in front of the aide. Mahmoud slowly looked down at the cards and coughed, spraying blue dust all over them.

"Pick a card, Mahmoud, any card."

Suddenly, the big man's arm lurched towards him. His fingers grasped Francois' throat, and the cards went flying. Almost effortlessly, he got up, holding Francois until they both stood. Francois felt his feet leave the floor as he struggled fruitlessly in Mahmoud's firm grip, gasping for breath. He tried reaching into his trouser pocket for the red bottle Imogen had given him, but knowing that even if he could, she had told him to move far away before using it, and he had no desire to spend the last few moments of his life on fire.

Mahmoud's grip tightened, but Francois continued to struggle, waving his arms about and shaking his legs in an effort to free himself. As angry as he was, Mahmoud had no wish to kill Francois, only incapacitate him and drag him back to Doctor Sadek.

Francois felt his strength fade as Mahmoud's fingers squeezed his windpipe closed, and finally, he lost consciousness.

"Put him down very carefully!"

Still holding onto Francois, Mahmoud turned his head at the sound of the loud, clear voice.

Twenty feet away stood Jayne, her legs planted slightly apart and her hands resting on her parasol handle.

A soft, familiar voice spoke in her head, "His name is Mahmoud."

Jayne shouted, her voice even louder than before.

"Mahmoud!"

At the sound of his name on the lips of a young stranger, Mahmoud dropped Francois, who crumpled to the floor in a heap, hitting his head on the floor.

Jayne slowly walked towards him, seeing an expression she often saw at such moments - a mixture of disbelief and confusion. Now, only a few feet away, she pulled at the parasol handle, revealing a six-inch blade and pulling it free of its secret sheath, which she threw to one side.

Weakened by Imogen's fog, Mahmoud's reactions were far too slow, allowing the girl to slip behind him and cut a deep gash in his thigh as she passed. He fell to his knees, grasping his leg and flailing his free arm around in a fruitless attempt to grab at her, but she was out of reach now and looking down at the splashes of blood on her white lace dress.

"Oh, look what you have done, you awful man!"

She ducked under his arm, knocked his Fez off and pulled his head back by the hair. He swore violently as she put her knee into his back and pressed the blade to his throat.

"You are big and strong, but I am not afraid of you or your harsh and most inappropriate language, Mahmoud. What would…"

The voice in Jayne's head returned – quiet, brief and precise.

"He has an older brother. Sokar."

Jayne nodded and smiled to herself.

"…what would Sokar think if he saw you now?"

Mahmoud tensed.

"What are you?" he growled indignantly.

"I am someone with a knife to your throat, and I promise you are far from my most pressing concern at this moment. I am going to release you, and you will walk away. If you do not, I will find you."

Jayne pressed the blade against Mahmoud's neck, using only enough force to draw blood. To his credit, he stayed very still as a small trickle of blood ran down his skin.

"Doctor Sadek. She is my duty."

"Her future is set, but yours is not."

Jayne felt his body tense again. The wound on his thigh was deep, but she had cut him quite deliberately and precisely. In time, he would heal.

"I do not believe you."

"You are a stupid man."

Jayne took her hand from his hair and slapped it on his forehead.

Speaking as if to herself, she shouted, "Show him!"

Mahmoud wondered who she was talking to, but then his body froze, and he lost all awareness of the world around him. Slowly, his mind filled with images of Doctor Sadek and what he quickly realised was her future – a future he wanted no part of. Then he heard a single word. It was soft and clear, and finally, he believed.

"Leave."

Jayne heard the word as well. She took the blade away from his neck, stepped back and looked up as Mahmoud stood and towered above her, still grasping his thigh. He looked down at the blood on her dress and then at the blade in her hand, scared for one of the very few times in his life.

"Please give my best to Sokar when you see him next."

He walked backwards for a few steps, then turned around and ran off down the corridor, limping badly. Jayne kneeled next to Francois, sitting him up against the wall. His chest rose and fell with a gentle snore as she tidied his hair.

"I came as fast as I could. I am sorry if he hurt you."

She leaned close and kissed him on the cheek.

"I will see you soon, you dear man – very soon."

Francois mumbled quietly.

"Not now, Monica...I have to be up early."

Jayne laughed happily as she checked her pocket watch, then walked off, picking up her parasol on the way.

Cabin B96 – Sunday, April 14th, 1908 – 11.35 pm

Penny lay on the floor under Imogen, red-faced and frustrated. Her anger had given her the strength to resist the older woman, but it was fading, and she was close to tears.

"It touched you, and it spoke to you! You are one of them! I am certain!"

Imogen sat astride Penny, holding her down easily, but the young woman struggled like an eel, forcing Imogen to adjust her position constantly.

"I deeply regret what I must do, Doctor."

"Must do?"

"I cannot explain why, but yes, I must."

"You are a thief!"

"Sometimes, but never without good reason. Despite the circumstances, I am glad to have met you, Penelope Sadek. I see greatness in you, much as a brilliant man once saw it in me."

With what remained of her strength, Penny tensed her body in a last futile effort to unseat Imogen.

"Oh, I do so wish you would stop patronising me, Imogen DiRossi! You are quite possibly the most insufferable and arrogant woman I have ever met."

Imogen considered the criticism.

"I have been accused of both before and on occasions, deservedly so, but I meant what I told you yesterday in Café Parisien - you must persist with your work. You are still young, just as I once was, but you will be great one day."

"First of all, I am already great, and secondly, I will find you, Imogen DiRossi! I will hunt you down and take back what you are taking from me!"

"I am almost certain that is not possible."

"Arrogance."

"Perhaps, but I have a rather excellent place to hide," smirked Imogen as she pulled her necklace out of her dress.

"This will have no lasting effect. You will sleep for a very short while, and when you wake, I will be gone."

"We do not dock in New York for two more days; until then, you have nowhere to go."

"It is a big ship, Pe…"

There was a deep rumble from below their feet. It lasted a few seconds, making the brass handles on the packing crates rattle, but then it was gone. Penny stopped struggling.

"What was that?"

"I have no idea. Goodbye, Doctor Sadek."

Imogen pressed her hand over Penny's mouth, forcing her to inhale a simple herbal concoction. It was one of the first things she had taught herself to prepare, and she had kept a small amount in her pendant since she was nine years old. It smelled like an old wooden cart and herbs and briefly induced unconsciousness.

Penny sighed into Imogen's palm as her tired, tearful eyes closed.

Wary of what had happened in the café, Imogen wrapped her hand in a handkerchief as she touched the clasp of the ancient bracelet. Harmlessly, it clicked open and fell onto the floor.

Moments later, Imogen left the cabin with The Serpent's Grasp and dagger wrapped in the leather pouch Penny had shown them yesterday. She walked back to where she had left Francois, finding him unconscious on the floor. She kneeled close to him and slapped his cheek with a little more force than was necessary.

"Francois! Francois!"

He woke suddenly, startled to find her face inches from his.

"Just once. Just once, Imogen, I would like to regain consciousness in some other manner. Also, you smell rather strongly of herbs."

Imogen looked into his eyes and moved her raised finger from side to side in front of them. Francois' eyes followed.

"You recently told me that I had a beautiful face. Surely, there are worse things to wake up to. There is bruising on your neck. What happened?"

Francois put his hand to his neck, remembering recent events and glanced up and down the corridor warily.

"An enormous Egyptian man tossed me about with almost no effort. He was somewhat agitated and spewing blue fog. I appear to have triumphed, however."

"Once again, I leave you alone and return to find you knee-deep in floor."

"Very amusing. It was an awful experience."

Imogen helped him to his feet, brushing him off as she did so.

"...and yet you are still here, and he is not."

"Please try to sound less surprised. Were you successful?"

Imogen held up the leather pouch and winked.

"Yes, but we must return to our cabin. Doctor Sadek will wake soon, and, like your Egyptian friend, she will not be in the best of moods."

"We simply hide in our cabin? Then what?"

"One problem at a time, Francois, one problem at a time."

Cabin B81 – Sunday, April 14th, 1908 – 11.50 pm

Imogen closed and locked the cabin door behind them, putting the leather pouch on the table. She looked down at her feet, shifting her weight from one to the other and back again.

"Mmmm…"

Francois, who had sat on the bed, watched her with

interest.

"What is it?"

"The ship is no longer moving."

He kneeled on the bed and turned around to look out of the window.

"Are you sure? It is too dark to see clearly."

Standing at the end of the bed, Imogen cupped her hands to the glass and looked out of the window.

"Yes, I can feel it. Also…"

Imogen took out her pocket watch, opened it and laid it on the table. She put on her spectacles and studied the face, adjusting its position.

"We are dipping at the bow ever so slightly," Imogen announced as she moved to the hamper and poured herself a glass of wine. She put it down on the table and peered closely at the glass.

"Come, look here."

The level of the wine was clearly resting at a very small angle.

"The ship is angled down a little over one degree."

Francois climbed off the bed and peered very closely at the glass. Imogen continued.

"Whilst I was in Doctor Sadek's cabin, I felt and heard

what I now suspect to be something hitting the ship, or possibly vice versa. Regardless of how it has occurred, I believe we have been holed below the waterline."

"We are sinking?"

"I do not know for certain, but it is possible that we are."

"What should we do?"

"To begin with, we must not panic."

"I confess, that was my first thought."

"You must breathe, Francois…with me…"

Imogen closed her eyes, took a deep breath, and released it slowly. Francois watched, finding it very difficult not to think about the cold, dark water, and then did as Imogen instructed. When he opened his eyes, her face was very close to his, causing him to lean back a little.

"Panic and anxiety will do nothing but cloud your judgement and blunt your reflexes. I need you to be at your best, Francois, if we are to triumph in our moment of shared adversity."

"I will do my best."

"Of course you will; now put on your scarf. We will learn more up on deck, where I suspect it will be very cold."

Cabin B96 – Monday, April 15th, 1912 – 12.02 am

Penny woke, looking up at the cabin light and tasting the forest floor in her mouth. It took her a few seconds to remember what had happened, but when she did, the anger returned quickly.

"Imogen!"

She sat up and regretted it almost immediately. Putting one hand on her forehead, she used the other to get unsteadily to her feet. In the corridor outside her cabin, she heard raised voices, which she thought unusual considering the hour. She opened the door just as a steward rushed past.

"What has happened, steward?"

"Nothing to be concerned about, Madam. There was a small problem in the engine room, nothing more. Please return to your bed."

At present, the steward knew no more than the passengers, but he had been told to assure everyone that all was well—this was the Titanic, after all.

"I was not in my bed. Why is the ship no longer moving?"

"We have stopped briefly, but it will not affect our schedule, Madam, I assure you."

Penny knew when she was being managed, and the young man obviously had no more an idea of what was happening than she did. She watched the steward hurry off down the corridor, suddenly feeling very alone.

Outside The First-Class Lounge – Monday, April 15th, 1912 – 12.18 am

Francois had followed Imogen up the grand staircase, hurrying in a way he hadn't been capable of since he was a small boy. For so long, his leg had ached and slowed him down, but now he easily kept up with his friend, even leaping up the last few steps two at a time. They walked out on deck to see crew members going briskly about their business, and the few passengers already there seemed mostly unconcerned.

Imogen looked over the side, opened her pocket watch again and rested it on the bulkhead.

"Almost two degrees at the bow, and we are listing noticeably to starboard."

"We must ask someone."

"...and what would we ask them? They will have orders to keep us calm."

"Then, we should perhaps get to the lifeboats."

"I have calculated that even fully loaded, the lifeboats on the boat deck above us could barely hold 1,000 people, and judging from the size of this vessel, passengers and crew number at least twice that. Also, as a woman, I will be ushered to safety without you, and…"

Imogen's voice trailed off as she considered her following remark carefully.

"…the only lifeboat I will climb into is one where you already sit, and the matter is not open to discussion."

"Imogen…"

"Hush. The matter is closed."

B Deck – Monday, April 15th, 1912 – 12.35 am

Several floors below, Berni Rosseau rushed down the corridor of B deck. He knocked loudly on each cabin door and waited briefly for a response before knocking again. Shouting politely, he relayed the same message to each passenger.

"Please make your way to the boat deck. Leave your belongings."

At the far end of the corridor, he saw Jayne walking towards him, case in one hand and parasol in the other.

"Jayne! You must get to the lifeboats. Hurry! There is a small chance that the ship will sink."

"There is every chance, Berni."

Realisation spread slowly across his face, and he lowered

his voice.

"You knew. This is the danger that you spoke of?"

Jayne nodded.

"Do what you must and see to your passengers. You have time, I promise. I will stay with you."

With haste, Berni finished waking the passengers with Jayne at his side. Most did as he suggested, but several scoffed at the idea that the unsinkable Titanic was in danger and refused to leave their cabins. Those who listened to him hurried up the staircase as Berni and Jayne watched from one side. In disbelief, Berni voiced his thoughts out loud.

"The Titanic is sinking. It really is."

Jayne leant her parasol against the wall, slipped her hand into his and looked at the staircase clock opposite.

"Yes. In a little over one hour and twenty-one minutes."

"Am I going to die?"

"Yes, but not today."

Despite their situation, Berni smiled as Jayne looked up at him. He was no closer to understanding her, but everything told him that he could trust her.

"Do you think I would have taken the time to become such good friends with you if you were to die a few days after we met? Worry not, Berni Rosseau; the world is not ready to lose such a lovely man just yet."

"I cannot go to a lifeboat unless a senior officer gives me permission, and that will not be until all passengers are safe."

"Women and children first," replied Jayne sadly as she looked up at Berni. "There are 2,220 people on board this vessel, Berni, and a great many are going to die because there are not enough lifeboats."

"But this is The Titanic! It is unsinkable, and we were told the boats would never be needed. If the ship were somehow disabled, we would simply wait for rescue. There would be music and dancing while we waited."

Berni looked up as the last passenger ran up the stairs, momentarily leaving them alone. It was quiet enough now to hear the ship creaking beneath their feet and the sound of raised voices from above.

"I should be up on deck, helping them, Jayne."

"Yes, you should, but I cannot go with you. I will be forced into a lifeboat against my will by someone who means well. No, I will stay down here for now and attend to a few important matters."

"You are sure?"

"I am sure, Berni, and now you must listen to me very carefully. The time has come for you to do exactly as I say."

Berni took a deep breath, ready to listen.

"At precisely 1.00 am, Starboard Lifeboat 3 will be lowered into the water with thirty-four people aboard, and you will be one of them."

"I cannot take a place meant for a passenger, especially if there are women and children before me."

Reaching up and touching his cheek, Jayne whispered gently.

"You are brave, Berni Rosseau, but your story is not yet finished. Come closer; I think you need a little push."

As Berni leaned down, Jayne pressed her palm on his forehead, and his eyes closed. His legs wobbled a little as he saw his immediate future.

"Oh my. What was that? What I saw…that will happen?"

"It will, but only with your help. On your way, Berni. I shall see you soon, I promise."

Berni walked a few paces, then hurried back, kissing Jayne on the cheek.

"Pardon me, Mademoiselle."

"Of course, Monsieur," she replied softly in French.

She watched him run up the stairs, then picked up her parasol and walked in the opposite direction.

Boat Deck – Monday, April 15th, 1912 – 12.48 am

Jayne pushed her way down the stairs against the flow of the other passengers. Several of them tried to grab her, but she shook herself free. Bursting through the door to the hospital, she found Heather Jacobs tucking the photograph of her son inside her overcoat.

"Jayne!"

"Heather, you have so little time! The ship is sinking, and you must get to a lifeboat."

"I will do no such thing. I will be on deck helping passengers. Why are you not with your mother?"

"I will be fine. Please, Heather, think of Joe."

"I have been assured that The Titanic cannot sink, and I have no reason to doubt it. The ship is merely disabled, and we need only wait for help."

"The ship will sink soon, and I do not want you to die."

"How could you possibly know that? Stop this nonsense and come with me."

Heather grabbed Jayne's hand and tugged at it, but defiantly, Jayne stood her ground and pulled against her. She took a small bundle of cloth out of her dress pocket and unfurled it. A small clock hand landed on the desk with a clang.

"What is that?"

"Pick it up."

"Why?"

In desperation, Jayne took hold of Heather's wrist and forced her to touch the clock's hand. Nothing happened.

"What is the matter with you, child? What is this nonsense?"

Yanking her arm away, the clock hand fell to the floor. This time, Jayne picked it up and tried to force it into Heather's grasp with her bare fingers. Again, nothing; there were no sparks, no strange feeling or soft voice in her head. Tears of frustration and sadness rolled down Jayne's cheeks as she threw the clock hand against the wall.

"No!"

Her voice trailed off as she fell back against the wall. Confused, Heather stared at her for a moment, remembering the moment she first saw Jayne and all that happened. Reaching for Jayne's hand, Heather pulled her up the stairs and past the surgery.

"Jayne! We must leave. We must go NOW!"

"It does not matter, Heather. None of this matters."

"What are you saying?"

"The ship is sinking!"

"If it really is, then we must get you to a lifeboat!"

Jayne stopped, forcing Heather to tug at her arm. Could it really be that simple?

"Of course! Yes...yes, we must," Jayne insisted.

She hurtled past Heather, seizing the moment as her companion paused, looking briefly confused by the girl's sudden change of behaviour. Then, she followed.

"Where are we going?"

"Starboard Lifeboat 3. Hurry!"

They reached the boat deck and emerged hand in hand from the door. Suddenly, they were forced to stop when a crowded mass of panicked passengers met them.

"Oh my!" said Heather, holding on tightly to Jayne's hand. A group of passengers pushed against them, but Jayne climbed onto a bench and walked along it, still holding Heather's hand and avoiding them easily. However, just as she leapt down, a larger group pushed against Heather, and she let go of Jayne. The seething crowd forced them further and further apart until Jayne could barely see or hear her.

"Heather!"

"Get to the lifeboat, Jayne, please!"

Heather's voice grew quieter, and even as she stood up on the bench again, Jayne could no longer see her. The deck was a writhing sea of people now, with hardly any space remaining. Without warning, someone grabbed Jayne and hoisted her high above the others.

"Come with me, Miss. Let's see if we can find you a life jacket. Have you lost your parents?"

The steward was large and very strong, and Jayne knew he had the best intentions, but this would not do.

"Please put me down!"

To his credit, he had found a path through the crowd, and Jayne now found herself near a lifeboat as it was hoisted over the side next to a group of frightened women and children. She wanted to help them all, but she knew she couldn't, and as soon as she was free of him, she ran away and down the steps to the deck below.

Boat Deck – Monday, April 15th, 1912 – 12.54 am

Berni tried his best to remain calm as he pushed his way through the crowd. Most were quiet, and some were still sceptical of the need to worry, even as the lifeboats were being lowered over the side - some of them not even full.

Berni noticed his friend, Terence, helping passengers nearby. They had joined the ship at the same time but had seen little of each other since leaving Southampton.

"Terence!"

Terence turned around and smiled at Berni, relieved to see a familiar face in amongst the chaos.

"Terence! What is happening? That boat is half-empty!"

"I am being told a great many different things, Berni, and I have been offered a great deal of money for spaces in a boat."

"You did not take it, of course?"

"No, I did not, but others have done so. Berni, what are we to do?"

"Your duty, Terence - nothing more and nothing less. Help as many as you can until you can help no more."

He patted his friend on the back, looking away quickly when he heard a scream. Twenty feet away, a crowd was rushing towards a lifeboat that was already being lowered. In their haste, they were crushing a young girl against the bulkhead. Berni pushed his way towards her.

"Hold on, Miss!"

Berni plunged into the crowd, pulling at arms and torsos to reach her. He lost his hat and was almost pushed to the floor, but he managed to put himself between the girl and the crowd.

"I am here, Miss. Are you injured?"

The girl pushed her face into his shoulder and her arms around him, grateful and relieved.

"No, I am just frightened."

Berni held the stranger close, gently patting her back. It was a moment of calm amid the increasing noise and panic around them.

"I am Berni. Berni Rosseau."

"My name is Elsie. Elsie Figgins. Thank you, Mr Rosseau."

"You are most welcome. We must get you to a lifeboat, Elsie."

"I am not a passenger; I must not."

"I happen to know that you must, Mademoiselle."

"You are French!" giggled Elsie happily. "I thought you were too dashing to be English."

Berni laughed and let go of Elsie, instead taking her hand.

"Come with me. You are my duty now, Elsie Figgins."

"I have never been anyone's duty before."

As the crowd rushed towards the boat, Berni led her away to the starboard side of the ship. Lifeboat 3 was already half-full and not only with passengers.

"There is already crew on the boat, Elsie. You will be quite alright."

"I am not crew, Berni. I serve tea in the café, and I am not at all important."

Berni cupped her cheeks, kissed her on the forehead, and then turned her to face the back of a large officer.

"Mr Murdoch, sir!"

First Officer William Murdoch turned around to see who had addressed him with such urgency.

"This is Miss Elsie Figgins, sir, and she would very much like a seat on this lifeboat."

Murdoch spared them a moment, smiling at the frightened girl.

"Would she now?"

Elsie bowed her head, almost embarrassed to be in such a position. Berni put his arm around her shoulder

"Yes, sir. She does not think she is important enough, but I disagree."

Murdoch smiled and put his hand on Elsie's shoulder.

"No more or less than any of us, Elsie Figgins. See to it, Mr Rosseau!"

Murdoch turned around to help others as Berni helped Elsie into the lifeboat. As she climbed in, an older woman reached out to help.

"In you get, my lovely. You sit with me, and we'll both be cosy and safe. I am Clara."

As she took hold of Elsie's hand, she let go of Berni's, and he stepped back.

"Thank you for your kindness, Berni Rosseau."

"You are most welc…"

Berni felt a hard push from the small crowd behind him, and he tumbled head-first into the lifeboat, narrowly avoiding Elsie. As he tried to stand, the boat tilted downwards, forcing the crew on deck to quickly lower the stern several feet.

"No!" shouted Berni, looking up at Murdoch as the boat was lowered towards the water. On deck, the crowd still surged and forced Murdoch to turn away from Berni to push back against them.

Able Seaman George Moore took hold of Berni's arm., steadying him.

"Not your fault, son. I saw what happened."

"I have left someone behind."

"We all have, son, we all have. You can help me help these people now. Will you do that?"

Berni thought of Jayne running about the deck and her promise to see him again soon, knowing that despite her assurances, he would never see her again. She had been right about so many things—why not this? He could still feel the tightness of her arms around him and her delicate scent when he kissed her on the cheek. George Moore's voice snapped him out of his thoughts.

"Will you, son?"

Berni looked at Elsie Figgins, sitting close to the woman passenger who had helped her aboard. Their eyes were closed, desperate to keep each other warm and safe. It was the second time he had seen this, something that brought him comfort.

"Yes...yes, I can, sir."

Moore patted Berni smartly on the back and moved to the back of the boat. Berni sat down next to Elsie, putting his arm around her. She was shivering, as he was, but he knew they would be alright.

"Everything will be quite alright, Elsie."

"I am not so sure. I am so cold."

"Then I will be sure enough for us both."

George Moore took the tiller as other crewmen took to the oars, slowly moving them away from the great ship. Berni looked up at the deck as the noise of panic grew quieter, thinking of those he had left behind, but his eyes were too cold to cry for a little girl.

CHAPTER TEN – COLD & DARK
A Deck – Monday, April 15th, 1912 – 1.00 am

Imogen was the picture of composure as they walked among the passengers rushing past them on their way to the boat deck. As always, her calm, decisive manner rubbed off on Francois, who followed close behind. When she stopped and sat down on a sun lounger, Francois quietly did the same.

"There will be no seat on a lifeboat for us both, so I see no reason to rush, Francois."

"No," said Francois as he rubbed his hands together - grateful for his scarf and recently purchased jacket. The cold of early morning had far more bite than the previous afternoon.

For a few minutes, they sat quietly, unable to ignore the sounds coming from the deck above, but both fully aware of what was soon to happen.

"A few hours ago, this was just another caper, Imogen - another daring adventure for us to remember over coffee and cake by the fire."

Imogen allowed herself a little smile.

"Yes. I must admit that I did not foresee this particular outcome."

"I do not expect you to anticipate everything, Imogen. Matters have taken a sharp left turn through no fault of yours."

"Thank you."

The Titanic's bow dipped more obviously now, causing unused chairs and loungers to slide slowly past them.

"Imogen…please go. Without me, you are more likely to find a space on a lifeboat."

"No, I am quite comfortable enough here with you."

"Please, do not sacrifice what little chance you have just to sit with me."

Imogen looked at her toes, considering her words.

"Until I met you, I had spent too much of my life sitting alone, Francois."

At the first attempt, Francois' words stuck in his throat, and he took a moment to steady himself.

"It is difficult to be alone in a busy café, but you have made me realise that I often was. How many others have waited so long for a friendship like ours?"

Imogen took the leather satchel from inside her dress and held it tightly, trying to focus on the apparent pointlessness of the last few days rather than her sadness.

"You are a ridiculous man, Francois Meyer, but I would rather not see tomorrow without you at my side if it is all the same to you."

Hearing the slight shake in her voice, Francois felt the most profound pain in his heart, already missing days with her that had yet to happen. There was still so much they didn't know about each other - enough to fill years spent by the fire, but Imogen's smile and gentle fidgeting told him all he needed to know for now.

"How long will it take?"

"Only minutes - perhaps ten", said Imogen as she took out her pocket watch and turned it over to look at a small thermometer on the back of the case. "The air temperature is freezing, so the water is likely to be a few degrees colder."

"Oh."

"I have seen hypothermia, Francois, and it is not how I wish to die."

"I would rather not die at all."

"No. If I were to choose how to end today, it would be with a glass of wine and one of your excellent card tricks."

Francois smiled, his mood lifting briefly.

"Alas, my cards are spread about the floor on B deck. Mahmoud was less than receptive to my offer of a show. Imogen?"

"Yes?"

"The numbers in my head. I must know how you did it."

"I am not gifted with magical powers, I promise you."

"There have been occasions when I have wondered."

He narrowed his eyes, and hers twinkled briefly.

"302".

"Imp. So, I end my days without an answer?"

"No. The simple answer, Francois, is that I have spent a great deal of time in your company in recent months. In fact, aside from my mother, I think I may have spent more time with you than any other."

"You last saw your mother when you were seventeen years old, Imogen."

"Yes. Please try not to be flattered."

Imogen sat back on the sun lounger and put her feet up, and Francois did the same. The sounds from above and the creaking of the ship faded into the background as they enjoyed each other's company for the last time.

"...and the great Nikola Tesla?"

"Although we write often, I have not spent a great deal of time in Nikola's company. In any case, the mind of a genius is complicated and..."

"Not as simple as mine?" interrupted Francois.

"...not as straightforward as yours. Once again, you do yourself a disservice, Francois. I study people, and I have had the opportunity to study you more than anyone else, that is all."

Francois almost had an answer to his original question, and he knew he must be satisfied with what he had. Above them, the voices grew desperate and became harder to ignore. They both sat up as a half-empty lifeboat lowered past them. Imogen listened to the bickering and complaining, watching the confused, frightened people fuss and panic.

"This is chaos, and I want no part of it."

"I have sometimes wondered what sort of man I would be in a situation like this."

She turned her head to him, comforted by his steady, familiar presence.

"You are behaving as you always do, Francois Meyer and I am glad you are here."

"You are?"

"Forgive me; I chose my words poorly."

Before Francois could answer, a third voice interrupted.

"Well, at least I lived long enough to hear that, Imogen. Today has been a mostly awful day, but you have given me a little hope."

Jayne Brewer leant on the bulkhead nearby, resting on her parasol handle to compensate for the tilt of the ship.

"Do I know you?" said Imogen sharply.

"From the stern, Imogen. She caught Berni's hat, and…yes,

who are you, and where are your parents?"

"I am Jayne - Jayne Brewer, and my parents are not here."

"You are on board alone?"

"In a manner of speaking, but that is not important at the moment."

Francois stood, straightened his jacket and then tightened his scarf. He offered his hand to Imogen, who took it and also stood.

"Unless I am very much mistaken, Imogen and I will shortly freeze to death in The Atlantic Ocean, something for which we are both prepared. You, my girl, must run upstairs to the boat deck and get yourself into a lifeboat."

"I will not, and although you will freeze, you will probably not die."

"Probably not?" enquired Imogen impatiently.

"It has only been a few days, but there is no harm in being optimistic, Iris," said Jayne with a wink. Imogen took a step back, much to Francois's surprise.

"Imogen?? Who is Iris?"

The young girl turned her attention to Francois.

"...and as for you, Frankie, have you forgotten what Luka told you in the park?"

Both Imogen and Francois stared at Jayne, mouths slightly

agape. Jayne moved closer, feeling her way along the bulkhead.

"I am not a fan of surprises, but I needed you to listen, and time is short."

"Who are you, child?" asked Francois, growing more frustrated by the second.

Imogen took out the leather satchel from inside her dress, having very quickly solved the puzzle.

"She is The Other, Francois."

"She is?"

Jayne smiled.

"She used to call me that, but I asked her to stop because it made me sound strange. I know what is in that satchel, Imogen, and I cannot take it. Indeed, I must not."

Imogen was clearly confused as she continued.

"I...touched it and experienced a hallucination of sorts, in which I was told to give this to The Other."

"You saw her?"

"Not exactly."

"Imogen saw our cat, Inglenook," said Francois unhelpfully.

Jayne giggled.

"I have never known her speak to anyone else."

"Who is she?"

"She is Ma'at."

"Harmony...balance...?"

"Very good, Imogen, although I am sure that is not her real name. She is my friend. She is wise and clever, and she knows things - not everything, but some things. Tell me, Imogen, did she say WHEN you were to give it to me?"

Imogen thought for a moment.

"She was not specific, no."

"Ma'at is not perfect. She is confused by the passage of my time, for instance. She talks to me for a while; then, she is quiet for a long time. When she returns, she is unaware of how long it has been for me."

"I am unsure what to do with this," muttered Imogen as she turned the satchel over in her hands.

"I suggest you tuck it inside your dress and keep it with you for now. I realise that is not much of an answer, but it is the only one I have."

Francois cleared his throat. "So...the ship is sinking, you say?"

"Yes, and if you stay here, you will be dragged down with it and likely never be seen again, which will not do at all. You must come with me, and we must find something that floats."

Jayne made her way towards the nearest door, holding it open and looking back at them.

"I understand the first-class lounge has some particularly fine wall panelling."

Imogen and Francois continued to stare at Jayne, still confused.

"Francois, who is Luka?"

"Luka? Who on earth is Iris?"

They looked at each other briefly, then followed Jayne inside and along the inner corridor to the lounge. Like the smoking room where they had first regained consciousness, it was exquisitely appointed, with pine panelling on the walls.

"Wait here."

Before they could reply, Jayne ran across the room and out of a door on the other side.

"What is happening, Imogen?"

"I have no idea, Francois. WHO is Luka, and what did she say to you in the park?"

"Luka was my friend when I was a boy, and…"

Francois hesitated, wondering how best to explain something that he hadn't stopped thinking about since

Jayne first mentioned her.

"...we were in the park, sitting on a bench. I was nine years old and had recently lost my mother. I was at something of a low ebb."

He sighed and closed his eyes, remembering the depths of a young boy's despair. He felt Imogen's hand on his back.

"Francois..."

"She...she told me that one day, I would find someone who needed me and that I would need that person, too. At the time, I thought she spoke of some future romantic entanglement, but now I am not so sure. We were alone, Imogen; how on earth could this girl know about that?"

"Entanglement? You have such a way with words, Mr Meyer."

"I do?"

"On occasion."

"... and Iris?"

"Should we survive our ordeal, I will introduce you to Iris."

At that moment, Jayne returned, dragging a large fire axe across the carpet. Although it was heavy, she didn't seem the slightest bit out of breath. As Francois took the handle and lifted it, her eyes widened, and she chuckled, almost as if enjoying a private joke.

"I have used an axe before, Jayne. I may be getting on in

years, but I work hard for a living."

"No, no, Francois, you look quite splendid. I just remembered something from long ago; that is all. You look every inch the lumberjack."

Francois smashed the axe into the wall, sending splinters in all directions. He swung it repeatedly, eventually finding enough leverage to pull the panel away on one side. He wedged the blade under the side, and all three of them helped pull it away from the wall. As they staggered back, it crashed to the floor. Francois looked up at the clock.

"How much longer do we have?"

Jayne also looked up at the clock and nodded.

"Twenty-eight minutes. More than enough, but we must hurry."

Imogen and Francois took hold of the panel and carried it towards the door, letting Jayne lead the way. She had to shout to be heard above the ship's creaking.

"Towards the bow, closer to the water!"

They hurried to catch up to her, both tired under the weight of the panel. Jayne stopped within sight of the bow - which was now totally submerged.

"Throw it over the side. It is not far - ten feet at most."

Imogen and Francois lifted it over the side and watched it fall into the water with an impressive splash. Below them, it floated close to the hull, occasionally bumping against it in the calm waters below. Jayne looked over, too, then took a step back.

"Swim as far away as you can - away from those in the water and well clear of the ship. The lights will stay on for some time yet, so you should be able to make your way."

Usually in control of events around her, Imogen was struggling with the situation.

"...and then what?"

"I am not sure, Imogen."

"You are not coming with us, are you?" said Francois.

"No. This is your moment, not mine. Ma'at was as sure about that as she was about your future."

Imogen was at Francois' side.

"We will not leave you to die, Jayne."

"I trust her, and she has told me that I cannot go with you."

Imogen climbed over the railing and sat with her legs over the side, though she felt guilty doing so. Francois pulled Jayne into a tight embrace and kissed the top of her head.

"Insanity, sheer insanity."

He felt her arms tight around him for a moment, then she pulled away and smiled up at him.

"I wish I could tell you everything, but my life is complicated. You must trust me, Francois - everything will be alright. Go."

Francois looked over his shoulder at Imogen, afraid to leave the little girl to what he knew would be certain death despite her reassurances.

Imogen could see that her friend was torn by the decision Jayne was asking him to make, so she took one last look down and then back to the girl, who nodded quickly and smiled. Francois saw the nod and turned to Imogen, who, at that moment, let go of the handrail.

"No..."

Immediately, he understood, and Imogen disappeared. As she fell, she made no noise, but upon hitting the icy water, she gasped in sudden pain. He rushed to the side and looked over to see her grab the panel and look up at him. Jayne moved next to him, also looking down at Imogen.

"Go. She needs you."

He put his hand to her cheek, then climbed over the railing and let go, hitting the water a few feet away from Imogen. The cold bit into him, taking his breath, as he swam the short distance between them and took hold of the panel.

Jayne leaned over to see them in the water, but they were both too cold and shocked to speak. She saw Imogen push against the hull, their feet splashing as they swam away, neither looking back.

Ma'at's voice returned.

"I am very proud of you, little one."

"Why could I not tell them?"

"Their fear will keep them alive. It has not been long enough to be otherwise."

"It feels cruel."

"I know, but they will know soon enough."

Jayne watched them until she could barely make them out, gripping the cold railings and trying to ignore the people in the water - all of whom she knew would die. She had seen so much in her extraordinary life, but the truth of what was to happen was almost too much to bear.

"You did not belong here, little one. It is not our place to change this."

"But we have changed things. Imogen, Francois and I...we were not here before, were we?"

"Many things have happened for the first time."

"Many?"

"Yes, but enough has happened as it did before. The moment is the same as it was."

The young girl drifted off for a few moments, the sounds of the ship and the people below fading away until the strangest sensation brought her back. She looked up and all around until she identified the source of the feeling. Then she saw her - fifty feet away and to the left, almost as if she had come from somewhere other than the ship.

The figure swam confidently, kicking her legs and making small splashes in the dark water. As Jayne watched, the figure stopped swimming and looked back towards the ship, smiling up at Jayne and waving.

"Oh my..."

Jayne waved back, happiness and sadness pulling her in opposite directions.

"It's me!"

After a few minutes, the girl swam on, disappearing into the darkness.

"All will be well, little one."

"How did this happen?"

"One day, the answers will be yours."

The ship suddenly lurched to port, forcing Jayne to grab the railing.

"Ma'at!"

"You must climb to the highest point quickly!"

Jayne looked towards the stern, seeing hundreds of passengers scrambling for the highest point above the water. Her world was suddenly loud and terrifying, but Ma'at's voice was as calm as always. They talked in the silence of Jayne's mind now, pushing away the chaos around her.

"I am frightened."

"I am with you."

"I really, really wish you were."

She pulled herself up the railing, ignoring the terror around her until she found something to cling to.

"I will not leave you."

"These people are all going to die."

She closed her eyes tight as the ship moaned and the people screamed.

"Yes."

In The Water – Monday, April 15th, 1912 – 1.25 am

Imogen and Francois were almost completely shrouded in darkness now, but the cries of the people nearby were impossible to ignore. The panel was keeping them afloat, and whether by accident or design, the decorative beading gave them both something to hang on to. Above them, the Bumble flitted about, seemingly unaffected by the cold.

"Imogen, I have a small confession to make."

"...and you are certain this is the most appropriate time to share it?"

"I have done something rather foolish, and I deeply regret it."

"You have ice on your moustache."

Francois lifted his hand from the panel and very quickly brushed his moustache, breaking the ice that had recently formed.

"Much better. Now, please…unburden yourself."

"On the way back from the barber, I visited the wireless room and sent a telegram to Monica."

"Oh, Francois…"

"What have I done? They will lose us twice."

"To quote the redoubtable Maria Dubois, 'what is done, is done'."

"Normally a phrase she reserves for the most minor mishaps, Imogen. But I appreciate your reassurance. I am sorry if I have disappointed you."

Imogen allowed herself a little chuckle.

"You ridiculous man. I am not your keeper; I am your friend."

Francois smiled.

"It seems the girl was correct - we are both frozen but still very much alive."

"Yes," she replied, her teeth chattering.

For a few minutes, they both watched the ship in silence as they floated in the freezing water. The bow had sunk even lower now, and the stern was high above the ocean.

"Despite everything, the lights are still burning..." pondered Francois.

"A brave crew. They have no doubt stayed aboard to keep the water pumps in operation and the lights on. Every minute they do so increases the chance of rescue."

"Who will come?"

"There will be other vessels nearby, but exactly how close, I do not know. If the ship stays afloat, those still aboard may survive until morning."

A rocket shot high in the air, briefly illuminating the dreadful scene around them. Francois closed his eyes as Imogen looked away. She allowed enough time for the glare to fade before opening her eyes and looking at her icy fingers. She knew they should be numb by now, but she felt her blood flow and warm her skin. The slightest stretch of her hand broke the ice.

"She knew, Imogen."

"So it seems. Were it not for everything else we experienced on board, I would not have believed her. Nevertheless, here we float."

Francois glanced up at the Bumble.

"Yes."

"Hello!"

The shout startled them both, almost causing Francois to let go of the panel.

"What the...?!"

The girl swam closer, her long, wet hair covering most of her face. Then she stopped, treading water nearby, half hidden in the darkness.

"I'm very sorry, but despite very specific instructions, I found myself on the wrong side of the bloody ship."

"Jayne?"

"Yes. Hello, how are you both?"

"We are...alive, but far from well," grimaced Imogen, her teeth chattering even more than before. "What caused you to reconsider?"

"Reconsider? Oh, I didn't."

Jayne fumbled under the water, eventually disappearing below the surface for a few seconds. She came back up holding a crinoline petticoat and threw it to one side in triumph.

"I took the time to take my shoes off, but not my petticoat!"

Jayne swam as close as she could to them, holding onto

the panel to steady herself.

"Instructions from whom?" said Imogen with a hint of impatience.

"You, Imogen. As usual, you were alarmingly specific but, alas, far more precise than my chosen method of travel."

Francois reached out and squeezed Imogen's hand.

"I cannot take much more of this, Imogen. My body is cold, and my brain is fit to burst. All I want is to…"

Behind them, the great ship roared, unable to take the weight of the water on its bow. The lights flickered briefly, then went out just before the deck broke in two. Even though they were some distance away, they could hear the screams of those still on board as the stern crashed back down into the water. Seeing the horror on their faces, Jayne addressed them sternly.

"Both of you - look at me and only me. That ship is sinking, and many will die, but this is not your time. You do not belong in this moment."

Francois ignored her, unable to stop thinking of those they had met onboard.

"Oh no…" he gasped

Jayne saw him look, then grabbed them both.

"Time to go…"

With a rush of silence, all three of them vanished, sending

pain through Jayne like she'd never felt before. The 15th of April 1912 struggled to cope with their sudden departure and the vacuum they left behind. The water was calm, but the space they had previously occupied churned and boiled with enough anger to smash the wooden panel into pieces.

Just moments later, the calm returned as if they had never been there in the first place.

RMS Titanic – Monday, April 15th, 1912 – 2.16 am

Jayne clung onto the frozen railing as hard as she could, closing her eyes and trying to drown out the cries of pain around her. Despite everything she had experienced before, this was by far the most harrowing.

An almighty noise ripped through the ship, sending tremors through her body as the bow plunged into the ocean, lifting the stern high above the water. Despite this, she could hear Ma'at chanting repeatedly in her head. As she listened, she felt her body grow warm and strong, and her heart beat faster and faster.

"You are always and forever, little one."

Jayne held on as the ship roared and broke in two, the sound almost drowned out by the screams of the people around her. The stern settled for a moment, then began to tilt down once again. Others fell past her into the water as she heard the ocean rush towards her, and a few seconds later, Jayne and the ship were gone.

The North Atlantic – Monday, April 15th, 1912 – 2.34 am

Lifeboat 3 moved slowly through the water with only the soft lap of the oars to break the silence. Almost everyone on board was quiet now, huddled together for warmth - scared that their salvation had been temporary and that they would now die a slower death in the lifeboat, waiting for a rescue that would never come.

"There's no one left, son; it's been too long."

Berni strained his eyes and cupped his hands around his mouth to call out.

"Hello!" He shouted into the darkness, "You are wrong, sir; I know you are."

Most on board had covered their eyes, hiding from the horror around them. Frozen bodies bumped gently against the side of the boat, testing the patience of Able Seaman George Moore.

"This is folly, Mr Rosseau, and it's more than these good people can bear. I am in charge of this boat, and I say that…"

Suddenly, Berni plunged his arm into the water, almost disappearing over the side. Reacting quickly, Elsie and two other passengers grabbed his legs and pulled him backwards. The fear of losing her new friend was too much, and she screamed at her companion.

"Berni! What are you doing?"

As they helped him back into the boat, he dragged with him the small, frozen body of a girl. George and the other crewmembers struggled to steady the vessel as Berni pulled Jayne's body close, desperate to warm her.

"She's gone, Mr Rosseau…long gone. Let her…"

Jayne's eyes fluttered open, and without ceremony, she spat seawater all over Berni. She grabbed his jacket and pulled him closer.

"SON OF A BITCH!!"

Elsie screamed and fell back onto Clara as Jayne clung to Berni, staring into his cold but happy face. Slowly, Jayne began to relax, taking deep breaths.

"You came back for me."

"Yes. How could I not?"

Berni tapped a finger on his forehead.

"I saw this moment when you touched me - I saw Elsie, and I saw you, pale and cold."

Jayne chuckled quietly

"Sometimes, Ma'at is a little too mysterious."

"Who?"

This time, it was Jayne who tapped her forehead.

"My friend."

Berni helped Jayne to a seat opposite the clearly terrified waitress.

"Elsie Figgins, please allow me to introduce Miss Jayne Brewer."

The woman said nothing but continued to stare, as did everyone else in the boat. Jayne realised there was little she could say to explain, so she didn't try. Instead, she held out her hand to Elsie as she sat down beside her.

"Hello, Elsie. Please do not be frightened."

Hesitantly, Elsie took her hand.

"Your hand…it is warm."

"It is? Perhaps it is just a little warmer than yours, Elsie."

"But you were in the water, and everyone else is…gone."

Berni wrapped a damp blanket around Jayne's shoulders and sat down next to Elsie, keeping his voice quiet.

"She is special."

Jayne smiled and squeezed Elsie's hand, warming the tips of her fingers with her secret.

"Almost as special as you, Elsie Figgins."

"Me? I am just a waitress."

"Just? People need tea and cake, Elsie. Tell me…do you also serve coffee?"

Elsie smiled, forgetting the cold for a moment.

"Why, Yes, of course."

"There is a café in Paris that serves the finest coffee and cake in all of France. It is such a happy and welcoming place, and they look after people just like you do, Elsie. I only take hot chocolate myself, but the smell of freshly brewed coffee…oh my."

Putting his arm around Elsie, Berni pulled her against him and rubbed her arm, sharing what little warmth he had. She smiled and attempted to laugh, but her voice cracked, and instead, she coughed.

Jayne looked around, the blanket falling from her shoulders as she leaned on one side of the boat; she scanned the horizon until she saw a faint light in the distance.

Berni followed her gaze, but his eyes were tired and unable to see more than the enveloping darkness.

"All we can do is wait, Jayne. There will have been ships nearby, and hopefully, they would have seen the rockets, but how close they are, I do not know."

She turned back, leaning forward slightly. Keeping her voice as quiet as possible, she pointed discretely at what she had seen.

"Carpathia."

"Pardon?"

"The RMS Carpathia."

Jayne wiggled her eyebrows happily, then leaned around Berni to look at the people huddled in the back of the boat.

"Could someone please tell me the time?"

Looking somewhat bemused, George Moore took out his pocket watch and replied, keeping a firm grip on the tiller.

"Seventeen minutes after three, Miss. Is there somewhere you need to be?"

Jayne giggled.

"I have a dollar to spend in New York, sir. A new dress and perhaps a bonnet if I can find one that I like."

"Is that right, Miss?"

"Yes, it is."

George was close to exhaustion, as were the men at the oars. Jayne had spent a life hiding the truth she knew from others, but these people needed more than just her gentle humour if they were to make it through the next few hours. Would it really matter so much if she gave them hope sooner than it had happened before? Ma'at may be disappointed in her, but that, too, had happened before, and it probably would happen again. Decisively, she stood up, making the boat rock as she steadied herself and pointed at what she knew to be their salvation.

"Look, sir! A ship!"

George turned his head to the light and then back to Jayne, who beamed and steadied herself on the side of the boat. He gave her the most baffled look, but relief stretched across his face.

"As I said, sir, I wish to buy a new dress and perhaps a bonnet. I am certain we cannot row all the way to New York."

"No, Miss, that we cannot. Mr Haggan, Mr Combes! The young lady has given us a new course. Look lively, now!"

With hope raising their spirits, the men at the oars pushed through the water until the boat swung around enough to point at the approaching ship. Jayne looked down at Berni and Elsie.

"Berni…move up. Let me sit between you. Quickly now."

He shuffled along the seat as Jayne squeezed between them, pulling them closer. She knew her body was warmer than theirs, and it would, at least, keep them awake. Berni rested on her shoulder, his voice trembling and quiet. He had finally decided to accept this strange girl at her word.

"How long?"

"About an hour, but…things may be different this time."

Bernie nodded, relieved.

"Jayne…?"

"Yes?" she replied enquiringly.

"What is that noise?"

They looked around, still holding onto each other, and heard a high-pitched buzzing noise approaching.

"Well, hello, my shiny little friend."

Hidden from the others in the boat, the Bumble flew in front of Jayne and hovered a few inches from her face. Berni watched in amazement as she gently reached out and plucked it from the air, tapping the top with her finger. The wings stopped flapping, and, with another tap, they vanished. She dropped the Bumble into the chest pocket of her dress, almost as if it was a boiled sweet she was saving for later. Scarcely able to make sense of all he had seen in the last few days, Berni muttered tiredly.

"I am not sure I can take any more of this, Jayne."

"Life is for living, Berni. The moment you understand it all is the moment you may as well give up."

Next to Bernie, Elsie stirred and opened her eyes slowly

"Is that a ship?"

Berni smiled and squeezed her gently.

"Yes, but I would be very surprised if they can see us yet."

Fireman Robert Triggs, resting from his turn at the oars, turned around. He was wary of lowering the mood but understood the circumstances better than most. Looking at Berni, he shook his head slowly.

Jayne contemplated the situation for a moment, then put her hand on her chest pocket, feeling the Bumble.

"I need a knife...a pocketknife. Please, who has a knife?"

A quiet voice spoke from the bow.

"I have a knife, but it is small."

"All the better," replied Jayne hastily.

The knife made its way back to her, passing from one pair of cold hands to the next. Taking out the Bumble, she pushed the point of the blade into a tiny, almost invisible recess. Berni leaned in closer.

"What are you doing?"

"I am...changing the way things were, but only in a small way. One more little push in the direction it was already going. Perhaps it is the right thing to do, perhaps not. Who knows? What is life without uncertainty?"

Berni watched as the Bumble began to glow in Jayne's hand, furrowing his brow.

"Ignorance?" he replied.

"Wonder!" she grinned back at him.

Jayne tapped the gold sphere twice and beamed as it hovered in front of her once more.

"Behold the science and genius of man, Berni Rosseau."

The Bumble glided away from them, glowing brighter as it did so. Jayne giggled and wiggled her fingers in a wave.

"Fly, my pretty...make your Papa proud."

It shot into the air, trailing sparks and light behind it. Everyone in the boat gasped with surprise as the Bumble soared higher and higher until it hovered a hundred feet above them. Jayne turned to look at Elsie, and her eyes shone as they reflected the golden glow from above.

"I think they can see us now, Elsie."

The young woman nodded in amazement. Suddenly, she saw several other lifeboats and dozens of scared, cold people looking into the sky. In the darkness, they might as well have been miles apart, but now, the ingenuity of a child and the mind of a man they would never meet had brought them together.

In the distance, RMS Carpathia ploughed through the still, black waters at seventeen knots - the very limit of its engines. It had been almost three hours since they had responded to the Titanic's call for help, and they had been nearly sixty miles away when their wireless operator had picked up their message.

On the bridge, Captain Arthur Rostron lowered his binoculars, his eyes still dazzled by the brightest light he'd ever seen in the sky.

"Mr Dean…I would be very grateful if you could assure me…"

"I see it too, sir!"

"I have never seen a rocket move like that."

"No, sir."

The captain raised his binoculars again, certain it would be the Titanic's survivors but confused about what he could see in the sky.

"Let them know we can see them, Mr Dean."

RMS Carpathia's foghorn sounded loud and long.

"Every five minutes and prepare to take on survivors."

"Aye, Captain!"

CHAPTER ELEVEN - THE POND

Place St Genevieve, Paris - Thursday, June 11th, 1908 - 8.25 pm

For a few seconds, there was only cold and darkness, then exhaustion and more pain. Jayne pushed down in the water, feeling her feet slip on mud as she clung to Imogen and Francois.

Jayne stood, struggling to hold onto them and keep their heads above water.

"Son of a...bitch!"

She cursed under her breath as she pulled them onto the stone path surrounding the pond, coughing up seawater onto the cobbles. Looking around, she saw the shadows of trees and the path surrounding the pond in Place St Genevieve, Paris. At least they were in the right place. Close enough anyway, and almost at the same time that they had left.

She spat out water again, smiled at the familiar sights and laughed in celebration.

"I am so clever...I am so...damned clever..."

As Jayne sat next to the pond, squeezing the water from her skirt, the familiar voice of Ma'at returned.

"They are well?"

"I think so. They are wet and cold, but..."

Gently pulling Imogen's shoulder, she rolled her onto her

side, feeling her heartbeat healthily in her chest. Jayne then did the same to Francois before falling onto her back between them.

"Yes, they are both quite well."

"…and you?"

"That was very difficult. It has been some time since I felt pain like that."

"I would never…damage you. You will recover soon."

"I always do, don't I?"

Jayne lay silent and caught her breath for several minutes before Ma'at spoke again.

"She is near?"

She sat up and looked toward the trees that grew around the park's edge against the wall.

"Oh yes, she is here – hiding behind a tree if you can believe such a thing."

"You must leave."

"Yes, I know. I need to sit before a warm fire, have a hot cup of tea, and change my underwear - not necessarily in that order. As before, I have enjoyed your company, Ma'at; it has been too long."

"It may be so again, but I will return."

"Unlike a certain someone nearby, I am very patient."

"Goodbye, little one."

"Goodbye."

Then, all she could hear were the boats on the river and the water lapping against the canal bank nearby.

Jayne signed and looked up at the moon, revelling in the peace and quiet for a moment, then she looked back at the trees, narrowed her eyes and felt a mind pushing back. Imposing her presence on that mind took little effort, but the results were immediate. There was a soft thud and the rustle of leaves as the hidden figure fell to her knees, putting her hands to her temples and moaning through gritted teeth.

Jayne took little pleasure in this, but sometimes it was necessary. She raised her voice only as much as she needed to.

"For one so proud and intelligent, you are so often foolish, Arnka. Behind a tree? Whatever were you thinking?"

"Get out…of my head…"

"In a moment. If you hurt them, I will find you. You know that don't you?"

The pained voice from the trees dripped with hate.

"You will try."

"You are such a dramatic old witch."

"…and you are an annoying little brat."

"Indeed, I am, but only sometimes. Tomorrow, when the sun rises, you will still be old."

Jayne left Arnka's mind, took one last look at Imogen and Francois and waved at the trees.

"Goodbye, Arnka. Remember what I said."

This time, there was no sardonic reply from the shadows, only a gasp of relief. Jayne walked away towards the park exit nearest the river. By the time she reached the stone arch at the far side of the park, she had faded away and left 1908 behind.

Arnka Søgard stepped from the shadows and into the light of the gas lamps, stretching her arms wide and flexing her head from side to side as she walked towards Imogen and Francois. Her blonde shoulder-length hair partially hid her sharp, angular features and bright blue eyes, but her long dress would probably never recover from her recent half-collapse into a pile of wet leaves, but it was a worthwhile sacrifice for what lay so near. She stopped and looked down at them, poking Imogen in the side with the tip of her umbrella several times.

"I have heard so much about you both, but from this distance, you certainly do not look very special."

She kicked Francois roughly, laughing to herself before leaning over to unbutton the top of Imogen's dress, smirking as she did so.

"Worry not, Imogen DiRossi; I am in something of a hurry and do not have enough time for anything more than business. Perhaps next time, things will be different."

Reaching inside, she pulled out the leather pouch, untied the suede laces and lay it on the path. The side of her mouth lifted into a sneer as she saw the contents glisten in the lamplight. The dagger was an unexpected boon, bejewelled and glittering. She picked it up and pushed it into the top of her boot before rolling up her sleeve to reveal a slim, pale arm.

Hesitating for a moment, she wrapped the bracelet around her wrist and closed it. It gripped her arm, but not painfully so, and aside from a strange warmth, she felt nothing. Considering what she'd been told about The Serpent's Grasp, she was more than a little disappointed. She took one last look at Imogen and Francois, then turned and walked away, pulling her sleeve down to hide the bracelet.

"I will see you both later."

On the cold, damp cobbles, Francois moaned, coughed, and turned on his back, lifting himself onto his elbows at the sound of the woman's voice and watching the strange figure walk away. He blinked several times and shook Imogen's arm.

"Imogen...Imogen..."

Without opening her eyes, his friend replied.

"I am quite well, Francois. Please stop doing that."

"I apologise, but you were very still."

"I am, however, wet, cold and…

She opened her eyes and sat up.

"…lying beside the pond behind the café."

Imogen looked about and took out her pocket watch.

"8.35 pm. I have no memory of how we came to be here."

"Nor I," muttered Francois, getting to his feet and offering her his hand. As she took hold of it and did the same, he grabbed his thigh, confused that there was no pain. Imogen glanced at him, concerned.

"I have often told you that you should not endure unnecessary pain in the pursuit of chivalry. I am perfectly capable of…"

"It does not hurt. It does not hurt at all, and where is my cane?"

As he turned his head to look, Imogen knelt and squeezed the top of Francois' thigh so quickly that he could do little but look down and watch.

"Not at all?"

"Well, you have quite the grip and have no doubt left a bruise, but other than that, nothing."

Imogen squeezed much harder, just to be sure.

"Ow!"

He pulled his leg away, stumbling back a few paces.

Imogen brushed the wet leaves from her dress.

"I have experienced memory loss before, but always alone. You remember nothing?"

"It is my birthday and…"

Imogen narrowed her eyes, hoping Francois' memory would nudge her own.

"You were lying on your bed. You were ill."

"Yes, but after that…nothing. Imogen, this is worrying."

"It is, but I am cold and wet, and for the moment, I think we should keep this to ourselves. Perhaps, in time, we will remember."

Imogen absent-mindedly patted down Francois' sodden lapel, making a soft, squelching noise.

"That will be difficult. Look at us! My suit may recover, but I fear your dress is beyond the help of even Monica's skilled hand."

"Clearly, you fell into the pond, and I leapt in to save you."

"What?"

"As we took an evening walk in the park, you slipped and fell into the murky depths of the duck pond, and I threw caution to the wind in a selfless act of bravery."

"I am deeply touched."

"Oh, hush, now come on, I would very much like some hot

coffee."

As Imogen walked towards the nearest archway out of the park, Francois followed, not far behind.

"Maria will insist that we undress on the doormat. We will not be permitted to wet the carpets," Francois warned as he hurried to catch up.

"A sensible precaution."

"The café may be busy."

"I should hope so, Francois. If we cannot fill a café on a cold Thursday evening, we have no business owning one."

"No, I suppose not."

Café Merle, Paris - Thursday, June 11th, 1908 - 8.45 pm

Maria stood in the café doorway, hands on her hips and barring the entrance to a very busy but now silent café.

Francois stood behind Imogen, leaning around her as Maria looked them up and down. Inside, most of the café patrons had turned around in their seats to watch events at the front door. They did so in almost total silence.

"Good evening, Maria. Do I smell a fresh pot of coffee?"

"Where have you both been? At the stroke of eleven this morning, I took up your coffee to find Inglenook asleep on

Francois' pillow and the windows wide open. Usually, I would assume the pair of you had been away on one of your escapades, but you have been absent all day!"

Francois looked at the floor and continued to drip on the doormat. Clasping her hands together, Imogen rose slightly on her toes.

"Francois fell in the pond."

Jacques LeGrande's unmistakable chuckle came from the back of the café. With a sigh, Francois looked up and nodded.

"It is true; I slipped and fell. Imogen jumped in and pulled me out."

The door opened wider to reveal Belle and Bryonie, both sipping a glass of red wine. Putting her hand to her mouth, Belle did her best not to laugh. Bryonie, who was more used to seeing members of both genders in compromising situations, gulped a mouthful of her wine and grinned from ear to ear.

"What fun!" she giggled just before Belle nudged her in the ribs.

Imogen glared at them both, then returned her gaze to Maria with as much dignity as she could muster.

"Francois and I will undress out here. Belle, please fetch my black robe and Francois' dressing gown from upstairs."

Francois looked behind him at the good people of Place St Genevieve as they went about their evening, wondering how much they would see in the light of the gas lamps. A few moments later, Belle returned, passing them their robes. Imogen shut the front door and turned her back to Francois, lifting her wet hair and baring her neck.

"I can usually remove my dress unaided, but the top clasp is still troublesome despite Monica's recent attention. If you would be so kind…"

"Surely you are not serious. Here? Outside?"

Once more, Francois looked behind him at the square, but Imogen brushed off his concerns.

"We are very wet, and it is cold, and as I said, I would very much like some coffee. Now, please stop fussing and help me out of my dress."

Francois saw to the top four buttons on Imogen's dress as she reached around, finished the job, and stepped out of it. Turning to face him, she began to unbutton her leather waistcoat.

"Monica will not be best pleased. My waistcoat and leggings are completely ruined. Please hurry, Francois."

With that, her waistcoat fell away, and she laid it on the nearest table. Even in the dark, under the light of two dim streetlamps, he could clearly see where the wet material of her undershirt clung to her body. Francois immediately glanced down and turned around quickly. Not for the first time that day, Imogen rolled her eyes.

"Oh, you ridiculous man."

Turning her back to him again, Imogen put on her robe and, with great difficulty, peeled off her leather leggings.

Meanwhile, Francois took off his wet clothes, folded them neatly and put on his dressing gown. He turned to face Imogen, realising she had been watching him for some time.

"My glasses."

"You have left them in the park?"

"Possibly, but...I just realised that I am not wearing them, and..."

Francois stepped back into the light of the closest streetlamp, slowly waving his hand in front of his face.

"Imogen!"

He stepped closer, something she often did to him, and smiled. Leaning back slightly, Imogen studied his eyes as they took in every detail of her face.

"Are you quite well?"

"I can see you!"

"Obviously."

"No, you do not understand. I can SEE you. Clearly!"

Imogen leaned a little closer, their noses almost touching.

"Whatever do you mean?"

"It is dark, yet I see every detail of your face and… you have a freckle."

She leaned back again as Francois touched the tip of his finger to a tiny freckle just above her top lip. Imogen gently took his wrist, lowered it slowly and frowned.

"Yes, as did my mother, in the same place."

"Between my reading glasses and my distance glasses, I have never seen it before. First my leg and now my eyes… what has happened to us, Imogen, and why can we not remember?"

"I do not know, but we cannot stay out here. We will catch a…"

"…cold," said Francois, completing her thought, "I had a cold! That's why I was in bed."

Imogen narrowed her eyes and nodded slowly, clearly remembering the same thing.

"First, Coffee, a fire and some dry clothes. We shall discuss this further upstairs. Are you ready?"

"Dignity is very overrated," said Francois as he adjusted his dressing gown, looked down at his bare feet and picked up his wet clothes.

"You might have drowned, Francois. I had no choice but to act quickly and with no thought for my own safety."

"We are sticking with that?"

"Yes. Yes, we are."

Before he could comment, Imogen opened the café door to enthusiastic applause from friends and customers alike. Standing behind the counter with her arms folded, Maria shook her head at them while Anton dried a large brandy glass and eyed them knowingly as they put their wet clothes on the counter and continued towards the stairs. They stopped at their usual table near the fire, where Jacques sat, drawing on his pipe and stroking Inglenook's head with a grubby finger.

"Good evening, Monsieur LeGrande."

He took his pipe out of his mouth and nodded at them in turn.

"Lady Imogen...Francois."

He chuckled as Imogen scooped up Inglenook from the table in front of him and swirled his half-empty glass of brandy.

Francois reached out and tickled under the kitten's chin.

"Hello, Inglenook."

The kitten lifted her head to allow his attention, then squeaked.

"She is very pleased to see you, Francois."

As they climbed the stairs, Inglenook stared at Francois over Imogen's shoulder with an intensity that continued to disturb Francois. Imogen began to stroke Inglenook's back slowly.

"Why does she find me so fascinating, Imogen?"

"She is hardly the first female to do so."

Inglenook squeaked again, blinked slowly and began to purr very loudly.

"Oh, for heaven's sake."

Café Merle - Thursday, June 11th, 1908 - 10.00 pm

Later that evening, Francois bid goodnight to Anton and Maria, watching them walk home across the square, just as he had done every night since they had moved out. It was only a short distance, and Place St Genevieve was a safe, friendly part of the city, but he never shut the café door until he saw them wave from the door of Madame Tomas' Bistro. He turned to address the final patrons of his café that night.

"It is long past your bedtime, ladies."

Belle finished drinking her warm milk, then put the cup down and stretched her arms high. On the table in front of her lay a small fortune in coins, and opposite her, a gently frustrated Bryonie Jewell.

Francois leaned down to see Bryonie's hand of cards.

"Only a fool plays cards with an angel, Bryonie. How much

has she taken from you this evening?"

"Almost two Francs, Francois!"

"You would fare better matching your wits with Jacques. He is almost as devious as Belle but grows less so with every glass of wine."

"Monsieur Meyer!"

Belle tried to look offended, but she knew Francois was mostly teasing. He winked at her and patted Bryonie's shoulder just as Imogen appeared at the bottom of the stairs.

"Belle has a serene disposition and a somewhat joyful outlook on life, Francois. I would hardly call that 'devious'. She has possibly the most perfect, unintentional poker face that I have ever seen."

"Thank you, Lady Imogen."

"You are trustworthy because you bestow trust on others easily, Belle."

Imogen pulled at the cuffs of her dress and, without breaking stride, held out her other wrist just in time for Boreas to fly from the counter and land on it. He touched his beak to the end of her nose as he settled.

"Good evening, sir."

The crow cawed, adjusting the position of his feet several times before flying to the top of the coat stand. Imogen sat at the counter and watched Francois rub his towel over it.

"He has such little respect for varnish, Imogen. Look at my counter."

"Our counter, Francois."

Imogen peered closely at the minor scratches in the well-worn wood of the café counter.

"They are everywhere, Imogen."

"You exaggerate."

"He might as well hack away at it with an axe..."

They straightened and stared at each other in silence for a few seconds. Then, Imogen looked at the scratches again, rubbing the largest with the tip of her finger.

"Imogen?"

"Why an axe, Francois?"

"It seemed apposite."

"Hardly. I have seen Boreas lift a great many things, but..."

Imogen's expression seemed to stare off into space for a moment.

"Francois, you swung an axe."

"When?"

"It's the strangest thing. I do not know, but I can see it."

"There is an axe in the cellar, but the blade is loose, and

despite his assurances, Jacques has yet to repair it. I have not lifted an axe since you first sat outside the...our café."

Imogen raised her eyebrow but dismissed the thought for now. She turned around on the stool to watch Belle count her winnings whilst Bryonie put the deck of cards back into her bag. Belle adjusted her hat in the mirror behind the counter and took Bryonie's arm by the door when she was finished. Placing his hand on the door, Francois opened it courteously.

"We would be happy to walk you both home, ladies."

Bryonie looked out across the square, then kissed Francois on the cheek.

"Thank you, but we will be fine. Few are brave enough to worry one of Madame Bonheur's young ladies, Mr Meyer, and anyway, I see Monsieur LeGrande hovering near the fountain, eager to escort us."

"You may tell him that his first cup of coffee tomorrow will be free if he sees you both home safely."

As the two young women walked away across the square, Francois bolted the door and checked the window locks. He turned around to see Imogen turning off the café lamps, one at a time, picking up the few remaining dirty cups as she did so. This had been Francois' sole responsibility for so long, but it pleased him no end to see Imogen adjusting to the life of a café owner so quickly.

"When exactly did Monsieur LeGrande last pay for a cup of coffee, Francois?"

"I am not sure, but I believe it was snowing. Brandy, Imogen?"

"Yes, please, barman."

Imogen took the dirty cups into the kitchen and began rinsing them in the basin whilst Francois took down two large brandy glasses from the shelf. She returned, standing beside him at the counter, just as he finished pouring the Brandy.

They clinked their glasses and took a sip, both taking a moment to enjoy the peace of their quiet, dark cafe.

"I am tired, Imogen, but I have no wish to sleep."

"Nor I. Perhaps you should bring the bottle."

Imogen opened the counter hatch, and Francois picked up the bottle as they climbed the stairs together. Turning left at the landing, they could already feel the warmth from the fireplace at the far end of the living room. Inglenook slept soundly in front of it, watched, as always, by the large, paternal crow from the top of the bookcase.

Café Merle, Paris - Thursday, June 11th, 1908 - 10.35 pm

The wind blew the rain against the windows of the living room, rattling the frames. Inside, Imogen and Francois sat on the long leather sofa in front of the roaring fire.

"That is all I remember, Imogen. Some twelve hours ago, you were sitting at your table, and I was on my bed."

Francois gripped his thigh again and squeezed as Imogen muttered, slightly impatiently, as she stared into the fire.

"You really should stop doing that, Francois."

"Imogen, it has ached since I was nine years old! Also, I see no point in looking for my spectacles near the pond tomorrow because I no longer need them."

"Forgive me, Francois. I find the unknown disquieting."

"Yes, I know you do. I am not terribly fond of it myself, but here we are."

Imogen contemplated as she continued to stare into the flames.

"Eleven years ago, I was shot... in the thigh. The bullet went straight through, and in the absence of a doctor, I treated the wound myself. I was in a great deal of pain and somewhat delirious, but I was successful."

Francois listened, remembering the bullet that had torn through his shoulder just a few months ago.

"I am sorry, Imogen."

"It was a long time ago and mostly forgotten. The scar, however, was particularly...impressive.

"I do not wish to see it," said Francois with an awkward chuckle.

"Even if I was so inclined, I could not

Francois paused, touching his fingers to his shoulder.

"As has mine. What has happened to us, Imogen?"

"We may have been drugged, but why? Such a thing is far from an exact science - even when age, physical size and health are taken into consideration, it is still extremely unlikely that we would both regain consciousness at the same time. As for our scars, your eyes and…"

She glanced down at his leg.

"Imogen…I confess that I am more than a little concerned. To have such a thing happen and have no memory of…"

The sudden tapping on the balcony window startled them both. Francois was on his feet first.

"What the…?

Outside, standing on the balcony in the rain, a little blonde girl in a white dress waved her fingers and smiled.

CHAPTER TWELVE - HELLO
Café Merle, Paris - Thursday, June 11th, 1908 - 10.55 pm

Keeping her eyes on the figure on the other side of the glass, Imogen stood up.

"Let her in, Francois."

"Are you sure?"

"She is a child, she is wet, and she is waving at us. If this is an attack on our home, I would suggest she has lost the element of surprise."

Francois slid the bolts across and opened the balcony door. The girl pushed past him, rested her sodden suitcase and white parasol against the fireplace, and warmed her hands in front of the flames. He tried his best not to sound sarcastic.

"Please. Come in."

If the girl noticed the tone of his welcome, she hid it well.

"Thank you."

She turned around, lifted her skirt a little and warmed her behind without the slightest sense of embarrassment. As she did so, Inglenook stretched and walked around her feet, nuzzling her damp ankles. Jayne looked down at the kitten and giggled.

"My dear little thing, did I drip on you? I am so sorry."

Imogen picked up Inglenook and stepped away, looking at the girl with suspicion.

"Who are you, and where are your parents?"

"They are not here."

"Clearly, but that is not an answer to my question."

"No, I suppose not. Did you know there was not a single taxi at the railway station? I was forced to run all the way here in the rain."

Francois glanced at the clock on the mantlepiece.

"There is only one taxi, and Clement Bidet is usually tucked up in bed with a brandy by now."

Imogen wrinkled her nose and looked a little incredulous.

"Bidet?"

Francois shrugged.

"Yes. A hellish time at school, I understand. Children can be very cruel."

"Quite so. Have I met Monsieur Bidet?"

"No. He and Anton do not see eye to eye on several matters, so he does come to the café."

"Vital matters?"

"Not in the slightest."

The girl watched them talk, her eyes flicking between them as if she were watching a game of tennis. There was a short pause before they both realised, and Francois resumed the conversation with her.

"Your parents may be worried, Miss. It is very late. We have a telephone if you would like us to call someone."

"They are not here, and they are not worried."

Francois huffed and folded his arms.

"Why were you on our balcony? We have a perfectly serviceable front door."

"You must forgive me; I am fond of a dramatic entrance."

"How on earth did you get up there?"

"I climbed a tree, and then I jumped. I am a girl of many talents, but sadly, flying is not one of them. Would it be too much of an imposition to ask for a hot drink?"

Francois was more than happy to leave Imogen to solve this latest conundrum.

"Coffee and cake for three it is, then."

"I would prefer hot chocolate if you have it."

"I am sure I can find some."

They waited in silence until they heard Francois reach the bottom of the stairs. At that point, the girl sat down in the chair nearest the fire. She gripped the arms, then lifted herself up and back until her feet dangled a few inches off the ground.

"You are being quite evasive, child. Who are you really, and what were you doing on our balcony?"

"I was getting very wet, Imogen."

If the use of her first name was an effort to intimidate, it failed.

"I do not know you."

"No, you do not, but you soon will."

"You speak as if we have no choice in the matter."

The girl narrowed her eyes, considering Imogen's words carefully.

"I am almost certain that you do not, but such things are best left to philosophers and other great thinkers. All I ask is that you spare me an hour or two of your time. You have already decided that I am no threat to either of you."

"I have?"

"Had you not, you would have already tried to remove me in an exciting and elaborate manner."

Imogen visibly considered this.

"Hmmm…it is my habit to do rather than try."

"Yes, yes, I'm aware of your talents, Imogen DiRossi, but I have no desire to put them to the test. That would not end well for either of us."

The girl's tone had changed only slightly, but there was enough intent in her words to make Imogen wary. However, the gentle rattle of a silver tray and footsteps on the stairs told them that Francois was near, so she would let things be for now. Jayne lowered her voice slightly.

"He trusts you, Imogen, and this will go much more smoothly if you listen to what I have to say and give it due consideration. Will you help me?"

Imogen had made her mind up long before the child had finished speaking. She thought of their waking up wet and cold by the pond and the unexplained healing of their injuries and scars. This girl's sudden arrival was obviously no coincidence.

"I will."

"I am pleased."

With that, the girl took a small box out of her pocket and placed it on the arm of the chair. It was wrapped in light blue tissue paper and was tied with a large white bow. Before Imogen could comment, Francois pushed the door open with his knee and set the tray on the table nearest the hearth. There were cups and three plates, each containing a large piece of chocolate cake. He passed a cup of hot chocolate and a plate to the girl, who grinned up at him.

"Thank you, Francois."

He glanced at Imogen briefly, assuming his name had come up during his absence.

"You're most welcome, Miss…?"

"Jayne. Jayne Brewer, and I am very pleased to meet you both."

Francois looked at the box on the arm of the chair for the third time, justifiably assuming that the gift was for him but too polite to ask. Jayne pushed the box closer to him with the tip of one finger.

"Happy Birthday, Francois."

He picked it up and sat down next to Imogen on the sofa, pulling at the white ribbon. Slowly, the box opened to reveal an almost luminous red bowtie. He beamed, then held it up to show Imogen, who thought it possibly the most garish thing she had ever seen.

"A bowtie, Imogen! and a rather splendid one!"

Imogen smiled, but for some reason, seeing something bright red around his neck troubled her.

"Yes, quite splendid. It will go well with your dark blue waistcoat."

"You think so? I was thinking the Harris Tweed would set it off rather well."

"I am almost certain that you wear the only Harris Tweed waistcoat in Paris, Francois. It is quite splendid enough already. Consult Monica if you wish, but I am confident that she will agree."

Imogen sipped her coffee and gave Francois a look that he knew signalled the end of the matter for now. Jayne chuckled into her hot chocolate, enjoying the gentle discourse.

"I chose it very carefully, Francois. I think it will go well with almost anything, but it is always best to ask those who often take your arm first. Imogen is your friend, and I have only known you for fourteen and a half minutes."

Jayne put her cup on the table and slid off the chair until her feet rested on the ground again. She straightened her dress and tidied her damp hair as best she could. Imogen watched her carefully, stroking Inglenook in her lap while Francois made quick work of his chocolate cake.

"You will both find what I am about to tell you very difficult to believe. You, in particular, Imogen, will struggle the most. You are a woman of science and fact, of mathematics and reality, but I am going to take a firm grasp of what you know and tear it asunder."

"Heavens," said Francois, dropping crumbs down his front.

Jayne winked at Francois.

"Quite so, Francois, and although you see life a little differently, you too will find what I have to say a little… fanciful."

"Fanciful is quickly becoming the norm in my orbit, Miss Brewer. Please continue, and I will do my best to keep up."

Jayne inclined her head in reply and took a deep breath.

"I understand that you have both had quite the day, and I would very much like you to tell me about it. I promise to listen and understand, no matter how much you think I will not."

Imogen's voice was calm, but Francois could hear an edge of discomfort in her voice.

"Several hours ago, Francois and I awoke beside the duck pond at the rear of The Café, and neither of us has any memory of how we came to be there. We both remember being in Francois' bedroom at approximately ten o'clock this morning, but after that...nothing."

"What were you doing in the bedroom?"

"I was attempting to repair our clock. It had been behaving rather erratically and..."

"Where is this clock now?"

"I have returned it to the mantlepiece, where it once again keeps good time."

"I will look at it, but I do not think I will find anything particularly unusual. It has clearly served its purpose. Please continue, Imogen."

"There is nothing more to add. We remember being upstairs, and then we found ourselves by the pond ten hours later."

Jayne looked thoughtful.

"Did you touch the clock?"

"Yes, but I have done that before on numerous occasions since I purchased it."

"How long ago was that?"

"Several days after I arrived."

Francois cheerfully interjected.

"March 19th - a Thursday. We also ate pastries in the park

by Eiffel's Tower, and I was accosted by a large crow."

Boreas squawked loudly, startling Francois and Jayne. Imogen looked up at the bird, winked, and then turned back to Francois.

"Francois?"

"Your arrival was somewhat of a turning point in my life, Imogen. I cannot help if the moment is seared into my memory. Also, I have to tell you that on this occasion, you are not entirely correct."

"I am not?"

"We BOTH touched the clock hands at the same time, Imogen. You asked me to hold one of the hands whilst you opened the faceplate."

Jayne and Imogen looked at him, both with a raised eyebrow, something Francois found quite startling.

"The two of you need not look at me like that. I am quite certain that we did. I am a simple man, but I do take a keen interest in things that happen in my bedroom."

Imogen looked back at Jayne, who folded her arms in satisfaction and took a deep breath.

"Imogen…Francois…I cannot precisely explain how or even why, but I am certain you have both travelled in time."

They both looked up at Jayne for almost a minute, trying to digest what she had said.

"…in time?"

"Yes, Imogen. I must also tell you that it was a journey you were supposed to make alone. It seems that dear Francois merely hopped aboard for the ride."

"I can only apologise, Imogen."

"Oh, hush. Miss Brewer…we also travelled from one place to another. Admittedly, it was not very far, but…"

"Yes, that is more unusual, but not unknown."

"This happens often?" enquired Francois.

"That would depend on your definition of the word 'often'. Until now, I am aware of thirty-nine similar events. You are the only two I know of who have travelled together."

"Thirty-nine?"

"Yes, and only twice before did anyone leave one place and return to another. Also, no one else has remembered anything of their journey. I hope that is not too troubling. They all continued to live happy, fulfilling lives once they returned home."

"You have met them?"

"Yes, all of them. It is what I do. It is what I am doing now, in fact. I explain as much as I can, make friends, and then move on."

Imogen was struggling with the facts and suspected that Jayne wasn't telling them everything. For now, though, she would be patient.

"I have a great many questions, Miss Brewer."

"Please, Imogen, call me Jayne. We are going to be such good friends."

"Very well, Jayne. There is...another matter, which I can only assume is connected."

"Yes, I was coming to that. How are you both feeling?"

"Rather well, actually. We are both, physically, very well indeed."

Jayne chuckled.

"A rather wonderful side-effect of the manner in which you travelled. Your bodies have...reset. I have tried many times to think of a better word to describe it, but simply put, you are as well as you have ever been. It seems that the act of tearing you from your present and depositing you in your future...repairs you."

"Francois no longer needs glasses, and we are both more than well."

"Yes, yes. I think it is quite lovely."

The girl's happiness was infectious, putting Francois so much more at ease.

"When I was nine years old, there was an accident, and I injured my leg very badly. The doctor told my parents I would never again walk properly, and although I have got by, it has ached my entire life."

"...and now?"

"It is healed, and the scars are gone."

Imogen took a moment to enjoy Francois' joy, then looked up at the cheerful girl in front of their fire.

"Was it the same for you?"

"Not exactly, but yes, I went on a journey of my own. I was walking with my dog, Alfie, and I came upon an overturned carriage. The driver and two passengers were dead, and I had no idea what to do. One of the passengers had dropped his pocket watch, and I thought it would be nice to put it back in his hand, but when I touched it..."

Jayne spread her arms to the side and opened her eyes wide.

"Whoooosh!"

Francois and Imogen both leaned back in surprise at her dramatic and unexpected gesture.

"For a moment, I felt great pain and saw the brightest flash; then everything was gone - the carriage, the bodies and even my dear Alfie. I ran back to the Village, only to be told that eight months had passed. I stayed with Father Hopper that night, and in the morning, he took me back to my Mama and Papa. Everyone had assumed I had been abducted and then returned. I did not understand what had happened to me and had no idea how to explain it to everyone, so I let them think they were correct."

Francois frowned in sympathy.

"You were also healed?"

"There was almost nothing wrong with me, Francois. I was a healthy child. Perhaps a grazed knee or a loose tooth, but nothing I would notice."

"So, we just accept what has happened and continue as before?"

"Yes. In the short term, you will have some difficulty sleeping, but that will pass.

Imogen considered this before stating, "I have some experience in pharmaceutical matters. Sleep will not be a problem."

"Yes, I know, Imogen, but this is a little different. You were both taken out of time and then put back rather suddenly. Your bodies need to catch up. I know it sounds a little silly, but in a few weeks, everything will return to 'normal'.

Francois collected the plates and cups, then stopped as a thought occurred to him.

"How did you know about us, and how did you find our home?"

"Mmmm…that is slightly harder to explain, but if I may…"

Jayne narrowed her eyes and looked directly at Francois. A warm tingle rose from his toes and travelled up his body until it settled behind his eyes. She raised an eyebrow and smiled. For a few seconds, Francois felt as happy and safe as he had ever been, then just as quickly as it had arrived, the tingle faded away. Francois beamed at her, unsure what to say.

Imogen had watched apprehensively, unsure of what was happening. Jayne turned her head and looked at Imogen, still smiling. The same feeling moved through Imogen, but she bridled at the sensation, surprising Jayne with the intensity of her resistance.

"Do not do that again!"

Jayne took a step back, and the sensations vanished as quickly as they had arrived.

"I apologise, but I have tried to explain myself before, and it is difficult. Imogen, you…stopped me."

"I was unprepared…and it was quite unpleasant."

"No, Imogen, you do not understand. No one has ever done that before, not even…"

Her voice trailed off, but the look of surprise remained. In truth, Imogen hadn't actually stopped her, but Jayne had never encountered such a strong, disciplined mind before.

Francois looked at his friend and wondered why he had felt so differently. To him, it felt like Jayne was holding his hand - a comforting, friendly sense of something he couldn't quite describe.

"I can sense our kind, Imogen. I know when one of us is near, and if I concentrate, I can make my presence known. It has never caused pain to anyone before."

"It was not painful, just unexpected. Perhaps I overreacted. Tell me, from how far away did you…sense us?"

"It is more difficult when it has only just happened, but there are two of you, so it was better. Perhaps three miles. I was on the train."

"But how did you know to come to Paris?"

"I was told about you both in a letter."

"A letter from whom?"

"I do not know exactly. She writes to me often - sometimes to tell me important things I must do and sometimes things I must not do. She seems to know a lot about the world, and I have never come to any harm doing what she says."

"She?"

"Yes, but that is almost all I know about her; I do not know her name, and I do not know where she is. She does always seem to know where I am, though, which I once found strange but not anymore. There is enough strangeness in my life."

"…and do you have a home?"

Jayne shrugged happily.

"I live where I need to be, and today, I need to be here. I will also need to be here tomorrow. May I please stay the night, Francois?"

"Yes, of course. I will check the guestroom, but I am sure it is fit. The bed may need warming, but that is all. There are fresh towels if you wish to take a bath."

"Thank you."

Francois left them alone.

"Please, Imogen, say what you need to say."

"There are things that you are not telling us."

"Yes, there are, but I have told you enough for now. I am aware that you have no reason to trust me, Imogen, but I suspect that you are a person who knows when they are being lied to. Am I lying to you?

"Hmmm…I do not think so."

"I am not, and I never will."

Jayne picked up her parasol and suitcase. She had seen the expression that Imogen now wore so many times.

"Do not think too hard about what I have told you both, Imogen. I know it is a lot to absorb, but you must focus on the here and now. You are both well, and you are home."

"A part of my life is a mystery to me, Jayne, a fact that I find almost intolerable."

On her way to the door, she stopped, put down her suitcase and patted Imogen on the arm.

"I know, but I promise that this feeling will pass.

Goodnight, Imogen."

"Goodnight, Jayne."

Café Merle, Paris - Thursday, June 11th, 1908 - 11.56 pm

After bathing, Jayne climbed into bed, sliding beneath the blankets and letting her toes find every cool corner before she finally settled. The guest room was small and comfortable, with the slightest hint of herbs and perfume in the air—clearly the lingering presence of its previous occupant. She pulled the bedclothes up to her chin and rested her hands on her chest, thinking about her evening.

Things had gone well and so much better than they sometimes did. In all the time she had been doing this, she had never met a pair like Imogen and Francois. On each of the previous thirty-nine occasions, it had been a lone, scared and confused individual. Closing her eyes, she took a moment to remember every single one.

With just a little concentration, she reached out to the ones who were close enough, knowing that they, too, would feel the touch of her mind and probably smile. It had taken her a long time to distinguish between them, but she had grown proficient, and even with Imogen and Francois so close and vibrant in her head, she could…

Arnka.

Jayne opened her eyes suddenly, angry with herself for forgetting. She had been so caught up in her sense of purpose and her two new friends that she had forgotten all about her.

As the train grew nearer to Paris, she'd felt Arnka and the unique, painful familiarity of her presence. She always pushed back, but it made little difference—Jayne could still sense her from farther away than any other, such was the intensity of her existence.

But now, she had gone. Staring at the ceiling, she whispered to herself.

"Where are you, Arnka?"

She closed her eyes and concentrated but sensed only Imogen, Francois, and one more on the other side of the city. Arnka was nowhere to be found.

Perhaps they had been travelling in opposite directions? If they had both been on a train, she would have been far away by now, so Jayne relaxed, knowing that if Arnka came near again, her angry mind would be strong enough to pull Jayne out of the deepest sleep.

Francois and Imogen would need to know about Arnka, but not yet. Jayne liked it here, and she already liked Imogen and Francois very much, so she would stay as long as they needed her to.

Beside Jayne, two envelopes lay on the bedside cabinet—one opened and one still sealed. She picked up the latter and traced the tip of her finger over the elegant script.

"Do not open until 1st April 1912."

She put the envelope down, whispering to herself as she did so.

"Three years, nine months and twenty-one days."

One more letter and one more mystery.

Café Merle, Paris - Friday, June 12th, 1908 - 7.24 am

Francois stood in the café doorway, sipping his first coffee of the day and watching Jayne Brewer twirling happily on the cobbles near the fountain. He had barely slept but seemed none the worse for it.

"Good morning, Francois."

Francois was still amazed by Imogen's ability to creep silently about the café, but after three months, he was confident that she enjoyed surprising him. As usual, he tried and failed to hide his shock as he spilt a little of his espresso into the saucer.

"Good morning, Imogen. Coffee?"

"Yes, thank you. Are you well?"

Francois turned his back, put his hands on his hips and gazed at the many jars of coffee beans on the shelf behind the counter.

"Once my heartbeat returns to a stable rhythm, I will be fine. To where shall Madame travel this morning? Kenya? Columbia? Ethiopia? Perhaps something to evoke memories of home?"

"I AM home, Francois. Also, coffee is not grown in Italy; it is only ground and blended there."

He turned around.

"This I knew. I was being…"

"Frivolous?"

"I was going to say mischievous, but…"

"Honduras."

"Pardon?"

"The red bag to your left. It is adorned with the image of a Collared Aracari."

"Ahh, yes. I always thought this was a Toucan."

"Toucans are blessed with a yellow or white face and chest - the Collared Aracari is not, Francois."

"A mistake I shall obviously not make again."

"I should certainly hope not."

Francois took the bag down, opened it, and sniffed the contents before pouring the beans into the grinder. As he turned the handle, Imogen leaned back on her stool to watch Jayne, who was now sitting on the edge of the fountain, talking to Jacques.

"Miss Brewer rose early."

"She was wandering the cobbles long before I came down. Anton and Maria saw her just after six on their way over to us."

Imogen leaned forward again, resting her elbows on the counter.

"I did not sleep."

"I am sorry to hear that. I finally stopped trying at just after three and came down to finish our weekly accounts - something that usually sends me off, but sadly, not on this occasion."

Francois paused and smiled at Imogen over his shoulder.

"Café Merle is thriving, Imogen."

She rested her cheek on one hand and smiled back at him.

"I do not need to look at your ledger to see that, Francois."

A few minutes later, Francois pushed a steaming cup of coffee towards Imogen. As was her habit, she lowered her face to the cup, closed her eyes and inhaled deeply.

"I trust Madame is satisfied?"

She raised a single finger, hushing him politely.

"I brim with optimism, Mr Meyer, however..."

She lifted the cup and took a delicate sip. As he did almost every morning, Francois folded his arms and waited patiently.

"Quite excellent. Perhaps you should consider a career in hospitality, Francois."

"The hours would not suit me, Imogen. As you well know, I am not one to rise early."

With that, the café door opened, and Monica entered, clutching a roll of dark blue cloth to her chest. Imogen turned on her stool, her mood lifted by the rush of caffeine.

"Good morning, Monica Byrne!"

Monica beamed, happy to see two of her favourite people.

"Good morning, Imogen DiRossi!"

Monica put the roll of cloth on the counter and climbed onto a stool, winking at Francois, who blushed. Imogen glanced between them, still not entirely used to the recent change in their relationship. There had been no official announcement, but there was undoubtedly more winking. Also, Monica had taken to speaking in a more hushed, lower register when addressing Francois.

"Good morning, Francois."

Francois glanced at Imogen before he replied.

"Good morning, Monica. How are you?"

"I am quite well, thank you."

Imogen finished her coffee, climbed off her stool and straightened her dress. She approved of their relationship, and the moment they acknowledged it formally, she would be publicly happy for them both. Until then…

"You must excuse me. I have business…somewhere."

Francois looked puzzled.

"Somewhere?"

"Outside. In the square. Perhaps a walk and a visit to The Post Office. I am sure I shall see you both later."

Imogen nodded and left. As the door opened and then closed behind her, the bell tinkled twice. Monica looked up at it, the only person who still wondered why it did so for no one else.

"Francois, Imogen has forgotten her…"

"Wait a moment."

Seconds later, Imogen returned, walked to the coat stand at the back of the café and took her hat from the hook. She nodded politely as she passed them both and exited once more. Monica leaned back on her stool and watched her walk away across the square.

"Is Imogen quite well?"

"She is adjusting to…us, Monica."

"But we have made no secret of our…"

Monica reached across the counter and squeezed Francois' hand.

"…love."

"Imogen is used to a certain formality, and we should respect that. I do not wish her to feel awkward."

"Then we shall tell her. Tonight, over dinner, perhaps?"

"Imogen does not like fuss of any sort, as you well know."

"Oh, Francois, she is my friend too. Do not worry."

"I cannot promise a lack of worry."

Monica raised herself up, leaned over the counter and kissed Francois.

"You ridiculous man."

Café Merle, Paris - Friday, June 12th, 1908 - 8.00 am

As Imogen made her way across the road and onto the square, Boreas flew from the café roof and swooped down towards her. She held out her wrist, and Boreas landed on it, his claws gripping her gently.

"Good morning, Boreas."

She hadn't noticed that Jayne was now sitting on a bench

nearby in the shade of the trees.

"He is such a handsome bird, Imogen."

Boreas squawked and flew to Jayne's shoulder, looking back at Imogen as soon as he was comfortable.

"He is very friendly, too."

"Actually, Boreas is usually quite particular in his choice of friends."

"As are you, Imogen. There is nothing wrong with being cautious."

Imogen sat down on the bench, resting both hands in her lap and glancing at Boreas as he watched the world go by from Jayne's shoulder.

"My friend Monica insists that he has an eye for the ladies."

Across the square, the pair watched Belle offer a flower to everyone who came near her cart. Jacques was sprawled across a bench, asleep and oblivious to the pigeon pecking at his foot. This was not the first time that Imogen had sat here and watched them. She already loved Place St Genevieve and the people who lived there.

"I am particularly cautious when it comes to my home and family, Miss Brewer."

"That was obvious from the moment I arrived, Imogen. I have travelled to many places, but to find such a welcoming, comfortable spot is quite rare. There is an ease between you and Francois, and now I find it out here as well. Are you truly aware of the high regard these people have for you and your friend?"

Imogen closed her eyes, breathing in the morning air, fully aware that Jayne was watching her.

"I have also travelled and will continue to do so, but now I have somewhere to come home to and people who will miss me. It is a new experience, but a pleasant one."

Across the square, Jacques woke up and shouted at the pigeon, sending his small corner of the world into chaos. Jayne giggled.

"Even Monsieur LeGrande?"

"Although they may not realise it, Jacques LeGrande and Belle Vellieux are the very heart of Place St Genevieve - possibly more so even than the crows."

Boreas squawked.

"Quite so, Boreas." she smiled.

"Imogen, when I arrived last night, it was my intention to tell you everything, but as the evening drew on, I began to suspect that Francois would hear it better from you. I hope you agree."

"We have been friends for only a short time, but..."

"There is a bond between you that suggests it has been far longer."

"I have wished more than once that we had met sooner."

"Well, you must have wished very hard, Imogen DiRossi."

"I do not follow."

"No, but you soon will."

Jayne sighed, ready to lift a weight from her small shoulders.

"Beside you sits a charming contradiction - not a unique one by any means, but a contradiction nonetheless. What do you see when you look at me, Imogen?"

Imogen turned to look at Jayne, raising her eyebrow.

"A child. Articulate, intelligent, personable and a little precocious, perhaps, but in my experience, that will be to your advantage later in life."

"I am slightly disappointed that my golden hair and sparkling eyes were not worthy of comment, but I am still flattered."

Imogen replied quickly, remembering herself at the same age.

"You are also pretty."

"Thank you, but I am not all I appear to be."

"No, you are not."

Jayne had learned long ago that no amount of preamble made what she was about to say any less bizarre. She looked across at the fountain, watching the never-ending trickle of water sparkle in the morning sun for a short while.

"Imogen...I found that overturned carriage and the bodies of those poor people in October 1789, not long after my fifteenth birthday. On the 24th of September this year, I shall be 134 years old."

Imogen's thoughts tumbled, even as she struggled to maintain her calm. It was an absurd statement, but try as she might, she couldn't dismiss it.

"I do not want to believe you."

Jayne turned to face Imogen.

"I have never heard that reply before, and you are only the third person to stay seated. Why do you not wish to believe me?"

"I am not sure, and that, in itself, bothers me."

"You have lived a life of patience and control, Imogen. Do not worry too much. Very soon, all will be well. I have told my story many times, and the result is always the same - only the time taken to accept it varies. I was twenty-eight years old when I first sat with someone in the same position as you, Imogen, and one day, I hope to find the perfect way to explain it all."

"Francois and I..."

"Yes. From the moment you began your mysterious journey, your bodies also ceased to age. I have no idea how long you were gone, but I suspect it was at least two days."

"Days?"

"Yes. I am reasonably certain that it takes at least two for your bodies to reset, and I must also tell you that the change is permanent."

"We cannot be injured?"

"You can still be injured, Imogen, and it will still hurt, but you will heal very quickly. For this reason, it is very important that you avoid doctors, as they will ask too many questions. Also, you will no longer become ill. Some of the more virulent diseases will...slow you down a little, but not for very long."

"We are immortal?"

"Not exactly, no. We are still vulnerable to serious injury, and more than one of us has been...permanently damaged, but we are somewhat resilient."

Jayne held both arms out in front of her, stretching her fingers and wiggling them.

"Personally, I intend to grow very, very old, Imogen."

"How...long will we live?"

"I have no idea. There are three Persistants older than me - one of whom is over 300 years old".

"Persistants?"

Jayne chuckled.

"Yes. Persistant, with an 'A' at the end. A rather clever friend of mine has devoted a great deal of time to understanding what we are. He has theorised that we are tied to this planet more firmly than everyone else - hence our permanence. Permanent, incidentally, was his second choice. I will introduce you to him one day but take care - Jack has an eye for the ladies and is very handsome."

"He is Persistant?"

"No, but he is like us in many ways."

Imogen frowned.

"This is very confusing, and I have so many questions, Jayne."

"Yes, and I will try to answer them all, but first, you must speak to Francois."

Imogen stood, seeing Monica leaving the café and walking the short distance to her shop.

"What of our friends?"

"That is for you and Francois to decide. If you genuinely believe that they will understand, then you may tell them. I must warn you, though, that the knowledge that they will grow old whilst you do not is a heavy burden."

"Francois and Monica...they are very close."

"Yes, I know. I can only offer you my experience, Imogen.

Francois must decide, and you must help him."

"Relationships are not my forte child, and to share this burden with him…I am not comfortable in such situations."

"Not many are. Take your time."

Imogen looked down at Jayne, swinging her dangling feet inches above the cobbles, and reminded herself that this was the oldest person that she had ever met. Jayne was still looking out across the square as she spoke.

"I am settled in my life, Imogen and one day soon, you will be too. At the moment, you are thinking the worst, but you have been blessed with an infinity of nows - you have time to read every book, hear every piece of music and learn…everything."

Changing her cadence, Jayne continued this time in fluent Italian.

"I must have my lemon tea and biscuits wherever I happen to find myself."

Imogen finally felt herself relaxing around the girl and replied in the same manner.

"Lunch is at noon, Jayne. On Saturdays, Maria makes Pea and Ham soup. It is quite excellent."

"I shall be there, Imogen."

Café Merle, Paris - Saturday, June 13th, 1908 - 2.15 am

For the second night, just as Jayne had said, Francois hadn't been able to sleep. He'd considered making the short journey to next door and waking Monica, but she would almost certainly mistake his intentions at this hour of the night. Tomorrow was a delivery day, and she needed to be up early, so instead, he had looked at her photo on his bedside cabinet and again marvelled at how a man's life could change in such a short time.

It was all Imogen's fault of course, but he wasn't angry at his friend. Her arrival, a mere three months ago, had changed all their lives for the better. It was their adventure at the château and Francois' brush with death that caused him to think more about his relationship with Monica and slightly less about his business.

After almost an hour, he'd climbed out of bed and rearranged his ties, waistcoats and shoes, but he felt no more tired after this than he did before. Now, he stood looking at the forty-year-old face in the mirror, searching in vain for the smallest piece of evidence that Jayne's story was true. At the doorway, Imogen cleared her throat quietly.

"I regret that what has happened to us did not happen soon enough to save your hairline, Francois."

He smiled, changing his position slightly to see her in the reflection.

"Monica assures me that it is a most distinguished look."

"Monica is in love with you."

"...and you?"

"I am not in love with you."

"You know perfectly well what I meant."

"She also told you that you suited a beret. No one suits a beret, Francois."

"Your point is well made, as always, Imogen."

Imogen remembered Jayne's words in the square.

"She said that we could tell those close to us but to be wary."

"How can I tell her, Imogen?"

"That, I do not know."

She moved closer, stepping into the light of his bedside lamp and rested a hand on his shoulder. Her beautiful face smiled at him beneath her loose, slightly untidy hair. She looked at herself and stroked her cheek with a single finger.

"The prospect of a changeless, constant face is… unsettling."

"I like your face, Imogen."

"...and I yours, Francois."

He sighed.

"She was in our heads."

"It was a little intrusive, but it added weight to her tale. I am certain that she is not lying."

"Then...so am I, but 1774, Imogen. Is that child really 133 years old? I confess she certainly does not sound like any other fifteen-year-old I have met."

Imogen smiled into the mirror.

"Had you met me at fifteen, you may think differently, Francois."

"You, Imogen? surely not."

A little of the day's tension lifted as they found comfort in each other's company.

"What shall we do?"

"Do? We shall live, Francois - live in perfect health for a considerably long time, it seems."

"Why does the idea trouble me so much?"

"Because it is an intriguing prospect fraught with complications. Looking as she does, Miss Brewer moves about the world with relative anonymity. You and I have a home, a business and friends - friends who will eventually notice that we do not change with the passing days. However, we will do nothing for now, and tomorrow, we shall discuss the matter further with Miss Brewer. In the meantime, we should sleep."

Francois sighed and patted the hand on his shoulder.

"I find comfort in the fact that I am not alone in this, Imogen."

"As do I, Francois. Now, into bed with you."

"I have been lying in bed for hours with no success."

"Humour me, Mr Meyer."

He kicked off his slippers and climbed into bed.

"I feel more than slightly foolish. Promise me that you are not going to read me a story."

Imogen grinned, sat on the side of his bed and took hold of the blanket.

"Why do you feel foolish?"

"Because my business partner is tucking me in. Some would consider that inappropriate."

"Oh, hush. I am tucking you in, not climbing in with you. Even if I wished to, your bed is not big enough, and I like to stretch out."

Francois pulled the blankets up to his chin.

"Also, I snore."

"On occasion, quite spectacularly so."

"I can only apologise, Imogen."

"Go to sleep, Mr Meyer."

Francois' eyes fluttered briefly, then his head rolled to the side, and he was fast asleep. She adjusted his blankets a little, then walked back to her room. Despite Jayne's insistence that it would make no difference, she had prepared the most robust sleeping draft she knew, and an hour before, she had taken as much of it as she dared. Not only was she as awake as she had ever been, but there were also none of the expected side effects - no headache, tingling of the fingers or dryness of the mouth.

So, she lay on top of her blankets and opened her book for the fourth time that evening. With Inglenook snoring quietly on the pillow next to her, Imogen DiRossi began to read, determined to understand why Mr. Sherlock Holmes entertained and fascinated her best friend so much.

Hotel Lambert, Paris, Room 187 - Saturday, June 13th, 1908 - 3.00 pm

Staring out of the third-story window, Arnka looked down at the people of Paris as they went about their business. Her face gave the impression that she despised every single one of them, but the truth was, they simply meant nothing to her. Their brief, pointless lives did little but annoy her and get in her way.

"Why do you waste so much of your time staring at them? They do not matter."

She turned around to look at the old woman sitting up in the bed, her back against a pile of silk cushions.

"I know. I watch them because it reminds me of how much better I am than them, Edith. Your mind is withering like a flower in the hot sun, and I grow increasingly tired of your drivel with every passing hour."

"My mind is as sharp as yours, Arnka Søgard, and as long as I am still useful to you, you will keep me in the manner to which I have become accustomed."

Edith patted down the blankets and leaned back even deeper into the pillows.

"How does it feel?"

Arnka held up her arm, letting the sunlight through the window fall onto The Serpent's Grasp. She twisted her arm, admiring its simple beauty.

"It is too heavy."

Edith pressed a wet handkerchief against her face, forcing air from her lungs in a laugh that turned into a deep, guttural cough. Arnka watched, detached and bored with what she suspected was more performance than genuine struggle. After almost a minute, the old woman took the handkerchief away from her face.

"Try not to look so superior, Arnka Søgard. You may be beautiful and wise, but you still fall to your knees in agony at the whim of a child. I told you that she would be there, and yet you were still not prepared."

"It is difficult to prepare for someone that can hurt me from the other side of the park."

"To you, everything is too difficult."

Agitated, Arnka looked away, rubbing the bracelet with the tips of her fingers and ignoring Edith's comment.

"I did as you asked, but you still have not told me why."

"For yourself."

"What?"

"The Serpent's Grasp - mysterious, beautiful and now…my gift to you."

"A trinket?"

"Yes."

As she grew more frustrated with the fragile figure in the bed, the bracelet seemed to tighten against her skin, making her head ache and her vision blur. Edith began to laugh - a dry rasp of a laugh that did nothing to lessen Arnka's anger. She climbed onto the bed, moving closer to the old woman and holding The Serpent's Grasp inches from her face. For the briefest moment, Edith looked terrified, but gradually, her weak smile returned.

"Pain at HER whim because you cannot hide. None of your kind can hide from her, but she does not care about them - just you, Arnka Søgard. Beautiful, wise and broken. She is the only thing left in the world that makes you feel less than perfect!"

Arnka pulled back a little, tired of the bracelet's weight and sick of Edith's foul breath on her face.

"Yes, get away from me, you ungrateful bitch."

Edith's laugh grew stronger.

"Without me, what are you? My truths and the things I know are worth everything to you."

Arnka climbed off the bed and fumbled with the bracelet's clasp.

"You are insane."

"Very probably, but she cannot see me, and as long as you wear that, she cannot see you either."

Arnka took her hand away from the clasp, turning to face Edith, and listened.

"From the moment you first wore that, she became blind to you. At this moment, she is less than five miles away, and for the first time in over a century, she has no idea where you are."

"Why did you do this?"

"Because I need you to do something else for me."

Arnka sighed, "What?"

"First, we shall have tea, and then we shall discuss Imogen DiRossi and Francois Meyer."

"You want me to kill them? They were changed only two

days ago. Could I at least wait until it was more of a challenge?"

"You enjoy killing far too much, Arnka, and if that was what I wanted, I am quite confident that you would do so without such an elaborate incentive. No, I want you to make them suffer."

"Is that all?"

"Yes. Frustrate them, annoy them and make them miserable. In time, you may hurt them, but not yet. Do you understand me?"

Arnka smiled in anticipation.

"Yes, but if I were to get lost in the moment and..."

"If you kill them, I will make you regret it in ways that even you cannot imagine."

"You?"

"Oh yes. First, prove to yourself that what I say about the bracelet is true, then consider what else I may know. You will come to heel and do as I say, Arnka. Besides, all I ask is that you be yourself. How many of your years have you spent making other people suffer?"

"Not enough."

"Quite. Now, I will have some tea."

Arnka pulled the sleeve of her coat down, covering the bracelet. As she opened the door, she looked back at Edith, who smiled at her like a kindly Aunt.

"What are they to you?"

Edith looked away from her and closed her eyes, sinking back into the pillows. After so long together, she knew exactly how to confuse and manipulate the younger woman.

"They are my end and…your beginning, Arnka."

CHAPTER THIRTEEN - NO LOOSE ENDS
LeGrande Antiques, Plymouth - Friday, September 22nd, 1957 - 11.10 am

Jayne took the last vase from the packing crate, spreading even more shredded paper over the shop floor. She held up a fine example of Wedgewood Blue Jasperware—unsigned but almost certainly the work of John Flaxman. Although styled after a Roman miniature, it was turned and fired two years before her birth. She ran her fingers over the two-centuries-old embossing and lost herself in the past.

"Well, well, my lovely. Has your journey been as eventful as mine, I wonder? Luckily, you are with me now, and I know the perfect place for you."

At her feet, Bessy-Lou pushed her snout into the pile of packing paper and emerged, wearing it like a wig. Jayne giggled.

"Oh, you silly dog."

She wiped the vase with her duster, climbed her small stepladder and placed it on a shelf near the counter. It would be a popular piece, and news of her acquisition would spread quickly. However, Jayne owned precious few items as old, and she had no intention of selling any of them. Climbing down and stepping back, she frowned, tilted her head to one side and spoke aloud to herself.

"One hundred and eighty years old, and you still have no idea, Jayne Brewer. Where are you when I need your eyes and good taste, Belle Veilleux?"

She moved the vase an inch to the right and rotated it slightly, still not satisfied.

"There, that will have to do for now. As usual, I have much to do and so little time."

"A curious thing to say, little one."

Happiness lit up her face at the sound of the familiar voice in her head.

"I was beginning to think you would never come back to me, Ma'at."

"Time has passed?"

It was both a statement and a question.

"You know very well that I could tell you exactly how long it has been for me, but I appreciate that it would not mean the same for you."

The reply was clearly too layered for Ma'at to comprehend, so she ignored it.

"It is time."

Three words, but Jayne had waited so long for this moment. Ma'at was so often distant and vague, but sometimes, she was brief and to the point.

"You have always said that I mustn't be where I already am, but I have already seen myself do this."

"It is inadvisable, but sometimes it is necessary, and it will be brief."

Jayne put down her duster and shook out her flared skirt.

"Your feet."

"What? Oh…of course," Jayne kicked off her heels, remembering, "It's going to be very cold."

Ma'at replied thoughtfully.

"Yes, but you will …persist," the eye roll almost perceptible in her voice.

Jayne laughed knowingly.

"You know Jack would be very flattered to hear you use that word."

"Yes."

There was an edge to Ma'at's reply, which made Jayne frown a little.

"He is kind and helps me sometimes. There are so few who understand what it is to be like us. Do not judge him too harshly."

The voice seemed to consider this, searching for the correct word but not finding it.

"Hmmm…he is…"

Jayne chuckled, amused by Ma'at's struggle.

"Yes…he is. I am ready."

"Take them home, little one."

Jayne took a deep breath and closed her eyes, feeling the present cling to her like a vice. She knew she had to relax. It was always easier if she relaxed.

"I am always and forever. But sometimes, I really, really wish I wasn't."

"I understand, little one, but I need you."

"I know you do. I just wish sometimes that you didn't."

Very slowly, she exhaled and opened her eyes. 1957 began to let her go just as the past took hold, pulling her into silent darkness. Noise returned with a rush, and Jayne fell nine feet into the freezing North Atlantic of 1912, swallowing a great deal of it in the process. Spluttering and splashing in the darkness, she felt her skin freeze and her hair turn to ice.

"Son of a bitch!"

Her body settled as it clung to life, protecting and warming her from within to the tips of her fingers. Treading water, she let her mind reach out, searching for Francois and Imogen in the darkness; opening her eyes, she laughed as she found them.

"There you are!"

The doomed ship towered above her as her arms swept away the freezing water in broad strokes. As she swam past the ship, doing her best to block out the cries of those on deck and in the water, she felt something new and remembered.

"Oh…yes."

She stopped and turned to face the girl on deck, remembering how scared she'd been - even with Ma'at near. Her younger self was too far away to hear, but she could…wave. She remembered waving, so she did - whispering to herself and desperate to reassure little Jayne.

"Look at me, Jayne. Think. Understand what it means. You are always and forever, Jayne Brewer."

She saw herself wave back and smiled before swimming on into the darkness. She heard Imogen and Francois talking before she saw them, chuckling at the familiar tone of their conversation. From twenty feet away, she shouted.

"Hello!"

LeGrande Antiques, Plymouth - Friday, September 22nd, 1957 - 11.25 am

Jayne fell to her knees on her living room carpet, the bottom of her dress still wet and her body exhausted - the closest to losing her grip on life as she had ever been. She had left Imogen and Francois thinking she was rested and ready, but clearly, she wasn't. In pain and almost desperate in the face of unfamiliar sensations, her mind cried out.

"Son of a bitch! Ma'at!"

"I am here."

"It hurts! I have nothing left."

"You must sleep."

Jayne tried to get to her feet, stumbling as she steadied herself.

"No, I will be…"

"Sleep, little one."

With a slight push, Jayne Brewer collapsed and fell asleep on the carpet.

LeGrande Antiques, Plymouth - Friday, September 22nd, 1957 - 5.20 pm

Jayne woke feeling a dog's tongue on her face and groaned. As soon as she stirred, the dog barked loudly next to her ear.

"Bessy-Lou!"

She got to her knees, still tired and sore and slipped out of her damp skirt. Picking it up, she walked towards her room, passing the kitchen, where she could hear quiet music and the bustle of activity.

"I am fine," she said, raising her voice to be heard as she

walked along the hallway.

"Of course you are, Miss. You looked comfortable enough lying there, and I could see your little chest rising and falling happily. I swear you are the only person I know who sleeps with a smile on her face. I won't ask what happened, but I am sure it was something exciting."

"A little, yes. By the way, we may need a new living room carpet."

Jayne heard a gentle huff from the kitchen, followed by the sound of the oven door closing.

"Dinner will be at seven. There is enough hot water if you need a bath."

LeGrande Antiques, Plymouth - Friday, September 22nd, 1957 - 11.40 pm

"It is long past time for your bed, Miss. Finish your tea, close your book and be on your way."

The housekeeper looked down at her with a friendly but frustrated expression.

"That recliner is far too comfortable if you ask me."

Jayne smiled up at the kind, old face.

"I didn't ask, and it is not a recliner; it is an Eames Lounge Chair. It was very expensive, and it cost a great deal of money to ship it here from The United States of America.

Besides, how could I not love a chair that had room for Bessy-Lou as well as myself?"

The golden labrador pressed her head into Jayne's hand at the mention of her name.

"Heaven knows what the neighbours think of us with our lights burning at all hours of the night. Can I get you anything before I retire?"

"No, thank you. Now, please go to bed. I will finish this chapter, and then, I promise, I will do the same."

"See that you do, poppet."

The housekeeper sighed, then slowly bent down and kissed Jayne on top of the head. She had done so for as long as she could remember and would continue for as long as she could, even though her bones ached more with every passing year. Jayne smiled contentedly.

"Good night, Elsie."

"Good night, Miss Jayne."

Elsie Figgins walked slowly and a little stiffly down the hall to her room, feeling every day of her sixty-five years but grateful for every single one.

EPILOGUE - ALMOND BISCUITS
Southampton, Tuesday, 9th April 1912 - 11.05 am

Jayne Brewer sat on a white, cast-iron chair outside the tearooms, resting her elbows on the table and trying to look like she was waiting for a responsible adult. Most of the time, the world ignored her until she wanted otherwise, and that was fine and nearly always convenient. She had stopped wishing everyone would take notice of her almost a century ago, but as she looked down at her feet and the inches between them and the floor, she wished again that perhaps Persistance could have waited until she was a little taller.

In her small, delicate hands, she held a letter - one that she had left unopened for three years, nine months and twenty-one days. Inside was another slightly smaller envelope on which another message was written.

"Be in Southampton by 11.00 am on Tuesday, April 9th, 1912. Buy a cup of lemon tea at the Greenslade Tearooms in Victoria Road, and then you may open this.

"Where are your parents, child? Are you lost?"

Startled, Jayne hid her surprise well and looked up at the rosy-cheeked face, offering her finest and most endearing smile. It was a performance that was so well practised that it took almost no effort at all.

"My Mama will be here soon. We would like two cups of lemon tea, but I will have mine first, as hers will be cold when she finally finds a bed jacket she is satisfied with."

Karen Greenslade put her hand on Jayne's upper arm and patted it gently.

"Of course, sweetie. Would you like a biscuit? They are fresh from the oven."

The sweet smell of baking had been evident from the moment Jayne had sat down, and she knew it would only be a matter of time before she took advantage of one of, if not the most convenient aspects of Persistance. She rubbed her tummy and grinned.

"Yes, please."

Ten minutes later, she opened the envelope and took out the single sheet of paper inside.

"My dearest Jayne, I trust that you have been patient enough to obey the instructions on the outside of the envelope and that I am now speaking to you on a cool, slightly overcast day in April 1912."

Jayne giggled, dropping biscuit crumbs down her dress.

"Once again, I must ask for your help and your trust. Tomorrow, a few minutes after midday, the RMS Titanic will set sail for New York, and you must be on board. At thirteen minutes past eight on the night of the 12th, Imogen DiRossi and Francois Meyer will arrive suddenly in The first-class smoking room."

She smiled to herself, excited and happy to finally understand.

"I regret that I have kept the details of Imogen and

Francois' mysterious journey on the night of his birthday in 1908 from you. As you read further, you will understand why.

Twenty minutes before midnight on the 14th, The ship will hit an iceberg. Two hours and forty minutes later, it will sink, taking with her 1500 passengers and crew. I know your first instinct will be to try and prevent this, but you must not. Indeed, even if you were to try, I believe this is beyond even your capabilities."

Jayne stopped chewing her biscuit.

"Shit."

The grey-haired, portly sailor at the next table turned his head sharply and laughed.

"Don't you like your biscuit? Don't let Mother Greenslade hear you."

Jayne smiled back, taking only a few seconds to fashion a suitable and believable response.

"It is a fine biscuit, sir, but it seems my uncle is coming to stay with us. He is somewhat fond of his gin."

She mimed drinking and swirled her eyes a little. The sailor laughed at what he seemed to think was the funniest thing he'd ever been told, made doubly so by the age of the girl who said it.

"Mother's ruin, child. You and your mother would do well to rid him of such a vice. You could perhaps introduce him to the warm glow of a daily tot of Rum?"

"Perhaps, sir," Jayne nodded as she returned to her letter.

"Your main concern will be Imogen and Francois' activities. I have arranged for a friend to meet you on the dockside tomorrow, and they will explain what needs to be done in more detail. In the meantime, finish your lemon tea and make your way to the offices of The White Star Line, where you will purchase two first-class tickets to New York - one for yourself and one for your mother. A mother is more likely to hide away in her cabin on a long sea voyage, and her fictitious nature is less likely to be discovered.

Good luck.

P.S. The gentleman sitting at the next table is called Tobias, and I am sure he would be grateful for your last biscuit."

She folded the letter and put it back in the envelope, drank the last of her tea, and got off her chair.

"Would you like my last biscuit, sir?"

The old sailor took the pipe from his mouth and smiled broadly.

"That I would, Miss. Thank you. If there's one thing Tobias Mahoney enjoys, it's an almond biscuit."

Jayne curtseyed and walked away.

Southampton, Monday, 10th April 1912 - 11.45 am

Dressed in her finest dress and bonnet, Jayne stood on the dockside and looked up at the massive ship. It was crowded and noisy, buzzing with the excitement of imminent departure. She put down her suitcase and tucked her parasol under her arm, checking her ticket again.

"Hello, little one."

Seeing that everyone around her was far too busy to notice her one-sided conversation, she replied out loud.

"Hello, Ma'at. I was told there would be a friend waiting for me, but I did not expect it to be you."

"Are you disappointed?"

"No, of course not."

"I am pleased. We have much to discuss."

She looked around, watching the excited faces of the people on the dockside. Knowing what was going to happen to so many of them upset her, but it wasn't the first time she had been asked to do things that were difficult or unpleasant, and she trusted that Ma'at would keep her safe. As she picked up her suitcase and made her way to the bottom of the boarding gangway, she stopped talking aloud and continued to converse in the privacy of her own thoughts.

"It would have been nice if the sun had shined."

"Some things are beyond even me, little one.

Printed in Great Britain
by Amazon